The
Smart One
and the
Pretty One

The Smart One

and the

Pretty One

Claire LaZebnik

5 SPOT

NEW YORK   BOSTON

Copyright © 2008 by Claire LaZebnik

5 Spot
Hachette Book Group USA
237 Park Avenue
New York, NY 10017

Visit our Web site at www.5-spot.com.

5 Spot is an imprint of Grand Central Publishing.
The 5 Spot name and logo are trademarks of Hachette Book Group USA, Inc.

Printed in the United States of America

First Edition: September 2008
10 9 8 7 6 5 4 3 2 1

Library of Congress Cataloging-in-Publication Data

LaZebnik, Claire Scovell.
    The smart one and the pretty one / Claire LaZebnik.—1st ed.
        p.   cm.
    ISBN-13: 978-0-446-58206-3
    ISBN-10: 0-446-58206-9
    1. Sisters—Fiction.   I. Title.

PS3612.A98S66   2008
813'.6—dc22

                                                              2007048631

Book design by Ellen Rosenblatt/SD Designs

For my father, Mel Scovell, who has always reminded me that "a writer is someone who writes," words that spurred me on to find a way to put *something* down on paper even when I had only little bits and pieces of spare time.

And by the way, Dad, I'm actually glad you made me memorize "The Love Song of J. Alfred Prufrock" when I was twelve. Turns out I really *do* measure out my life with coffee spoons.

Acknowledgments

Writers routinely (and often mechanically) thank their editors and agents, so I wish I had a way to prove to everyone how crucial the notes, support, and advice were that I got from Emily Griffin, Alexis Hurley, and Kim Witherspoon. People will just have to take my word for it, I guess. I'm grateful to all of them and just wish I had a better and stronger word than "grateful."

The support I've had professionally is matched by that at home. Rob reads everything I ask him to, no matter how busy he is, and his notes are always right (damn him). Even when I try to ignore them, sooner or later I have to give in and admit that it'll be a better book if I just listen to my husband. Aubry Dennehy continues to cover my back and make all our lives better in all sorts of ways.

The Smart One and the Pretty One is a novel about sisters being there for each other. I know firsthand how supportive sisters can be, since I have three wonderful ones. My thanks to Julie, Alice, and Nell for always looking out for their little sister. To Ted, too, the lone male sibling.

Finally, what keeps me going is the enthusiasm of my biggest fans, the ones who spend their free time setting up Web sites and Wikipedia pages about me, who pass my books along to anyone who might be remotely interested in them, and who follow my career with passion. The fact that I gave birth to them all doesn't diminish my gratitude. Thanks, Max, Johnny, Annie, and Will. You're what matters.

The
Smart One
and the
Pretty One

Prologue

One evening, when Ava Nickerson was eight years old, her parents betrothed her to Russell Markowitz, the son of their friends Lana and Jeffrey Markowitz. The adults seemed to find the idea of an arranged marriage between their kids very funny, but the whole thing embarrassed Ava, especially when Mr. Markowitz called her his "daughter-in-law" and tried to get his teenage son to embrace his future bride. "Come on, Russell," said Mr. Markowitz, who had a genial smile and small, shrewd eyes. "Do an old man a favor and give us some proof for once that you're batting for the right team."

Ava didn't know what he meant, but the phrase "batting for the right team" stuck in her head, and since the Markowitzes drifted out of her family's life soon after that visit, she only ever remembered Russell Markowitz as the kid who played baseball and had annoying parents.

Chapter 1

Your sister is on the phone," Jeremy said as Ava approached his desk and snagged a Hershey's Kiss out of his candy dish. Jeremy was a perfectly good assistant in other ways, but his endless supply of chocolates made him an indispensable one, in Ava's opinion.

Ava looked at her watch. "She wants to talk *now*?"

"Should I tell her you'll call back?" he asked. Jeremy had sweet big brown eyes and thick, tousled hair. There was something slightly babyish about his round chin and full lips that made Ava feel mildly maternal toward him, though he was only a few years younger than her.

"No, it's all right. I'll take it." Ava went into her office, shut the door, and punched the speaker button on her phone.

"Transferring," Jeremy's voice said, and then there was a beep and Lauren's voice came out of the speaker. "Ava? Are you there?"

"Yep. Just got here." She shrugged off her coat.

"Really? So late?" Lauren's voice had the breathy quality of a young girl, but she lingered on her *s*'s in a way that was oddly sultry. The combination suited her: in person she managed to be simultaneously childlike and alluring, with wildly curly dark hair, big eyes, a pointed chin, and a small, curvy figure.

In theory, she and Ava resembled each other—they were both small and dark-haired and anyone could immediately identify them as siblings—but Ava, whose hair was straight and who knew herself to be neither childlike nor alluring, didn't see it at all.

"It's nine a.m.," Ava said. She hoisted her heavy briefcase onto her desk. "Three-hour time difference—remember?" She extracted her laptop and a few folders, which she arranged in a neat pile on her desk, squaring the corners.

"Yeah, I know. I just figured you got up with the sun and made it to the office by six. Hey, A?"

"What?"

"How seriously do you have to take letters from a collection agency?"

Ava digested that for a moment and then the weight of it made her sink into her desk chair. "You want to start at the beginning?"

"Not really."

A pause. "Okay, then it depends a little on how many you've gotten and how much time has passed since the initial notice, but . . . I'd certainly take them pretty seriously. Who's sending you the letters?"

"Who isn't?" Lauren said with a little laugh. "I'm up to my ass in debt, Ava. No, deeper. Up to my ears."

"Why?" Ava said. "I mean, you rent your apartment, you have a job, you don't have kids—"

"My job *is* the problem," Lauren said. "I can't go out there and buy stuff for the boutique without seeing things I want for myself."

"Wanting something and having to own it are two different things."

"Not for me."

"Well, that explains why you're up to your earholes in debt," Ava said. "So do you need me to lend you some money?"

"No, no," Lauren said. "I don't want your money. Unless, you know . . . you feel like you want to—" She cut herself off. "No, really, I don't. But I thought maybe if you wrote some of these debt collectors—you know, on your letterhead—maybe used some legalese, sounded official—"

"And tell them what exactly?" Ava said. "That you're above the law and shouldn't have to pay money you owe?"

"Would that work?" said Lauren with a hopeful little laugh.

"You need to talk to a debt counselor, Lauren. Someone who'll contact your creditors, consolidate all your debts, and set up a payment schedule for you. Do you want me to get some names for you?"

"Would I still have to pay it all back?"

"Of course."

"What about declaring bankruptcy? Don't people do that all the time?"

"It's a morally corrupt way to avoid accountability," Ava said seriously.

Another little laugh. "But besides that—"

"It should only *ever* be a last resort," Ava said. She stood up, which made her notice a small stain at the bottom of her sweater that hadn't been visible in the mirror of her badly lit bedroom that morning. "I'll e-mail you about the debt counselors as soon as I get some references. In the meantime, cancel all your credit cards and stop buying stuff. Make yourself a strict budget and stick to it. And if you can't stand being around beautiful, expensive things, get a different job. Did I mention that you should stop buying stuff?"

"I get it," Lauren said. "How are *you* doing?"

"Fine," Ava said. "I got my TiVo fixed."

"Woo-hoo. It's an exciting life you lead."

There was a knock on the office door and Ava walked over and opened it. "It had been broken for a while," she said, raising her voice so Lauren could still hear her. "I was missing all my favorite shows." Jeremy was waiting outside the door, a steaming cup of coffee in his hand. She mouthed her thanks as she took the cup, then said out loud, "I need to get to work, Lauren."

"Yeah, okay," Lauren said. "Bye. Oh, wait—one last question. I almost forgot."

"What?"

"Hypothetically . . . A landlord can't just suddenly evict you for not paying your rent, right?"

Ava groaned.

Lauren's boss had asked her to cover the boutique that afternoon. Normally Lauren was the one who went to trunk shows and designer showrooms while her boss manned the store, but Saralyn had promised a friend with a new handbag line that she would check it out herself. Lauren didn't mind. She liked working with customers. She knew what looked good on people and enjoyed creating outfits for them. And once she had put them in something really spectacular, she was often inspired to try on something similar, so she frequently ended a day in the store with a bag of her own purchases—bought, of course, with her employee discount.

It was a fairly slow weekday, and after she had helped a preteen and her mother find something they could agree on for the girl's first middle school dance—the girl wanted it to look sexy, the mother didn't, and Lauren got them to compromise on a tube dress that was form-hugging but didn't actually reveal anything—she was all alone in the store until a young man entered.

He was probably about twenty-eight, in good shape, and wearing a blue wool suit and a dark red tie. He could have wandered in from any of the financial or legal offices that surrounded their downtown store. She wasn't crazy about his goatee, but it didn't matter: any guy who came into their store was taken, or he wouldn't be shopping there.

"Hi there," she said, looking up from the sweaters she was refolding and stacking. "How are you doing?"

"Great." He studied her briefly. Lauren was wearing a very short skirt with go-go boots and a tight heather-brown cropped sweater that was much shorter than the crimson tissue tee she wore underneath. "I have a feeling you'll be a big help," he said with a pleasant nod. "You're so stylish. I need a present for my girlfriend."

"What's the occasion?"

"Birthday," he said. "It's today, actually."

"Today?" Lauren said. "You sure put it off till the last minute, didn't you?"

"I kind of forgot." He gave a sheepish smile. "She had to remind me this morning."

"Ouch," she said. "That's why BirthdayAlarm-dot-com was invented, you know."

He held out his hands in a gesture of supplication. "So long as I get it in before midnight, I'm okay, right?"

"Don't worry—we'll find her something fantastic. Did you have anything in mind?"

He indicated her outfit. "How about that sweater you're wearing? I wouldn't mind seeing her in that."

She adjusted the sweater slightly. It was one of her favorites. For that month. But she hadn't bought it at the boutique. "You sure you don't want to go with jewelry? You don't have to worry about size and everyone loves to get it."

"You know best."

"Let me show you what we've got." She circled around behind the jewelry counter, which was also the cash register stand, and sorted through the necklaces hanging on the wooden display tree. She slid a long silver link chain off a branch and held it up. "This is really popular right now. It's extra-long, but it can be doubled up if she wants to wear it choker-length. I bought one myself a couple of weeks ago."

"How much?" he said.

She squinted at the tag. "A hundred and twenty-nine dollars."

He gave a low whistle. "That's a little more than I was hoping to spend."

That was actually fairly inexpensive for their store. "Okay," Lauren said, slipping the necklace back into place. "We'll find something else." She poked through the other necklaces, checking the price tags, and then pounced on one that was less than a hundred dollars and very simple, just a teardrop red stone hanging from a delicate silver chain. It wasn't exciting but it was completely unobjectionable.

She slid the necklace off the post and laid the stone across the palm of her hand. "This is it," she said. "This is the one you want." Men shopping for gifts liked to be led to a decision—that much she had learned from her years of selling to them.

"It's pretty," he said obediently. "How much?"

"Eighty-nine."

"You know what would help?" he said. "If you put it on. So I could see what it looks like. Would you mind?"

"Not at all," Lauren said, but the clasp was a tricky one and the little hook kept slipping out of the link.

The guy said, "Let me help," so she handed the necklace to him and gathered her long hair in one hand to bare her neck as she turned her back to him. He leaned over the counter that was between them and strung the chain out above her chest, then brought it around to the nape of her neck. His fingers brushed against her skin—possibly more than was necessary, but she wasn't sure and decided to ignore it.

Once it was fastened, she turned again with a bright smile, letting her hair drop back into place. She touched the necklace to reassure herself that the stone hit just below the hollow at the base of her neck. "There," she said. "How beautiful is that? If you don't buy it for your girlfriend, I might have to buy it for myself. And I can't afford to go around buying myself any more jewelry, so you'd better take it."

"It looks great," he said. "But I'm not sure the necklace can take the credit. I bet everything looks good on you."

"Hardly." She reached up behind her neck again. Fortunately, it was easier to undo the clasp than to fasten it. "Shall I wrap it?"

"It's a go," he said with a nod.

While she was tying a ribbon around the box, another customer walked in. Lauren looked up and said, "Hi—be right with you," and the woman said "Take your time" and wandered over to the sweaters.

"There you are!" Lauren said, slipping the box into a bag and handing it to the guy. "I hope she enjoys it."

"Me too," he said and took the box out of the bag and held

it out to her. Lauren stared at it uncomprehendingly. Then he said, "It's for you."

"Excuse me?"

"It looked so good on you," he said. "I think you should have it."

"You're so funny," Lauren said, trying to pass it off as a joke, give them both an out. Flirting with a male customer was one thing—it was practically in her job description—but the flirting was supposed to end as soon as the charge was approved.

Apparently he hadn't read the rulebook. "No, really. Take it." He put the box on the counter between them and pushed it toward her.

"I can't." She folded her arms. "Take it home and give it to your girlfriend. She's going to love it."

"If you're not comfortable taking a gift from a stranger, then give me a chance to get to know you. Have dinner with me tonight."

"I doubt there'll be enough birthday cake for all three of us," Lauren said.

"That's not what I meant—"

"I know." She gave the box a backhanded slap. It flew across the counter and the guy had to make a dive for it before it hit the floor. She took advantage of the moment to escape from behind the counter and quickly hail the new customer, who had some question about hat sizes.

The guy lingered for a little while longer, trying to catch her eye, but she pointedly ignored him, and eventually he gave up and left, carrying the little box with him.

At least his girlfriend would get a pretty necklace, Lauren thought, though she suspected it might get thrown back in his face sometime in the not too distant future.

A few weeks later, Ava returned to her office from a meeting to find that her father had sent her and Lauren a joint e-mail. The subject line said, "Serious news."

The entire body of the e-mail read "Your mother has cancer. Call home."

"Oh my God," she said out loud and grabbed the phone. Her parents' line was busy: her father refused to get call waiting because he thought clicking over to a new call was disrespectful to the original caller.

She kept trying, dialing with trembling fingers that fumbled and hit the wrong buttons, but the line stayed busy. After a few minutes of this, Jeremy buzzed in to tell her that she had a call.

It was Lauren, who didn't bother to greet her, just said, "Have you spoken to Mom and Dad yet?"

"Not yet. I was in a meeting and only just got Dad's e-mail. My God, Lauren, *Mom* . . ."

"I know, I was freaking out, too, but it's okay." The normal-ness of Lauren's voice was the most reassuring thing Ava had ever heard. "I can't believe Dad told us like that. The man is insane. Mom's fine, Ava. They just found a few cancer cells in one of her breasts—I mean, literally, we're talking a few *cells*. They'll blast them with some mild chemotherapy and she'll be fine."

"Are you sure?"

"Positive. I talked to Mom about it. She was actually laugh-ing at me for being so upset. Dad sent that e-mail without even asking her. Anyway, you should call them, of course, but don't worry. Everything's okay." Her voice broke on the last word and there were little sighing sounds. It took Ava a few seconds to realize that her sister was crying. "I'm sorry," Lauren said, her voice thick. "I've been doing this ever since I got the e-mail, even though I know everything's fine. I think it was the shock of thinking Mom *could* be that sick."

"I know what you mean," Ava said. "But she's not, right?"

"But what if something goes wrong? Or there's a next time and it's more serious? They're getting old, Ava." She took an audible deep breath. "Anyway, you should call Mom now. But remember—*don't overreact.*"

"I wouldn't dream of it," Ava said. She hung up on Lauren and called home.

Her father answered. "Finally you call."

"I only just got your e-mail a few minutes ago," she said. "But I spoke to Lauren and—"

"You called *her* before you called us?"

"Your line was busy," Ava said. "And *she* called *me*, which by the way is what normal people do when they have to give scary bad news. They pick up the phone—they don't send mass e-mails telling people their mother has cancer."

"I had to do it by e-mail," he said. "You know how touchy you girls are. No matter who I called first, the other one would have been hurt."

"That's not true," Ava said.

"It is true," he said. "Lauren called us right away, you know."

Ava let out a slow breath between her teeth. "May I talk to Mom?"

"I think you should," he said seriously and put her mother on the phone.

Her mother sounded oddly cheerful. "It's good to hear from you, sweetie!" she said. "How are things at work?"

"Fine," Ava said. "How are *you*?"

"I'm so fine it's embarrassing," Nancy said. "I'm sorry about that e-mail. Your father wanted you girls to know as soon as possible that I'm dealing with this *thing*, but it's really nothing all that serious."

"Tell me exactly what the doctor said."

"He said I have a few cancerous cells in my breast. It's hardly even a lump—just the beginning of one."

"How'd they find it?"

"Oh, something showed up on a mammogram and then they did a biopsy and it came back positive."

Ava felt vaguely that a good daughter would have already known that her mother was having breast cells biopsied, but she hadn't. She wondered if Lauren had.

Her mother was still talking. "—the thing about this family," she said. "I love you all dearly, but little things become big ones. First your dad with that over-the-top e-mail, and then Lauren calling up sobbing as though the world had ended and insisting on coming home—"

"She's coming home?" Ava said. "She didn't tell me that."

"Day after tomorrow. I told her not to, but she insisted. She's been living across the country from us for years and suddenly she can't be apart from me for one more day. She can be so melodramatic."

"Yeah," Ava said. "I've met her."

"But since she *is* coming, I thought we could all have dinner together Friday night. Can you make it?"

"I've got to check," Ava said, pulling her keyboard closer so she could get to her online calendar.

"You have to come," her mother said. "It's my dying wish. You have to honor your mother's dying wish to get her family together."

"That's not funny," Ava said.

"It's a little bit funny," her mother said. "See you on Friday."

Chapter 2

"T ime for a toast," Lauren said, standing up. She was wearing a silk slip dress, which she had layered over a pair of wool and silk capri leggings, a look that practically screamed "autumn in L.A." to her—which is why she had bought the whole outfit right before flying back home. She raised her glass to Nancy. "To our mommy. Because we love her and should remember to tell her so even when she's not sick."

"Hear, hear," Ava said, raising her own glass to her lips.

"To my wife," said their father. "Whose health is precious to us all." He drank.

"Had to rewrite me, didn't you, Dad?" Lauren said.

"She's not *my* mommy," he said.

"I liked both versions," Nancy said.

Lauren looked at her mother's familiar, very pretty face, framed by fire-red hair (L'Oréal Preference Intense Dark Red, she knew now as she hadn't as a child), and felt a sudden ache. She had barely seen her mother in the last few years, hardly spent any time with her since going off to college in New York. Once she had moved across the country, she pretty much only ever bothered to call home when she was walking somewhere, which meant she was usually distracted and in a rush. But that fear she had felt when she read the e-mail her father sent, the fear that had sent her flying across the country to see her mother immediately—*that* had shaken her up, made her realize that knowing her mother was always waiting for her back home was what allowed her to roam freely, and that if she ever lost that base, she would come crashing down, alone and scared.

The doorbell rang as they set their glasses down. "Who would come by *now?*" Jimmy said. "It's dinnertime."

"Probably a solicitor." Nancy pushed her chair back.

"I'll take care of it," Lauren said. "You sit." She ran to the front door and threw it open. A young Asian girl stood alone there, wearing what was unmistakably a school uniform: a blue and white plaid jumper and a white polo shirt. She had long straight black hair pulled back by a matching plaid headband. "Hey, who ordered the little girl?" Lauren called out.

Nancy emerged from the dining room. "Oh, hi, Kayla!" she said. "How are you? Kayla lives next door," she said to Lauren, gesturing toward the south side of the house.

"I'm very well, thank you," the little girl said. She spoke very gravely and precisely. She held up a large yellow envelope. "My mother said I could come ask you about this. My school is doing a walkathon. Would you be willing to sponsor me? It's for a good cause."

"Of course," Nancy said. "Let me just get my purse." While she went to get it, Lauren and Kayla were left alone again.

"It's a good thing to do," Lauren said, feeling that, as the adult, she was responsible for making conversation. "Raising money for charity."

"Uh-huh," Kayla said.

"What *is* the cause?"

Kayla stole a glance down at the big yellow envelope she held in her hand. "Cerebral palsy?" she said.

Nancy returned with her purse. As she opened it and pulled out her wallet, Lauren said to her, "I thought the whatstheir-names lived next door. You know. The ones who had that yearly Halloween party."

"They haven't lived there for years," Nancy said. She handed Kayla a couple of bills. "Here's twenty dollars, sweetie."

"Thank you." Kayla carefully tucked the money into her envelope.

"I want to sponsor you too," Lauren said with sudden conviction. "Just let me get some money." She ran to the family room to get her purse. She took out her wallet and opened it up—and realized she only had two dollars left.

"Shit!" she said out loud, desperately searching through all the folds of the wallet, hoping she would find a twenty hidden and forgotten somewhere. But those two dollars were it. She could write a check, but her checking account was completely depleted and bouncing a check to a charitable organization probably guaranteed you a seat by the fire in hell. Lately she had been charging everything—she would deal with the repercussions later—but she doubted Kayla could accept a credit card.

She threw her purse on the sofa, angry at it. She had wanted to make the little girl like her, and now she was going to look like an idiot.

Then she spotted Ava's handbag.

"Here!" she said, running back into the foyer a minute later. "Take this." She thrust thirty dollars at Kayla.

"Wow, thanks," Kayla said and put it in the envelope. Then Nancy told her to say hi to her parents and they watched as Kayla crossed their front yard and was safely welcomed back inside her house.

"Man, she's cute," Lauren said as Nancy closed the door.

"You should see her little brother. I may have to steal him one day and raise him as my own. We lent them our power drill once, so I think it's fair."

"What was all that about?" Ava asked as they returned to the dining room. She had stacked a bunch of dishes while they were gone and was on her feet, about to carry them into the kitchen. Jimmy was still sitting at the head of the table, sipping his wine. Lauren had never seen him clear a dish in her life.

"The little girl next door was collecting for some charity," Lauren said.

"Kayla?" Ava asked Nancy, who nodded. "I love that kid," Ava said. "She's like a forty-year-old CEO in an eight-year-old's body."

"Oh, I had to raid your wallet, A," Lauren said.

"What do you mean?"

"I didn't have any cash, so I borrowed thirty bucks from you."

"Borrowed?" Ava repeated. "As in you'll pay it back?"

"One hopes," Lauren said cheerfully. "You should have seen her earnest little face—I had to give her *something*."

"It's easy to be generous when it's not your money," Ava said.

"I would have been generous with my own money. I just didn't happen to have any. And you're a rich lawyer."

Ava turned to their mother. "You see why this is annoying to me, don't you?"

"She certainly should have asked you before taking your money," Nancy said. "But at least it's for a good cause."

"See?" Lauren said. "Everyone wins."

"Except me," said Ava. "I'm out thirty dollars and Kayla thinks *you're* the generous one."

"Oh, who cares?" Lauren said. "She doesn't even know us."

"That's not the point," Ava said.

"What is?"

"I don't know," Ava said. "But if I ever find you in my wallet again without my permission . . ." She didn't bother to finish the threat, just picked up the stack of dishes and headed into the kitchen.

"Oh, I'm scared now," Lauren said with a laugh. She looked up to find her father glowering at her. "What?" she said.

"You don't *think*," he said. "You don't ever stop to think."

There was no answer she could make to that familiar refrain, so she just slumped in her seat feeling misunderstood and waited for someone to serve her dessert.

Another glass of wine took care of any lingering resentment Ava might have had, and a couple of hours later the girls were sprawled out companionably in the family room, their parents already gone up for the night.

"This house is so cozy and wonderful," Lauren said with a contented sigh. "You've never seen my apartment, have you? It's a studio and it looks out on a brick wall and the whole building smells bad. It sucks, Ava. This is how I grew up"—she gestured around at the pretty, warm, slightly messy room they were in— "and now I live in a shithole."

"If Dad heard you using that kind of language—"

"He's asleep," Lauren said. "And I'm twenty-six years old. And he's asleep." She put her wineglass down and hugged her knees to her chest—she was perched precariously on the edge of a low ottoman, despite the fact that there were several comfortable armchairs and a sofa in the room. "The point is, when I come back here and remember how nice it is, I wonder why I'm living there and not here."

"Uh, maybe because you're an adult?" Ava said. "Growing up means you stop living with your parents."

"Guess I'm not grown up, then."

"You can say that again," Ava said and then suddenly sat upright. "Wait a second. Are you trying to tell me something?"

"You mean like that I quit my job and I'm moving back home to live for a while?" Lauren said. "Nah. It's nothing like that."

"Oh, good," Ava said. "Because I thought maybe—"

"I got *fired* from my job and I'm moving back home to live for a while. Completely different. Oh, and I also got evicted from my apartment."

Ava's mouth fell open. "Seriously? What happened? How did you get fired?"

"My boss found out I had some credit problems."

"She can't fire you because of that," Ava said. "That's not right."

"Oh, she didn't," Lauren said. "Not exactly." She unfolded her legs and reached for her wineglass again. "My boss— *ex*-boss—Saralyn—she's not a bad person, but she can drive you crazy. She thinks she has to turn everything into a morality lesson. I mean, I *know* that if I spend more than I make I'm going to end up in debt. I don't need some idiot boss lecturing me like I'm four years old."

"So what did you do? Get mad and quit?"

"Not mad so much as—" Lauren stopped and shrugged. "Well, *she* started the truth-telling, not me. If she wanted us to be brutally honest with each other, *I* certainly wasn't going to hold back."

"Oh, God, Lauren. And you also managed to get evicted at the same time?"

"Not exactly," Lauren said. "That was an exaggeration. But the landlord was getting pretty nasty. He even turned off my hot water."

"That's illegal," Ava said. "Even if you haven't been paying rent, that's illegal."

"Well, it's also possible I just forgot to pay the gas bill." She laughed and Ava did too, but the laugh ended in a sigh. "I've already shipped all my stuff out here," Lauren said. "I just shoved it all in boxes and called UPS—Dad paid for that. So I'm out of there."

"But you love New York."

"Loved," Lauren said. "Past tense. I want to try L.A. again."

"Okay," Ava said. "If you want to move back home for a little while, fine."

"Thanks for the permission," Lauren said with a roll of her eyes, which Ava ignored.

"But you need to have a plan and a definite move-out date. How long do you intend to be here?"

"Jesus, I don't know," Lauren said. "I'll see what happens."

"I have an idea," Ava said. "I just need a pen." She jumped to her feet and tugged a cabinet door open. A bunch of papers flew out and swooped down onto the floor. "Whoa!" she said. The cabinet shelves were bursting with shoeboxes and baskets and stacks of old pictures and drawings and photos and school essays—all the paper relics of their childhood. "What a mess," she said, shoving a stack of photos back from its precarious placement at the edge of one shelf.

Lauren got up and came over to her side to peer in at the mess. Glancing sideways, Ava noticed that with neither of them wearing shoes—they had both kicked them off at some point that evening—they were roughly the same height. Usually Lauren wore very high heels, so Ava always thought of her little sister as being significantly taller. But she actually wasn't.

A photo had fallen on the floor. "Look," Ava said, picking it up. "This is exactly why you shouldn't be living at home."

"Why? Who is that?"

"Fiona. Dad's aunt. Look at her—she was a good daughter who lived with her mother her entire life. When Rose died, Fiona was like fifty-five and had never been married and had barely ever left the house she was born in. She inherited enough money to do whatever she wanted. So what did she do? Stayed in the same house, hardly ever went out, never got married, and died a decade later, the most boring person who ever lived."

"You give her a run for her money."

"Shut up. The point is she never had a life because she didn't have the sense to move out of her mother's house when she was still young."

"I'm nothing like her," Lauren said. "I moved out of my mother's house and I've had plenty of boyfriends. Besides, back in those days, if you lived with your mother, it was because no guy would marry you. Now tons of people move back in with their parents—"

"And never leave again," Ava said. "It's not a positive step, Lauren. Learn from Fiona."

"Fine, I've learned." Lauren snatched the photo out of Ava's hand and shoved it in the cabinet. "Boring cautionary tale over now. Scary great-aunt goes back in the closet where she belongs."

"Of course, that could have been the problem right there," Ava said thoughtfully. "Being in the closet, I mean—it is possible she was gay at a time when that would have been unacceptable."

"Some girl-on-girl action for Great-Aunt Fi," Lauren said with a smirk. "Now there's a thought."

"Not one I want to dwell on," Ava said. "Anyway, the point is, if you're going to move in with Mom and Dad, you have to agree to a checkout date. One you'll stick to. Which is why we're going to put it down in writing. If I could just find a pen . . ."

"Forget it." Lauren slammed the cabinet shut. Some pieces of paper that hadn't been pushed back far enough got caught in the door and she pulled them out and tossed them on the table. "I don't need to put it in writing. Do you really think I want to live with Mom and Dad forever?"

"No," Ava said. "But—"

"End of discussion." Lauren threw herself onto the sofa— lying down the long way, so there wasn't room for Ava. "Let's do you now," she said. "In the interest of sisterly . . . interest. Let's talk about how you're almost thirty and you haven't had a decent boyfriend or the prospect of one since—when? Law school?"

"Lauren—"

"It *was* law school, wasn't it?"

Lauren always knew how to push her until she had to rise to her own defense. "Of course not. I've had relationships since then." Ava sat on the little orange slipper chair she always thought of as their mother's, since Nancy tended to sit in it when they were all in the family room.

"Name one."

"Michael Rodriguez."

"Michael Rodriguez?" Lauren's forehead wrinkled in thought. "Oh, wait. He was the one who did that weird thing with his cat, right?"

"I can't believe you remember that story," Ava said. "I can't believe I *told* you that story."

"What was it again?"

Ava hesitated, then sighed. "Whenever he took a shower, he'd let his cat lick him dry. Well, parts of him, anyway."

"Which parts?"

"He was a nice guy," Ava said defensively.

Lauren laughed. "I never said he wasn't. So anyway, how long ago was Michael?"

Ava thought. "Three years?" she said after a moment. "Yeah. Three years." She slid way down in the chair. "I can't believe it's been that long since I've dated anyone even halfway decent. And Michael *was* a little weird. The cat was weird too, come to think of it. It had these little squinty eyes—" She made a face. "Why are we even talking about this?"

"Let me take you out," Lauren said, suddenly sitting up. "The night is young. We could hit some bars—"

"Are you *kidding*?"

"Come on, it'll be fun. The worst thing that happens is you and I have a drink and some laughs. The best thing that happens is you meet some handsome young doctor who falls madly in love with you—"

"Make him a pilot," Ava said. "I've always wanted to date an airplane pilot."

"We'll go to a bar near LAX," Lauren said. "Got to be pilots there."

"I was joking," Ava said. "I don't meet guys in bars, Lauren."

"That's because you don't go to them."

"No, it's because I don't look like you."

"You look a lot like me."

"Not in the ways that matter."

"Let me make you over," Lauren said excitedly. "I'll do your hair and face and lend you an outfit. I'll make you look so hot the guys'll be lining up—"

"I'm tired," Ava said. "I just want to go home."

Lauren stamped her foot. "Why do you always have to be such a loser?"

"Says the girl who's about to move back in with her parents."

Lauren stuck her tongue out at her sister.

"A brilliant comeback," Ava said.

"Sorry. Guess we can't *all* be straight-A geniuses."

"Too bad for you," Ava said. "Good night."

As Ava left the room, Lauren immediately and automatically reached for the TiVo remote, accidentally knocking off the papers she had tossed on the coffee table earlier. They fell to the floor and she reached down to pick them up.

It was, she thought with amusement as she glanced through them, a classic Mom stack of papers, completely random: there were a couple of childish crayon drawings, a manual for the DVD player, a photo of Lauren on prom night (wearing too much makeup, she had to admit—she had a heavy hand with eye shadow at that age), a page torn from a Spanish-English dictionary, and, finally, some sort of handwritten document that Lauren stopped to examine more closely.

In her mother's slightly loopy handwriting were the words:

We, the parents of Ava Carrie Nickerson and Russell Douglas Markowitz, do hereby agree that our two children are betrothed to each other and upon reaching maturity, or some semblance thereof, will be joined in matrimony to live Happily Ever After. We also agree to be good in-laws and to share them on the major holidays and not try to make the grandchildren love one set of grandparents more than the other.

The document was signed at the bottom by her mother and

someone named Lana Markowitz—presumably Ava's intended mother-in-law.

Lauren heard footsteps and assumed it was Ava coming back for some reason, so she called out, "You have to see this!" but it was Nancy who entered, wearing the same crimson silk bathrobe she had worn every morning to make coffee for as long as Lauren could remember.

"See what?" she asked with a yawn.

"What are you doing up? I thought you had gone to bed a while ago."

Nancy flopped down on the sofa next to her. "I've been having trouble sleeping since the diagnosis."

"Are you worried?" Lauren slid closer and leaned her head on her mother's shoulder.

Nancy put her arm around her and squeezed. "Not in the light of day. It's just in the middle of the night that my mind runs on and I start imagining crazy things like you girls getting married and having kids without me." She said it lightly enough, but Lauren's heart contracted.

"You'll be there," she said.

"Oh, I know," said Nancy. "I expect to be. But, just in case I'm not—?"

"What?"

"Promise me you'll pick out Ava's wedding shoes? If she wears a pair of those ugly Aerosole pumps she's always got on—just in *white*—I swear I'll come back to haunt you both."

Lauren laughed. Her mother wasn't a real clotheshorse, but she did love a beautiful pair of shoes, and it wasn't the first time she had expressed pain over Ava's determinedly utilitarian approach to footwear. "I promise," she said. "But you'll be fighting that battle at my side."

"So what *is* that?" Nancy asked, flicking at the piece of paper Lauren was still holding.

"Look." Lauren handed it to her and Nancy read it, holding it far from her face and squinting at the writing even though the room was fairly bright.

She gave a short laugh. "I had forgotten we did that," she said, dropping it on the table.

"Who *was* Russell Douglas Markowitz, anyway?"

Nancy pushed off the pretty velvet mules she wore for slippers and curled her feet up under her, snuggling down into the cushions with Lauren. "His father worked with Dad for a while back in the late eighties. Dad liked Jeffrey—he was a very entertaining guy, very smart and funny—so we got together with them a bunch of times, but I never really hit it off with the wife."

"Why not?" Lauren rubbed her cheek against her mother's silk-covered upper arm.

"I don't know. We just didn't click. She didn't have much of a sense of humor, for one thing, which, given how funny Jeffrey was, made for an odd marriage and ultimately a divorce."

"I don't get it," Lauren said. "Why would you want to marry Ava off to one of her kids if you didn't really like her?"

"I didn't *mean* it." Nancy shrugged sheepishly. "I needed several glasses of wine to get through an evening with Lana Markowitz, so I was probably a little tipsy when I wrote that."

"I'm shocked," Lauren said. "Such goings-on in my own home."

"I do remember thinking the boy was sweet, though."

"Are you still in touch with them?"

"Not for years. They both moved away after the divorce."

Lauren yawned, and Nancy gently pushed her upright. "You should go to sleep, Lulu. It's late and you're still on East Coast time."

"Okay." She stood up. "Just tell me one thing: am *I* engaged to anyone I should know about?"

"Not that I'm aware of," Nancy said. "You have anything to tell *me*?" Lauren shook her head. "Anything at all?" Nancy persisted, almost pleadingly. "Doesn't have to be an engagement. Could just be an interest. Or even a breakup."

"There really isn't anything or anyone worth talking about," Lauren said.

"I feel like I know so little about your life these days."

"You're not missing anything." It was true, though, that Lauren hadn't told her much about the last few guys she had dated, well aware that they weren't the kind of men she would ever end up bringing home to meet her parents.

Nancy said wistfully, "When Bobby Cho kissed you in Extended Day, I was the first to know."

"That was fourth grade, Mom."

"I know. I miss how you girls told me everything in those days."

"Not *everything*," Lauren said. "I never told you what Bobby Cho did the *next* week at Extended Day."

"What?" Nancy asked, a little too eagerly.

"On second thought, I'd better keep it to myself," Lauren said. "Good night, Mom."

"Now I *really* won't be able to sleep," Nancy called after her as she left the room.

Chapter 3

Hey," Lauren said, sticking her head around Ava's office door and peering in. "Jeremy said I could come on in."

"I'll just be a sec," Ava said. "Make yourself comfortable." She bent back over her work.

"Thanks." Lauren came in and wandered around the room for a moment. She picked up the one framed picture Ava had on her desk. "Hey, it's me!"

Ava looked up. "That was at Aunt Jeanie's wedding. Remember?"

"Not really. Mom let me wear a torn tutu to a wedding?"

"You wouldn't take it off." Ava dropped her pencil. Clearly she wasn't going to get any more work done. "There was a huge fight and you said you wouldn't go to the wedding unless she let you wear it."

"I loved that tutu." Lauren put the picture back down. "Can we go? I'm starved."

"I ordered in for us." Ava pressed the buzzer. "Jeremy? Is the food here yet?"

Jeremy's voice said, "Not yet. Do you want me to check on it?"

"No worries. Just meet us in the red conference room when it gets here." Ava stood up. "Come on, Lauren. There's someone I want you to meet."

"Ooh," Lauren said, jumping down from the edge of the desk and catching up with her at the door. "Is he cute? And if he is, why not keep him for yourself?"

"All will be explained in time," Ava said.

"I hate you when you're mysterious," Lauren said as she swept by her.

Ava just smiled at her back. And then she sighed.

Carolina Hernandez was waiting outside the conference room for them, looking every inch the professional in a well-tailored, formfitting navy blue suit. Ava greeted her and they shook hands and then Ava introduced her to Lauren, who looked suddenly wary. And very young. Maybe it was the pink babydoll tunic top she was wearing over tight blue jeans, but sandwiched between two older women who were both wearing fairly formal dark work clothes, she looked like a teenager who had been forced to accompany her mother to the office and couldn't wait to run free at the mall again.

"So," Carolina said once the greetings were over with a nod toward the conference room door. "Shall we—?"

"Shall we *what*?" Lauren asked warily.

"Get started."

Even more suspiciously: "Get started doing *what*?"

Ava said brightly, "Carolina is a debt counselor, Lauren. She's going to help you consolidate your debts and set up a payment schedule so you can work toward restoring your credit rating."

"Ah," Lauren said.

"Lunch is on the way." Ava took a step back. "If you two don't need me, I'll wait for you back in my office."

"We shouldn't be more than a half hour or so," Carolina said over her shoulder as she headed into the conference room. "It was sweet of you to get us lunch, though." She put her briefcase on the table and briskly popped it open, then began taking out various papers and a laptop computer.

Ava took another step back, but Lauren put her hand on her arm, stopping her. She said in a quiet falsetto, "Gee, Lauren, why don't you come on in at lunchtime and we'll go grab some sushi or something?" Then, still quietly, but back to her regular voice: "Why didn't you just tell me you were doing this?"

"Honestly?" Ava said. "I wasn't sure you'd show up if I did."

"It's not that I mind meeting with her," Lauren said. "But you could have been up-front about it."

"Could I have?" Ava said. "Really?" There was a short silence. "Go on," she said. "Just get it over with. Carolina's very nice and you'll feel so much better when things are in order."

"Maybe," Lauren said. "But you're a bully and a jerk."

"I'll see you when you're done," Ava said.

As she went down the hallway, she ran into Jeremy, who was carrying a stack of sushi-filled plastic containers. She swiped her own order (a spicy tuna roll) out of his hands and sent him on to the conference room with the rest.

As she went back to her office, she felt vaguely uneasy. *Should* she have told Lauren ahead of time? But she had too much work to waste time worrying about something that couldn't be changed now.

There was a knock on her door about an hour later and Carolina beamed as she and Lauren entered. "We made a lot of progress today," she said.

"Good." Ava glanced at Lauren, who didn't meet her eyes. "So do we have a master plan?"

"We're getting there," Carolina said. "Lauren's going to get me some of the information I still need, right, Lauren?" She sounded a little bit like she was talking to a small child, and Ava winced.

But all Lauren said was "Yeah, I'll get it all together."

Carolina smiled and her teeth sparkled. Bleach, Ava thought. And not just over-the-counter Crest Whitestrips bleach. The real thing, done in a dentist's office for hundreds of dollars. Those were some white teeth. "You are going to feel so much better once we've taken care of this," Carolina said to Lauren. "Bet you're feeling better already, aren't you?"

"Oh, I'm great," Lauren said flatly. "This is a whole new me."

"In that vein," Ava said, "and while I've got Carolina here to weigh in, I have another idea to propose—"

"What's that?" Carolina asked.

"When I was doing some research about debt online, I read that a lot of people make a vow these days not to buy anything that's not a necessity for a certain length of time, like six months or a year." Ava snuck a glance at Lauren, who was now staring, stone-faced, at the opposite wall. "Going cold turkey gives you time to get back on your feet, pay off all the bills, start putting some money in the bank account. If you cut off all temptation, it's just easier to, uh . . ." She searched but ended up with a somewhat lame "resist temptation."

Carolina was nodding away, her glossy black hair swaying with each enthusiastic bob. "It's a fantastic idea," she said. "It's like dieting—sometimes it's easier to cut out your danger foods altogether than to try to eat them in moderation. For some people, money *is* a danger food." She dazzled them with her teeth. "For me, it's M&Ms."

"I hear you," Ava said. "So what do you think of the idea, Lauren?"

Lauren said slowly, "Let me get this straight. You're saying you want me to write out a little contract promising not to buy anything for the next year?"

"You could also do it on one of those Web sites," Ava said. "If that seems less weird to you."

"Weird?" Lauren repeated. "I wasn't thinking it was *weird*. Infantalizing, yes. Embarrassing, maybe. Patronizing, definitely—although that would be more your issue than mine. But it's not particularly *weird*."

There was a short, uncomfortable pause. Then Ava said, "I'm just trying to help. You have a problem, Lauren. You can't control your spending. Carolina can help you dig yourself out of your current situation, but it won't do any good in the long run if you don't make some real changes in how you deal with money."

"And you think I have to sign my name to a scrap of paper to make a real change?" Lauren said. "You think this"—she mimed her signature, moving her hand through the air—"is going to make the difference between my being responsible or not?"

"The world runs because people sign their names to pieces of paper," Ava said. Her cheeks were flushing hot—she could feel them—and she had to fight the urge to back out of the room and flee. She hated any kind of personal confrontation, even with her own sister. "That's all everything comes down to— business deals, purchases, political arrangements, marriages—

everything. All day long I make sure that the pieces of paper my clients are signing their names to are going to improve their lives and their businesses and not destroy them—because those little pieces of paper have the power to do both those things. So don't act like I'm belittling you just because I'm suggesting you put something in writing, Lauren. I have every reason to know that it matters."

"Oh, right," Lauren said. "You're the important lawyer who knows about contracts and never gets into debt. I'm the loser sister," she said to Carolina. "She's the successful one. In case you hadn't noticed yet."

"I wouldn't say that," Carolina said. Nothing seemed to upset her composure. Ava envied her that. "You guys both seem pretty amazing to me. And you are so lucky you have each other. I have two brothers and I would have killed to have a sister. It's a really special relationship."

Lauren grinned suddenly and Ava felt herself breathe out with sudden relief. She hadn't realized until then that she was basically holding her breath. "Yeah," Lauren said. "It is. No one can get as far up your ass as your sister."

Amusement won out over horror and Ava laughed out loud as a small expression of distaste flickered momentarily on Carolina's face.

Ava asked Lauren to stay after Carolina left. "I already wrote up a rough draft of the document for you," she said. "It's just a jumping-off point. See what you think." She held it out to Lauren, who took it and glanced at it disdainfully.

"Define 'necessity,'" she said.

"Toilet paper. Not that you'll need it if you're living at Mom and Dad's, but eventually . . . Anyway, that and soap and tooth-paste and food. But not fancy high-end restaurant food. Paying thirty-five dollars for a plate of pasta is out."

"Unless someone else is paying," Lauren said. "I am allowed to let someone else buy me things, aren't I?"

"So long as you don't start turning tricks for Stuart Weitzman shoes."

"Hadn't thought of that," Lauren said. "But now that you've suggested it—"

"Not a suggestion," Ava said. "Definitely *not* a suggestion. Anyway, most drugstore stuff is probably okay, except you can't run out and buy a new blow dryer just because it's fancier than the old one—no replacing anything that still works or could easily be fixed. You can go to the supermarket, of course. But you have to stay out of clothing stores. And absolutely no Internet shopping."

"You are really starting to piss me off." Lauren dropped the paper onto Ava's desk. "I'd be the first to admit I don't always handle money well. And you were right to set up the thing with Carolina. I do feel better actively taking care of the situation. But I don't need to sign some stupid fake-legal document to keep a promise."

"How can it hurt?" Ava said. "It'll be a good reminder—"

"You're going to hold it over my head," Lauren said. "Every time we go anywhere, every time I so much as *look* at a sweater in a window display, you're going to be whipping this thing out—"

"I won't," Ava said. "I promise."

"Can I get that promise in writing?"

"Sure," she said. "Unlike you, I love to sign 'fake-legal' docu-ments." She picked the document back up and thrust it at Lauren. "I'll witness your signature."

"Oh, dear *God*," Lauren said and snatched it from her. She pressed so hard while she was signing that her pen tore the paper. "Is it still legal if it's torn?"

"Yep," said Ava. "Not that it's likely to stand up in a court of law to begin with. But you know what I mean. It still *counts*." She signed her own name. "Thank you. You've made me feel much better. You want a copy?"

"Not really."

"Good, I'll make you one." She lifted the fax machine cover.

Lauren said darkly, "I will get back at you for this, you know."

"For caring about you and trying to help?"

"For being up my ass," Lauren said.

"That's a disgusting expression."

"The question is," Lauren said, "what would be the best revenge?"

"Living well?" Ava suggested. "Oh, wait—you're not allowed to do that anymore."

"Then I'll just have to find another way, won't I?"

"Why do you need to get revenge on me?" Ava said. "All I want is to help you."

"Yeah," Lauren said with a maniacal little grin. "Me too you."

⟨●⟩

Jeremy buzzed in to say that Brian Braverman was coming in to talk to Ava, and a moment later a bald man in glasses and a conservative wool suit entered the office. "There you are!" he said to Lauren as if they were old friends. "Did I catch you on your way out?" Then he spotted Ava over her shoulder and took a step back. "Oh, dear, forgive me. For a moment, I thought you were—"

"I'm her sister." Lauren held out her hand. "Lauren."

"Brian Braverman." He shook it warmly. "It's remarkable how much you two look alike."

"Really?" Ava said, dubiously studying Lauren.

"You could be twins." He turned back to Lauren. "How long are you in town for?"

"I'm not sure yet. A while."

"Wonderful." He rubbed his hands together. "How lovely for you both. Nothing like family. Well, forgive me for interrupting—"

"Lauren was just leaving," Ava said. "I'm all yours."

"Oh, don't make your sister leave on my account. I just wanted to ask you for a favor. I've got to leave early today for a meeting with the rabbi—it was the only time we could get— and I was wondering if you could take over a client meeting for me at five."

"Shouldn't be a problem," Ava said. "Let me just check to make sure I'm not forgetting anything." She went over to her computer and hit some keys as she peered at the screen.

"My daughter's getting bat mitzvahed next week," Brian explained to Lauren. "You wouldn't believe how much work it entails. The decisions, the meetings, the writing of speeches, the weekend tutoring. The bills." He gave a theatrical sigh. "Especially the bills. But it'll all be over soon."

"It's going to be great," Ava said from over by the desk.

"I hope so. Oh, and you should come too." He touched Lauren's arm. "It'll give you a chance to get to know some of the people your sister works with every day. You weren't bringing anyone else, were you, Ava?" Ava shook her head. "Well, there you go. Now you have a plus one."

Lauren said, "Are you sure it's okay?"

"Absolutely. The more the merrier. Ava, I insist you bring your sister."

"Fine with me," Ava said.

"Really?" Lauren said.

"Yeah. Brian's right—it'll give you a chance to meet people."

"It'll be a great party," Brian said. "Fun for all ages. I've tried to leave all the details to my wife, who's much better at these things than I am, but I can tell you that I heard a rumor about an ice cream sundae bar."

"Well then, count me in," Lauren said. She added, "Best part is this gives me a chance to buy a whole new outfit. I've had my eye on the most amazing dress—"

Ava's brows flew together in a frown. "Lauren—"

"I'm kidding," Lauren said. "I'm kidding." She took her leave of them both and left the office pleased with herself.

Chapter 4

"I don't know why they called it a lumpectomy," Nancy said. "There wasn't actually a lump. A clump, maybe. But not a lump."

"A clumpectomy?" Ava said uncertainly. The three Nickerson women were camped out in Nancy's bedroom, watching the Audrey Hepburn movie *Funny Face* on TV. Lauren had gone with her parents to the hospital for Nancy's procedure, and Ava had joined them at home as soon as she got off work. Once he realized he was outnumbered three to one and that the evening's entertainment was an exceptionally girly movie, their father had fled to the relative safety and quiet of the downstairs.

"I keep telling her she should be taking advantage of the situation to get implants," Lauren said to Ava. Lauren was sitting on the terry-cloth armchair in the corner of the bedroom. A few years earlier, a decorator had convinced Nancy that white terry cloth would give the room "an adorable boudoir feel." Within three months, the chair looked like it was covered in an old, worn towel. But the upholstery had been expensive, so Nancy had just kept it that way.

"It's a little hard to justify new breasts when there's barely a dent taken out of one of the old ones," Nancy said.

"Aw, come on," Lauren said. "Can you imagine how excited Dad would be if you just showed up one day with a pair of 34 double-Ds?"

"With his blood pressure, the shock could kill him. I'll make a deal with you, Lulu—if I actually have to get a mastectomy at any point, I will get the loveliest, most voluptuous implants you've ever seen. But until and unless that moment arrives, may I please enjoy my old friends here?"

"All right," Lauren said. "But can I get implants if you're not going to?"

"I don't think they qualify as 'necessities,'" Ava said. She was lying on the bed next to her mother, her feet hanging awkwardly off the side since she hadn't bothered to take her shoes off.

"Tell that to every actress on TV. No boobs, no job. Hence the term 'boob job.'" Lauren stood up. She was wearing long sweatpants that were slung low on her hips, fit her snugly in the thighs, and widened toward her ankles. She looked very stylish and chic even though she was theoretically dressed down. Ava wondered how much the sweats had cost Lauren—probably a lot more than the skirt *she* was wearing, which was a plain dark blue and not particularly stylish or chic or even flattering. It had, however, been available online. And it was machine washable and, through some miracle of modern science, never wrinkled. "Mom, you want anything?" Lauren asked. "A glass of water? Something to eat?"

"I'm fine," Nancy said with an aimless wave of her hand. "Enjoying being lazy and watching TV. I almost never do that."

"You eat dinner yet, A?" Lauren asked.

"No, and I'm starving."

"Me too. Want to grab something to eat?"

"We could just order in," Ava said, looking to her mother for her opinion. But Nancy's eyes were closed.

"I need to get out," Lauren said. "I've been either here or at the hospital all day."

"Why don't you go pick something up for us? I came to see Mom."

"Don't stay for me," Nancy said, her eyes flickering open. "I took a Tylenol with codeine right before you came, and in all honesty it's a struggle to stay awake."

Ava sat up. "Why didn't you tell me?"

Nancy smiled apologetically. "It seemed rude when you only just got here."

"That's stupid, Mom." Ava jumped to her feet and tugged the white cardigan sweater she was wearing into place. "If you need to sleep, you should sleep. Lauren and I will go grab some dinner and come back."

"Just give me a sec to change into real pants." Lauren headed toward the door.

"That will be your fifth wardrobe change of the day," Nancy said sleepily. "Or is it the sixth? I may have lost count somewhere."

Lauren turned back. "It's important to dress appropriately for each activity." Using her fingers, she ticked off items as she listed them. "You have your exercise clothes, your hanging-around-the-house clothes, your going-to-the-hospital clothes, your going-out-to-dinner clothes—"

"I get up in the morning and get dressed," Ava said. "That's it."

"You sure you want to give me style tips?" Lauren said with a meaningful glance at Ava's current outfit.

"Oh, shut up and get dressed," Ava said.

Nancy was asleep and snoring by the time Lauren came back, fully dressed, shod, and ready to leave.

◖◗

"So where are we going?" Ava asked once they were in her car. Lauren had begged for a turn behind the steering wheel— "I never get to drive; it's just a chore for you and it's fun for me"—and Ava had reluctantly agreed to let her, not really having any reason to say no except for the fact it was *her* car and it felt weird being in the passenger seat.

"There's this new restaurant in West Hollywood," Lauren said as they turned onto Sunset Boulevard. "It's supposed to be great."

"Why go that far? There are plenty of good restaurants in Brentwood."

"I want to try this one. It sounds really good. And we're in no rush."

"But Mom—"

"Will be asleep until tomorrow."

"It's a waste of gas and time."

"You have a Prius," Lauren said. "And we can talk on the way there and back. Sister-bonding is not a waste of time."

Short of wrestling Lauren for control of the car, there wasn't really a lot Ava could do but accept the destination. "It better be good," she said.

"It'll be better than that disgusting sushi I had to eat at your office," Lauren said.

"What was wrong with the sushi?"

"The side order of humiliation that came with it."

"Oh, I had to pay extra for that," Ava said.

The restaurant was exactly what Ava *hadn't* wanted: a crowded and unevenly lit monument to excessive minimalism, filled with aging hipsters and young actresses out with much older men whose eyes were glued to their BlackBerries.

"We'll never get in without a reservation," she said hopefully as they left their car with the valet and entered.

"We'll get in," Lauren said, walking ahead of her. She murmured something to the host that Ava, a few feet behind her now, couldn't hear, and the host, a slim, handsome man with a shaved head, nodded and said, "Right this way. They're waiting for you."

"Who's waiting for us?" Ava said as they followed him.

"Them." Lauren pointed to the table where the host was already indicating two empty places.

Two unfamiliar women and two unfamiliar men looked up at them. One of the men stood up, and Lauren held her hand out to him. "Hi!" she said. "I'm Lauren."

"Of course you are!" he said, and to Ava's surprise—given the fact he had needed her to identify herself—he pulled Lauren to him and gave her a quick but enthusiastic hug. He was a tall guy with sandy-colored hair and he wore a charcoal-gray suit with a dress shirt and tie. "And you're Ava, right?" he said, turning to her. She nodded and was immediately swept into a similar embrace. "Wow," he said, releasing her and stepping back. "Look at you two. How long has it been? Fifteen years? Twenty? You were like this tall—" He put his hand parallel to the floor, about three feet off the ground.

"You remember us?" Lauren said, looking pleased.

"Absolutely. You"—pointing at Ava—"were always sitting in

corners reading and you"—at Lauren—"were always dancing around in a pink tutu shouting at everyone to look at you."

"I was cute, wasn't I?" Lauren said.

"But where's the tutu? I hardly recognized you without it."

"Sorry," she said. "It's at the cleaners."

"Excuse me," Ava said to the guy, "but I'm lost here. Who *are* you?"

Lauren said, "This is Russell Markowitz, Ava. His parents were friends of Mom and Dad's."

"Oh, right," Ava said, recognizing the name but no less confused. If Lauren had arranged a dinner, why hadn't she told Ava so ahead of time?

Russell ushered them closer to the table. "Let me introduce you to everyone," he said. "My buddy Cole Masterson and his wife, Rachel . . ."

Cole, a beefy guy with a buzz cut, wearing khakis and a jacket and tie, lumbered to his feet and shook hands with both girls. "Pleasure to meet you," he said. He looked like he had been a lineman back in high school. Maybe even in college.

His wife had very long, layered hair that was shiny and carefully textured so it looked like it belonged in a fashion magazine photo, and her makeup application had strayed far beyond anything natural into what she no doubt deemed glamorous but Ava felt verged on trashy. She nodded at the two girls politely enough but something about her face gave the impression that she had just smelled something unpleasant. She wore an empire waist top that emphasized her curvy figure and round shoulders.

Russell moved on to the other woman, putting a proprietary hand on her shoulder and informing them that her name was Corinne Sutton.

Corinne was blonder, younger, and thinner than Rachel, but

her hair was similarly layered and piece-y. She wore enough skill-fully applied makeup to make her big blue eyes look even bigger and bluer and her enviably sharp cheekbones look even sharper and more enviable. She was the kind of blonde men would al-ways notice. She was wearing a spaghetti-strap dress that was cut so low that it was clear that, unlike Ava's mother, Corinne had been more than happy to take advantage of the surgeon's ability to bestow what nature had begrudged her. She delivered a tune-less "Welcome" to the girls.

"Come sit," Russell said, pulling out a chair for Lauren. Cole did the same for Ava, who hesitated, looking from one man to the other.

"We don't want to intrude," she said.

"Why do I get the feeling you didn't tell your sister about this dinner?" Russell asked Lauren.

"I get that feeling too," Ava said, glaring at Lauren, who shrugged and plumped down in her chair.

"Thought it would be more fun as a surprise," Lauren said as the men took their seats next to them. Each side of the table now went girl-boy-girl with the two sisters directly across from each other at one end. "I wanted to see if Ava would remember you."

"Do you?" Russell asked Ava.

"Well, not immediately obviously." On closer study, his face did feel vaguely familiar to Ava, but she could have passed him on the street without recognition. "I think it's coming back to me a little, though. You had a big brother, right?" He nodded. Ava suddenly remembered something else. "And you were really into baseball!"

He gave her a funny look. "No. Never. I wasn't what you might call a sporty kid. Much to my father's constant and fre-quently vocalized disappointment."

"Oh." She was embarrassed she had gotten it wrong. "Maybe I'm remembering your brother."

"Maybe. Baseball wasn't really his game—he was all about basketball back then—but he was definitely the athletic one and I was the scholar. At least according to family legend." He put his hand on his flat stomach with a proud smile. "Now I'm in better shape than he is."

"Ava's the smart one in *our* family," Lauren said. "Which is probably why our parents did *this*." She pulled a piece of paper out of her purse and held it up with a dramatic flourish.

"What is that?" Ava said. The others all leaned forward curiously.

"A contract," Lauren said, looking around the table with evident pleasure at having everyone's complete attention. "Written by our parents years ago—ours and Russell's. It says that you and Russell are engaged to be married."

"Really?" Russell shifted closer to her so he could look at it. "That's so funny."

"It's why I tracked you down," Lauren said. "I mean, once something's down in writing like that, it's legally binding, right?" She winked at him.

Cole laughed. "Sounds like you're committed, my man."

Russell shrugged. "Sure does."

"I don't understand," Corinne said at his other side.

He took the paper from Lauren and showed it to Corinne, who leaned her body against his as she looked at it. "What's to understand?" he said. "I'm engaged to *her*"—he indicated Ava. "Didn't know it until now, but I wouldn't dream of going against my mother's wishes. You know how I respect my mother."

Corinne made a little sarcastic noise at that. "Will that make me your mistress?" she asked, cuddling against his arm. "If you get married again?"

"Sorry," Russell said. "I'm not the cheating type. I believe in monogamy. Serialized monogamy. You'll just have to get in line."

Lauren laughed at that, but Corinne pulled away from his arm and sat up straight in her seat again, not looking particularly amused.

"Can I see it?" Ava asked. Russell handed the contract to her and she read it swiftly. When she looked up, she realized everyone at the table was watching her. She could feel the blood rising in her neck and cheeks.

"It's pretty stupid, isn't it?" she said. "I don't know what they were thinking." She wished they'd all stop looking at her. She wanted to kill Lauren. And her parents.

"Are you trying to nullify this?" Russell snatched the paper out of her hand and held it to his heart. "Claiming they weren't of sane mind when they wrote it?"

"It's so *silly*."

"You're hurting my feelings," Russell said. "She's clearly trying to get out of it," he announced to the others. "Do you think it's my looks? Is it my looks?" he said, turning back to Ava. "Am I that big a disappointment to you? I mean, two minutes and you want out already?"

"Smart girl," Corinne said. "Run while you can."

"There you go," Russell said to Ava. "Right from the horse's mouth."

"Don't call me a horse."

Lauren said, "Don't mind Ava. She's a lawyer. It's in her nature to look for loopholes. On the other hand"—she shot a look at Ava—"she loves her contracts."

It suddenly became clear to Ava why they were there: Lauren had said she would get revenge for that meeting with Carolina—and here they were.

"You do realize that you'll be wife number three for this guy?" Cole said to Ava.

"Seriously?" Lauren said before Ava could respond.

"Yep."

"You've already been married twice? Then is she—?" Lauren gestured at Corinne, who immediately tossed her head in the opposite direction and reached for her orangey-pink cocktail.

Russell shook his head. "Number two? No."

"He got rid of number two a long time ago," Cole said.

"Happiest day of my life," added Russell.

"I thought that was supposed to be the wedding day," Lauren said.

"Clearly you've never been divorced."

"Just so long as you're not completely done with marriage *yet*," Lauren said, with a nod toward the piece of paper he still held.

"I thought I was." He smoothed out the contract and looked at it again. "But I guess this changes everything."

Corinne said suddenly, "We should order our food. I'm starving."

Rachel immediately said, "Me too. Where's the waiter?"

Lauren ignored them. "Your attitude worries me," she said to Russell. "If you're going to marry my big sister, I think you need to show a little more enthusiasm."

"Give me time," he said. "I've known about the engagement for all of five minutes."

"Me too," Ava said.

"You didn't know about this before?"

Before she could answer, the waiter approached their end of the table. "Would you ladies like something to drink?" he asked.

"We can't stay long," Ava said with a pointed look at Lauren. "We promised our mother we'd be home soon—"

"Was it my imagination or did she just say, 'I think I hear my mother calling'?" Russell asked the others.

"She did," Cole said.

"We have plenty of time," Lauren said. "Don't listen to her. We'd each like a glass of Chardonnay," she said to the waiter, who nodded and turned away.

"Stop him, Cole!" Rachel said, grabbing her husband's arm and pointing to the waiter.

"Hold on," Cole called out to the waiter, who turned back.

"We'd like to order now," Rachel said. "We're very hungry. And our party is *finally* all here."

"Let me just get their drinks and I'll be right back," he said.

"I hate this place," Corinne said as he walked away.

"It's especially bad tonight," her friend said meaningfully.

"Lauren," Ava said in a low voice. "We should go." The other women so clearly didn't want them there that she couldn't see why Lauren wouldn't just leave. The joke was over now, wasn't it? Lauren had successfully embarrassed her and gotten her revenge. It was time to go.

"Aw, don't be in such a hurry to leave," Russell said. "We have so much to plan—the venue, the date, the caterer, the music, the divorce . . ."

The wedding talk wasn't doing anything to improve the mood of the other women. Or hers. Ava wished he'd stop with it.

But Lauren insisted on egging him on. "I think you should wait on that last bit," she said. "It seems like bad luck to plan the divorce at the same time as the wedding."

"All right, then," he said. "We'll wait until after. But there's still so much to do. By the way, I'd just as soon not wear a tux, if it's all the same to you girls. Feels like bad luck to go black-tie the third time around. But it's the bride's call. We can figure it all out once we've ordered." He cocked his head at Ava. "Unless you still hear your mother calling?"

"Don't worry about her," Lauren said. "Of course we're going to join you for dinner." She put her finger up. "But I'm afraid I'm going to have to insist on a black-tie wedding."

"Shouldn't that be your sister's call?"

"Trust me," Lauren said. "You don't want to leave the fashion choices up to Ava."

"Ouch," Russell said with an exaggerated wince.

Ava was barely listening to them at this point, too distracted by the way Corinne and Rachel were now leaning across the table to talk in a low voice to each other while they shot little sideways glances at her and Lauren. Their hatred was almost palpable, but she didn't blame them. How would *she* feel if she were dating a guy and some random woman came in and announced she was engaged to him? Even as a joke, it was in bad taste. And Russell had deliberately made the situation worse by flirting with Lauren and being rude to Corinne.

She looked across the table at Lauren, who was laughing at something Russell was saying, saw how adorable Lauren looked with her curly hair and pretty top and how both men seemed captivated by her. The other women's hostility only seemed to inspire Lauren to work even harder for the men's admiration and attention: it just made Ava want to flee.

But then, Lauren was equipped to go toe to toe with these women. Lauren, like them, was stylish and flirtatious and hip. A restaurant like this—a hot spot—was her natural element. You could plunk her right down between Corinne and Rachel and no one would sing, "One of these things is not like the other" (except, Ava thought loyally, Lauren was prettier and fresher than the other two). But stick Ava in there, with her dowdy clothes and un—made-up face and air-dried hair, and the imaginary spectator would do a double take.

Not that she minded. She didn't *want* to fit in with women who looked like that, who thought that fashion magazines held all the secrets to success. Let them spend hours on their over-styled hair: she would do something better with her time. She didn't envy them or want their companionship.

But that knowledge did nothing to make her feel less self-conscious, and the realization that even people she held in contempt could nonetheless make her feel embarrassed and awkward drove her crazy with frustration.

Ava slumped down deeper in her chair, wanting desperately to leave. The only good thing was that no one seemed to be expecting her to contribute to the conversation: Lauren was perfectly capable of doing all the charming and talking for the both of them.

Shortly after their entrees had been cleared, Lauren excused herself to go to the ladies' room and Ava immediately jumped up and followed her. As she passed by the other end of the table, Corinne gave her a very deliberate once-over, raising her eye-brows as she took note of the cardigan and skirt. She looked back across the table at Rachel and said, "Oh, that reminds me. I have to go to Target soon—I'm running out of toilet paper." Rachel snickered obligingly.

Ava flushed and darted after Lauren.

She caught up as Lauren was entering the bathroom, which

was blessedly empty. Once they were inside the door, Ava said, "Can we please go home now?"

"Aren't you having fun?" Lauren said, rearranging a few of her curls in front of the mirror.

"No. I want to go. You should have heard those women just now, Lauren."

That caught Lauren's attention. "Why? What'd they say?"

Ava repeated the insult for her. "I honestly don't care what she thinks. But I don't want to spend any more time with these people. Can we—"

"I can't believe her. If *I* were wearing something that tacky, I wouldn't go around criticizing other people's clothes." She patted Ava's arm. "Don't worry, A. I'll get back at them. They won't know what hit them."

"I don't want you to fight with them," Ava said. "I just want to go home. This whole thing has gone on long enough."

"But the guys are cool even if the girls aren't."

Ava crossed her arms. "I'm leaving. If you don't want to come with me, find another way home."

"Okay, fine, I'll go," Lauren said. "Am I at least allowed to pee first?"

Ava gestured impatiently at a stall and Lauren went inside. She waited in the bathroom for her to finish: she wasn't about to go back to the table by herself.

Once they had returned there together, Lauren announced that she and Ava were leaving.

"Really?" Russell said, rising to his feet. "Why so soon?" Lauren just pointed to her sister, and Russell said, "She hears your mother calling again, doesn't she?"

"We have to go," Ava said flatly.

"But you'll stay in touch, right? Now that we've re-connected?"

"Are you free on Friday?" was Lauren's immediate response.

He glanced down at the end of the table. It wasn't clear if the other women could hear them or not: they were watching, but the restaurant was pretty noisy. Russell said in a low voice, "Friday night's good."

"Great." Lauren moved around the table. "It was so nice meeting you all," she said. As the women raised listless hands in farewell, she stopped for a moment and pointedly studied Corinne's outfit, then turned back to Ava with a clearly audible "Oh, that reminds me—I have to stop at Forever 21 and get a joke gift for my friend."

Corinne's jaw fell open and Rachel's face mirrored her friend's, but before they could say anything, Lauren spun around on her heel, took Ava by the elbow, and walked with her out of the restaurant. "That felt good," she said.

((●))

While they were waiting for the valet to bring their car around, Lauren said, "Wow. Wasn't Russell totally cute? I mean, not handsome cute, but interesting cute—but then I kind of like big noses. What did you think?"

"I think I hate you," Ava said.

"Why?" Lauren said. "Because I sprang something on you without telling you first? And made a big deal out of a little piece of paper? There's been a lot of that going around lately. Have you noticed?"

"This is totally different," Ava said. "I was trying to help you. You're just trying to embarrass me."

"I needed a debt counselor and you need a boyfriend," Lauren said. "We're *both* just trying to help each other out. That's what sisters do, right?"

"A boyfriend?" Ava said with real outrage. "Is that what this is about? You're trying to find me a *boyfriend*?"

The valet drove up with the car, and Lauren said, "Let's go."

Once they were both seated and the valets had closed their doors, Ava said, "Where did you find that stupid contract, anyway?" She pulled away from the curb with a quick and furious jolt that made the tires squeal.

"Seat belt not on yet," Lauren sang out. "Thanks for caring." She fished behind her and buckled it in quickly. "It fell out of the cabinet—remember when we were looking for a pen at Mom and Dad's?" She put a finger to her temple in exaggerated thought. "Now, why were we looking for a pen again? Oh, right! It was because you wanted me to sign a piece of paper saying I'd move out of their house by a specific date. Because— stop me if I'm wrong about this—you believe that signing a piece of paper makes things come true. Like, for example, a mother's wish that her daughter marry a specific young man. That would count, right?"

Ava said through clenched teeth, "If I smashed your side of the car into a pole, I could say it was an accident."

"What are you so mad about?"

"That was the single most excruciating hour of my life," Ava said. "Having his friends stare at us. Watching you pull out that fucking contract."

"My God," Lauren said with delight. "You swore. I don't think I've ever heard you swear before. I mean, 'shit' maybe when you hurt yourself—but not 'fuck.' Not like that, in the middle of a sentence, an actual adjective—"

"Oh shut up," Ava said wearily.

"This could be really good for you. He was *cute*, Ava. That's kind of cool, isn't it? That he was actually what you'd want him to be?"

"I didn't want him to be anything," Ava said.

"I thought he was perfect for you."

"Did you notice? He *has* a girlfriend."

Lauren waved her hand dismissively. "He's *so* not into her. You could blow her away in an instant."

"In my whole life, I've never blown anyone away," Ava said. "And anyway, that's not the point. Did you see what she looked like? That's the kind of girl he likes."

"We just have to teach him to appreciate someone like you."

"Why?" Ava said. "Because our parents made a joke two decades ago?"

"Because you've taught me the value of a signed piece of paper," Lauren said with mock gravity.

"Oh, will you just let it *die*?"

"Not until after Friday night," Lauren said.

Chapter 5

Some guy was yelling at the nurses. Apparently his mother was supposed to have been put in a private room for her chemotherapy but was instead being asked to sit in the more public general seating area, where about half a dozen reclining chairs and corresponding IVs were separated from one another only by optional curtains. Nancy had been settled in one of the reclining chairs and her bag started about ten minutes earlier, and Lauren was sitting on a stool at her side. A young girl who was there with a much older man—a father? grandfather? hard to know—caught Lauren's eye and rolled her own in the direction of the yelling guy. Lauren grinned at her, two strangers bonded by their disapproval of another stranger's bad behavior.

"For God's sake!" Yelling Guy had backed one of the nurses up against the wall. "What does it take to find someone who's actually competent around here?" He was fairly young—probably in his early thirties—clad in khakis and a button-down shirt. His thick dark hair was cut short and he looked like he worked out a lot, which added to the menacing quality of his stance. His mother was sitting on the edge of one of the reclining chairs a few feet away, looking exhausted and completely detached from whatever battle he was fighting. With a little thrill, Lauren noted the bag at the woman's side: it was Hermès and retailed for several thousand dollars.

"I'm sorry if there was a misunderstanding," the nurse said, squaring her shoulders. She was short but had an impassive strength to her that would have intimidated Lauren. "We never promise a private room in advance."

"You should have told your colleague that," he said. "The one who promised me one last week."

"What was her name?"

He looked around, like he might spot her. "I don't know," he said. "She had red hair. She was probably about your age." His eyes flickered across her face and he added deliberately, "Maybe a little younger."

The nurse scowled. "Well, whoever she is, she had no right to promise you a private room. They're strictly on a first-come, first-served basis for *all* our outpatients, and we're full up today. These chairs are very comfortable and we can draw the curtain around her if—"

"I don't want a fucking curtain," he said. "I want a private room."

"Please keep your voice down and watch your language. Show some courtesy toward the other patients."

He put his face even closer to hers, forcing her to draw back. "I'll do that when you show some courtesy toward my mother."

Lauren was rooting for the argument to escalate into some real drama. She was bored. With any luck, the guy would get so belligerent that security guards would be called in.

Unfortunately for Lauren, the nurse chose to defuse the situation.

"I'm sorry," she said, firmly pushing the young man to one

side and stepping around him so she could address his mother directly. "I really am, ma'am. If we had a private room available, there's nothing we'd like better than to see you happily settled in there. But since we don't, why don't we just make you comfortable here and get the drip started, so you can be back home and in your own bed ASAP?"

"That's fine," the mother murmured. She was bone thin and sallow but still beautiful, with elegant cheekbones and wide-set gray-blue eyes.

"You should have a private room," her son said to her. He looked a lot like his mother, except he radiated health. And fury. No, not fury—Lauren amended that—more like frustration so great he was going to explode with it. "They promised last week. You heard that nurse, didn't you? She said—"

His mother put up her hand. Her fingers were so thin that her knuckles looked far too big for them. "It's all right," she said. "I don't care. I just want to get through this."

"I can make them give us one," he said. "I'll go to the head of the hospital if I have to."

"Please, Daniel. Let's just get through it and go home." Slowly and carefully, she swiveled her body, moving her legs up and onto the leg rest part of the recliner. The casual slip-on shoes she wore—basically slippers with a thin leather sole—didn't fit with her elegantly tailored pants and silk top and were the only noticeable sartorial concession she had made to her illness. Well, that and the scarf around her head, which was probably there to hide thinning hair but was so pretty and so artfully arranged that it looked like something Jackie Onassis would have tossed on to walk the streets of New York. All she needed were the big sunglasses.

The woman's son moved over to support her and guide her into place. His body's violent energy seemed to soften into an anxious tension as he bent over her. "I just want to get done and go home," she said again.

"All right," he said. "All right." He brushed some hair off her forehead and let his fingers rest against her temple a moment. Then he turned back to the nurse. "Can you at least get this thing going?" he said, his voice strident again. "Can we please just move quickly for once?"

"I'll do what I can," the nurse said. "But I can tell you on behalf of the entire staff that a pleasant tone of voice and a little respect would go a long way toward generating some goodwill."

"Respect has to be earned," he said. "Making a promise to someone who's sick and then not keeping it—"

"Daniel," his mother said. Her voice was soft, but he immediately turned back to her. "I'm thirsty. Could you get me something to drink?"

"I can bring you some water," the nurse said. Man, she was clueless, Lauren thought. Even from where she was sitting, it was clear that the mother was trying to get rid of the son, give him some time to calm down.

Sure enough, the mother said, "Thank you, but what I'd really like is some juice—there's usually some in the snack room. Daniel, would you mind—?"

"Of course," the guy said. "I'll be right back." He moved off. As he did, he noticed Lauren staring at them all and narrowed his eyes at her.

As soon as her son was out of earshot, his mother took hold of the nurse's arm. "Don't be mad at him," she said. "He's just worried."

"Everyone here is worried," the nurse said, a little stiffly. "There's no need to take it out on the staff. We're doing the best we can."

"I know you are," the mother said. "He does too. He just

wants to take care of me so badly. He hates that he can't control this."

"Maybe he should see one of our social workers," the nurse said. She pulled on her patient's arm, straightening it out, turning it palm up, running her finger over the most prominent veins, all with a practiced efficiency and detachment. "They're very good at helping people deal with their anger and pain. Let me know if you want me to schedule an appointment for him." She gently stretched the skin on the inside of the woman's elbow between her thumb and forefinger and studied it, shaking her head. "Too many punctures. Have you talked to your doctor about getting a port put in?"

The woman reached up tentatively to touch her own collarbone. She let her fingers trail down to the skin a few inches below it as if checking to see that the flesh there was still untouched. "He wants me to. But it seems so . . ." She hesitated before saying, "Permanent."

"I don't see that you have any choice," the nurse said. "Your veins can't take any more sticking. I'm going to let him know that it has to be done."

The woman nodded briefly and closed her eyes.

The nurse resumed her work in silence. Lauren checked her own mother's IV bag, which was only a quarter empty. Nancy was watching the TV that hung down from the ceiling, either feigning interest in the talk show that was on or genuinely absorbed by it. "Mind if I stretch my legs?" Lauren said.

"Of course not." Nancy looked up at her. "I'm sorry this isn't more entertaining."

"Yeah, what's up with that?" Lauren said. "I was expecting nonstop laughter here."

Nancy said, "Go."

Lauren found the snack room on the other side of the floor.

There wasn't much to the place; it wasn't even really a room, just a sectioned-off area with a small dorm-sized refrigerator on the floor, a hip-height counter that ran around the edges, a bunch of drawers and shelves under the counter, and a coffeemaker, microwave, and toaster on top of it.

The area was empty except for one person: the guy who'd yelled at the nurse. He was frowning down at a couple of small packets in his hand, as if their contents offended him. As Lauren entered, he looked up and waved them at her. "Partially hydrogenated cottonseed oil," he said. "That's all these cookies are made of. That and sugar. I thought the goal here was to make people healthier. Why would they have these?"

"Yeah," Lauren said. "Sick people shouldn't be putting *poison* in their bodies." She smirked. "Oh, wait—isn't that *why* they come here?"

"Ha," he said. He didn't exactly seem amused, but he did look at her with a little more interest now, pausing to take in the tight jeans, the formfitting T-shirt, the long curly hair she was wearing pinned up in a loose knot with painstakingly arranged tendrils escaping. "Is that gallows humor?"

"Just trying to keep myself amused." She opened the mini-refrigerator and took out a bottle of water. "I'm bored out of my mind."

"I noticed." He tossed the two packets of cookies back in a big tray of assorted snacks. "I saw you staring when I was talking to Nurse Ratched over there. Hope our argument kept you entertained."

"It was kind of hard not to stare," Lauren said, unscrewing the bottle cap. "You were talking pretty loudly."

"They drive me nuts here," he said. "Every time we come, they fuck something up. The nurses are morons." A nurse passing by the area shot him a dirty look over the top of the partition.

He returned the favor and she went on with an audible snort of disgust. "The part that drives me nuts is that one will make a promise and then the others will act like *I'm* the irrational one for believing it. Bad enough we have to keep coming here, but to be treated like we're idiots—" He shook his head.

"How many times have you been here?" Lauren asked.

"You mean specifically for chemo? Or in general?"

"Chemo, I guess."

"This is our fifth time," he said. "You?"

"First."

"Who's the patient?"

"My mom. She has breast cancer. It's not too serious, though. You're here with your mother, too, right?"

"Yeah," he said and rooted aimlessly through a basket filled with bags of chips.

Lauren said, "She looked pretty wiped out."

"She is." He picked up a juice box. "I should get this to her. She was thirsty." Lauren waited, an eyebrow raised skeptically, and he sighed. "Or maybe she wasn't. She knows I hate watching them put the IV in. Ever since this one time . . . The nurse couldn't get it in right. She just kept digging and digging in there with the needle and my mother actually fainted from the pain." He smiled humorlessly. "That nurse no longer works here."

"You got her fired?"

"I don't know. They may have just moved her to a different part of the hospital. All I know is she isn't anywhere in sight when we come. But if she ever again walks into a room where my mother's being treated, I'll—" He stopped.

"What?" Lauren said. "What will you do? Now I'm curious."

He considered her. "You're still looking to be entertained, aren't you?"

"Desperately."

"I have an idea." He opened up a drawer and pulled something out: a deck of cards. "I found this the other day."

"Terrific," Lauren said. "Let's play."

He wanted to be within sight of his mother, so they went back to the chemo area and found some chairs across the hallway from where their mothers were reclining. There weren't any real tables, but Lauren pulled up a stool to play on while the guy took his mother the juice and made sure she was comfortable.

"Okay," he said once he had rejoined her and they'd both sat down. "What'll it be? Lady's choice. Five-card stud, Texas hold'em, Omaha?" He riffled the cards expectantly.

"Texas hold'em," she said.

He made a face. "Should have guessed."

"What's that supposed to mean?"

"Everyone plays that now," he said. "Every socialite and soccer mom. It's hip and adorable to play Texas hold'em. Which goes against the whole idea of poker. It should be grimy, dirty, low-class, played only by the lowest form of what's barely humanity—"

"I could spit tobacco all over the cards, if you like," Lauren said.

"It would be a start." He stacked the cards and evened out the edges with his fingers. He had long, slender fingers. Lauren wondered, idly, if he played the piano.

"So how'd you end up with mom duty today?" she asked. He didn't strike her as the caregiver type.

"I do it every day."

"Why you?"

"Short answer is there's no one else."

"Are your parents divorced?"

"No. My father's dead."

Lauren winced. "Sorry."

He shrugged. "It was a long time ago."

"You have any siblings?"

"One younger brother. He moved to Costa Rica two years ago. If he calls my mother once a month, it's a miracle."

"Do you work?"

"I have a job back in New York."

"So what's going on with that?"

"I took a leave of absence."

"That was good of you."

The guy—what was his name, anyway? His mother had said it, but Lauren had already forgotten what it was—looked annoyed. "Good of me?" he repeated. "She's my mother, for God's sake. What choice did I have?"

"Everyone has a choice. Your brother didn't come running."

"My brother," he said with a disgusted roll of his eyes. "I *had* to be here. End of story. My life will wait for me."

Lauren wasn't bothered by his abruptness. It seemed more honest than rude to her. Well, maybe a little of both. But she didn't mind other people's rudeness: she never took it personally. "What do you do back in New York?"

"I'm an investor."

"And you can just take a leave of absence from that?"

"From the office, yeah. I'm still working—most of what I do I can do on the computer from here. And the time difference helps. I get a lot of work done early and then I'm available the rest of the day to help my mother." He made three piles out of the cards and then stacked them up again, each one on top of the next.

"You fly back and forth a lot?"

"When I need to," he said. "Stuff comes up. But I don't like to leave her alone, so it's usually just a twenty-four-hour thing. I spend more time on the plane than I do in New York."

"And did you always know you wanted to play with money?" Lauren asked.

"Well, not *always*," he said. "I mean, when I was five, I didn't walk around saying I wanted to work for Morgan Stanley. But I've been on a pretty steady track since college."

"What *did* you walk around saying you wanted to be? I mean, when you were five?"

He grinned with a sudden and surprising charm. "A professional poker player."

Lauren pushed her chair back. "That does it. I'm not playing with you *now*. You'll beat the pants off me."

"I like the image," he said. Their eyes met briefly. Then, almost as if in direct response to that shared look, he shifted away and looked across the hallway at his mother. You could see his eyes tracing the length of his mother's arm and the tubing up to her IV.

"It's got to be pretty scary," Lauren said. "What you're going through."

He looked at her with a sudden savage embarrassment, then settled back in his seat and rapped the cards loudly on the stool. "Are we playing or not?" he said.

"We'll need something to bet with."

"They have M&Ms in the vending machine. Go get some." He started to deal the cards. "You need change?"

"I'm good." Lauren stood up. "Hey, hold off on that dealing until I get back. I don't trust anyone who deals when my back is turned."

"Nor should you," he said, gathering the cards he had dealt back up. "I was planning on cheating."

"Really?"

"Nah, I'm just joking," he said in a tone that made her wonder.

He was a much better poker player than Lauren, and the discrepancy between their abilities seemed to bother him.

"Why the hell did you keep betting?" he said after winning a particularly huge pot. "You knew I wasn't going to fold and you had a crappy hand."

"They're just M&Ms," Lauren said. "Why not take a risk or two?"

"You've got to think like they're twenty-dollar chips."

"Why?"

"Because otherwise there's no point to playing at all."

"I thought we were playing to pass the time."

"We are," he said. "But it's more fun and more interesting if you take it seriously."

"It's more fun if you have fun." Lauren stretched her arms, arching her back a little and surreptitiously watching his reaction. The move—a classic, and usually effective—was wasted on him: he was looking across the hallway, checking on his mother again. She let her arms drop to her sides. "Want to play something else?"

"Let's take a break." He threw the cards on the table. "Your mother's bag is almost through."

"Should I go over there?" Lauren started to rise, but he shook his head.

"The nurses will take care of it. It'll be a while yet—they'll flush her out with some extra liquids first."

"Oh." She fidgeted. "You want to grab a cup of coffee?"

They went back to the snack area. Lauren pushed a button on the coffee machine that dispensed exactly one cup's worth of coffee into a Styrofoam cup. She handed it to the guy, who stared at it absently. "My mother always drank a ton of coffee," he said. "Cups and cups, all day long. Then, months ago, she stopped suddenly. She said it made her stomach feel funny. She thought it was because she was getting older—just couldn't handle the acid anymore. But it was the cancer. It was already affecting her, only no one knew it. Not until the real pain started."

"So it's stomach cancer?" Lauren punched at the coffee machine again and filled up a cup for herself.

"No. Pancreatic. Stage four. Inoperable."

"I'm sorry," Lauren said, turning with her cup of coffee. She didn't know much about cancer, but the little she had read online had made it clear that stage four was bad. "All of this must be so overwhelming."

He looked around and past her. "You see milk anywhere?"

"How's this?" She fished a little plastic container of creamer out of a bowl full of them and tossed it to him.

He made a face as he caught it. "You know what this stuff is made of? Corn syrup and partially hydrogenated oils. Not a drop of real milk in it."

"Maybe there's some in the fridge." Lauren put her coffee on the counter, squatted down, and peered into the refrigerator. "So are you some kind of health food nut? That's twice you've complained about bad fats."

He dropped the creamer onto the counter. "Years ago, a friend of mine read an article about how bad partially hydrogenated oils are for you and wouldn't stop talking about it—this was way before everyone else started worrying about them. She convinced me my blood would just stop flowing if I ate any. So I try to avoid them. But it's not like I eat tofu and broccoli every day. I enjoy my hamburger and fries as much as the next guy."

"So long as they're not cooked in trans fats."

"Exactly. Or so long as I don't know that they are. When it

comes to french fries, I observe a strict 'don't ask, don't tell' policy. Especially if they're hot and salty."

Lauren stood up with a small carton of milk and knocked the fridge door shut with her knee. "I eat everything."

"Everything?"

She handed him the milk. "Except flan. I have a deep-seated fear of flan."

"It's scary stuff," he said. "I don't blame you." He opened the milk, sniffed it carefully, then poured a little into his coffee before offering the carton to Lauren.

She shook her head. "I like coffee creamer. Think I'll die young?"

He gestured around him. "Nice joke to make *here*."

"Oh, come on," she said. "Give me a break. I didn't mean—"

He put his hand up. "I was kidding. Make any joke you want. If you can't laugh at this fucking shitty situation . . ." He didn't bother to finish. Instead he said, "You know, the more time we spend together, the more awkward it's going to be when I admit I have no idea what your name is."

"I don't know yours either," she said. "But I heard your mother say it. Let me see if I can remember." She sipped her coffee, frowning in thought. "Is it David?"

"Daniel."

"Hey, I was pretty close. Want to guess mine?"

"I'm at a slight disadvantage," he said. "Never having heard it at all."

"So? You could still guess."

"That's stupid," he said. "I could guess for hours and still not get it."

"I could give you the first letter—"

He made an impatient noise. "Just tell me the name, will you?"

"It's Lauren."

"I never would have guessed that," he said.

The coffee was old and sour, even with the creamer. Lauren gave up on it and tossed it into the plastic-lined trash can. The cup had been pretty full and coffee sloshed over all the garbage. "I better go check on my mom."

"Do you know when her next appointment is?" Daniel asked as they made their way back to the chemo area.

"In a week, I think."

"We're back then too. We're on a twice-a-week schedule for six straight weeks. Which doesn't even include the checkups with her oncologist. I spend half my life on the freeway between Encino and here." He stuck his hands in his pockets and then said, "Sounds like there's a good chance we'll run into each other again next week. Maybe we could play some more cards."

"I'd like that," Lauren said.

"You should practice playing poker until then," he said, and she couldn't tell if he meant it as a joke or not. "So I don't keep beating you so easily."

"I don't mind."

"I do," he said. "It would be more fun with a challenging opponent."

"Well, then, I'll try to improve my skills," Lauren said. "For your sake."

"Hope to see you next week then," he said and walked off, toward his mother's chair. He sat down on the stool next to her. She opened her eyes briefly and managed a smile before closing them again. For a moment or two, Lauren just stood there watching Daniel watch his mother absorb the poison that would make her sicker for now and probably wouldn't ever cure her.

Chapter 6

Ava wasn't the kind of boss who kept track of how many personal calls her assistant made on any given day or whether he was five minutes late coming back from his lunch break or anything like that, but right now her door was open and she could hear him talking on the phone, and it felt like the call had been going on forever. She was dying for a cup of coffee. She could have buzzed in and interrupted him at any time, of course, but a cup of coffee didn't seem important enough to make him hang up—just important enough to make her aware he had been on the phone for at least half an hour.

Finally, she called out, "Jeremy? Got a sec?"

He immediately stuck his head around the doorway, phone clasped against his chest. "Sorry, Ava. I'm right here. What do you need?"

"I'd love a cup of coffee when you get a chance. No rush."

"Sure. I'll get it right now." He held the phone up. "Can you talk? It's your sister."

"My sister? Is that who you've been talking to all this time?"

"Um, yeah?" he said uncertainly.

"Oh. Okay. Could you please shut the door, too?" As the door swung shut, she picked up the phone. "Lauren? What were you talking poor Jeremy's ear off about?"

"I was just saying thank-you to him."

"For what?"

"For tracking down Russell's address."

Ava sank into her desk chair. "Oh, God, Lauren. Tell me you didn't tell my assistant about that stupid, *stupid* contract."

"Of course I didn't. I just said that you and I were curious about an old friend and he offered to see if he could get any information about him online. Is Jeremy gay, by the way? He's cute enough to be. And he's just so darn *sweet*. But I can't quite tell."

"Hold on a second," Ava said. "I'll ask him. Or maybe I'll just speculate on the phone about it really loudly so he can hear me."

"It's a perfectly reasonable question," Lauren said. "Don't get all huffy. I just thought the subject might have come up. He might have mentioned a boyfriend. Or a girlfriend. Either one would answer my question."

"Jeremy and I have a professional relationship, Lauren, which means I don't ask him questions about his personal life, and I don't expect him to hunt down men's addresses because my sister thinks I need a date."

"You should," Lauren said. "He's very good at it. He sent me all of Russell's contact info within a few hours."

"Did you tell him what it was for?"

"Not exactly. Anyway, forget that for now. I was calling to ask you something."

"What?"

"Would it be okay if I came to stay with you for a little while?"

Ava blinked a couple of times. Then she said, "Excuse me?"

"Hey, you're the one who keeps saying, 'Only losers live with their parents.'"

"What did Dad do this time?" Ava asked wearily. She settled against the back of her chair and crossed her legs.

"He won't stop lecturing me," Lauren said. "And not for the reasons you'd think. I mean, the guy should be lecturing me about finding a job and getting out of debt, right?"

"That's certainly why *I* would lecture you."

"I know! But guess what Dad's deal is. He thinks I should go to *dental hygienist school.* Seriously. Last night, I was trying to watch TV and he turns it off and says, 'I've been thinking. You're never going to be the kind of professional success your sister is—'"

"Oh, God," Ava said with loyal disgust, but deep down she felt a small rush of pleasure at hearing that her emotionally withholding father viewed her as the family success.

"It's not like it's the first time he's pointed out how much smarter you are than me. Anyway, then he says, 'So I've been thinking about it and you need to acquire some skills that will ultimately bring you in contact with the right kind of men. You'll never make money, so you better marry it.'"

"That's a little harsh."

"No kidding. Then he says, 'I've figured it out. You have nice thin fingers, so I think you'd make a decent dental hygienist. And dentists earn good money while working much more regular hours than doctors.' Which I guess means better husband material. Anyway, he even said he'd pay for the whole thing."

"That's kind of nice of him."

Lauren snorted. "Oh, please. Can you imagine me as a dental hygienist? Or even married to a dentist? Could the man know me any *less?* Anyway, you know how he is—if he gets an idea about something, that's it, that's the solution, nothing else will work.

He's figured out my future and he's damned if I'm going to mess up his plans by, say, finding another job as a clothing buyer and actually doing what I *like*. He's been researching dental schools on the Internet. I mean dental hygienist school—apparently I'm not smart enough to become an actual dentist." She paused. "Or maybe no girl is—I'm not sure if it's personal or sexist. Or which would be worse."

"Tell him you don't want to do it."

"I intend to," Lauren said, "but he's not going to take it well. That's why I need an escape route."

"So either I let you move in with me or you have to become a dental hygienist?" Ava said.

"Exactly."

"You do have those nice thin fingers."

"Yeah," Lauren said. "And they're just itching to do a dance inside some stranger's mouth." She shuddered audibly. "Ew."

"Ew," Ava agreed.

"So can I? Please?"

"Let me think for a sec." Ava chewed on the side of her thumb, trying to do the calculations in her head. Company in the evening might actually be nice. But Lauren could be messy. And it meant she'd have no privacy. But then again she had nothing to be private about. Out loud, she said, "You'd have to sleep on the living room sofa—I'm not sharing the bedroom."

Lauren squealed with delight. "Oh, thank you, A! This is going to be great."

"Hold on." Ava had thought of something else. "You can't move *all* your stuff in—I don't have room." The UPS truck had visited their parents' house and deposited so many boxes of clothing and accessories that Nancy had insisted Lauren move most of them to the garage without unpacking them. "Just take what you need. No, better yet—take what *I* would need under similar circumstances."

"How about we compromise somewhere in the middle?"

"It's a small apartment," Ava said.

"We'll be so cozy there."

Ava didn't answer.

Lauren moved in on Friday. When Ava got home from work that night, Lauren had a pan of brownies baking in the oven, and they agreed that brownies could count as dinner when topped with vanilla frozen yogurt, which, Ava pointed out, provided both calcium and protein.

They made up a bed for Lauren on the sofa and she curled up happily under a fleece blanket, claiming it was far more comfortable than any bed she had slept on in recent memory. Ava felt happy as she got ready for bed that night. It was nice to have someone to say good night to.

But a few hours later, when she was woken up by voices in the next room and groggily came out to investigate, only to find an instantly contrite Lauren watching TV—"Sorry, didn't realize it was too loud"—she felt a little less serene and optimistic about the whole arrangement and wondered instead how long it was likely to last.

The Braverman bat mitzvah started at ten the next morning. At nine-thirty Ava was showered and dressed and ready to go, but Lauren was only just getting out of the shower. As Lauren emerged from the apartment's only bathroom wrapped in one towel and drying her curly hair with another, she stopped at the sight of Ava and said, "*That's* what you're wearing?"

Ava looked down at her dress, which was green and belted and unstained, and said, "What's wrong with it?"

"It's a party, Ava. Don't you want to look a little more"—she searched for a moment—"like you're going to a party? Wear something that you wouldn't wear to work? Maybe put your hair up?"

"It's a party that everyone I work for or with will be at," Ava said. "It's basically a day of work with catered food and some dancing." She sorted through her small box of jewelry and extracted a pearl choker that her grandmother had passed down to her on her twenty-first birthday.

"But it's still an excuse to dress up and wow people." Lauren took her clothes into the bathroom but left the door open so Ava could hear her. "Why do you always dress like you're fifty years old?"

"I don't," Ava said, but she dropped the pearls back in the box with a slightly guilty start. "I dress like a lawyer. Anyway, I'm not like you. I don't think getting dressed up is fun. I think it's a pain."

"Come on," Lauren said. She emerged from the bathroom in a pair of blue and white striped boy-short underpants and an off-white lace-trimmed camisole. The two undergarments didn't match at all, but somehow they looked right together anyway. "You're a girl, aren't you? Every girl likes to get dressed up for a party."

"Not me," Ava said. "It's a chore. Like cleaning the bathroom."

"The problem is you don't *have* the kind of clothes that make getting dressed up fun," Lauren said. She pulled a dress off its hanger and tugged it over her head. It slipped right into place.

It was a dark blue that wasn't quite navy and it had a deep V-neck that showed off just the right amount of the lace trim on her camisole. She instantly looked smashing and very stylish. "Let me loan you something."

"It's 'lend.' 'Loan' is a noun."

"Miss English Major. Seriously, A, I have a dress that would look so great on you—" She started to sort through the hangers.

"No, thanks," Ava said. "I'm perfectly happy with how I look."

"Really?" Lauren said in a tone of utter disbelief. "Well, wait until you see this."

"Forget it. I don't have time to get changed, anyway. Hurry up."

Lauren crouched down and sorted through some shoeboxes she had stacked on the floor of Ava's closet, seized on one with a shout of joy, and extracted from it a pair of silver high-heeled sandals. "There you are, my beauties!" She jumped to her feet, clutching them to her chest.

"Please tell me you're not hugging your shoes," Ava said.

"I love these shoes."

"How can you love a pair of shoes?"

"Are you kidding me?" Lauren stopped in the act of pulling the shoes on to stare at her, balancing unsteadily on one leg. "I mean, are you insane?"

"Oh, *I'm* the insane one because I'm not having a love affair with my footwear?"

"It's so sad," Lauren said. She twisted her leg so she could prop one foot up on Ava's bed and do the strap. "There should be some sort of intervention for people like you—"

"People like *me?*" Ava said. "I'm not the one who's in debt because I can't say no to a pair of shiny sandals. Come on, Lauren, hurry up."

"Just let me put on some makeup and I'll be ready to go." She went into the bathroom and spent what felt like an eon to Ava brushing and smoothing and clinking while Ava paced outside the door, impatiently glancing at her watch. "Want me to do you?" Lauren called after a few minutes.

"No, I'm fine," said Ava. "I just want to get going."

"Almost done," Lauren said. When she emerged a few minutes later, she had arranged her hair in Pre-Raphaelite curls down her back, with just the front pieces pulled back and twisted together and then pinned so they merged with the rest. Her skin looked flawless, and her eyes were now smoky and dramatic. She did look very beautiful, and as Lauren checked her reflection one last time, Ava deliberately moved out of the mirror's sightline, knowing that a side-by-side comparison wasn't likely to increase her self-confidence as she headed off to try to be social.

⸎

"That was endless," Lauren said to Ava as they emerged from the temple sanctuary into the foyer at the end of the two-hour bat mitzvah service. "Would it be wrong to thank God that our family isn't religious?"

"Maybe not wrong," Ava said, "but certainly confusing."

"Ooh, this'll help." Lauren snagged two little Dixie cups off of the table where the rabbi had just blessed the wine. She handed one to Ava and took a sip, then made an awful face. "Oh, good Lord, it's *grape juice*." She put her cup back down on the table and hailed a waiter going by with a tray of filled wineglasses. "Is that the real thing?"

"Pinot Noir," he assured her.

"Hallelujah!"

"Hey, you *are* religious!" Ava said.

"What do you know—I've been born again." Lauren swiped two glasses off the tray and handed one to Ava. As she drank, she turned to study the crowded room. "So are you going to introduce me to people? Are there any cute guys at your firm?"

"Some." Ava leaned toward Lauren and lowered her voice. "There's this one guy who all the women think is gorgeous. Peter Rogers. He's over by the bar. Do you see him? He's wearing the red tie and talking to that bald guy."

Lauren casually sipped at her wineglass as she swiveled just enough to see the guy Ava meant by looking out of the corner of her eyes. "Oh, yeah," she said. "Totally hot. What's his story?"

"He's new," Ava said. "I don't know much about him."

"Have you spoken to him?"

"Yeah. I asked him to press the fourth-floor button on the elevator once. It was a real moment."

"Let's go," Lauren said, moving in his direction.

"Wait." Ava grabbed her by the arm. "You can't just go walking up to him for no reason."

"Sure I can." Lauren shook her off and kept moving.

Ava pursued her. "Seriously, Lauren, I have to face him every day and if you—"

"You really have to learn to relax," Lauren said and walked right up to Peter Rogers and the bald guy. "Hi!" she said brightly, and they returned the greeting with equal warmth. "So here's a question for you—"

"Yes?" the older man said with an expectant smile.

"I was reading the Bible back during the ceremony and now I'm doing a survey, trying to see how many people know the answer to a simple biblical question. Ready?" They nodded. "Okay. Today's question is 'Who slew Cain?'"

"Abel, of course," Peter Rogers said.

"Careful." The older man winked at Lauren. "You've got to

get up earlier in the day to trick *me*. No one slew Cain—Cain slew Abel."

"Oh, right," Peter said. "The mark of Cain."

"They *don't* have to get up early in the day to trick *you*," the other man said with a fond smile.

"Apparently not." He gave a good-natured shrug.

"Everyone falls for it," Lauren said. "Except for you." She nodded toward the bald guy, who smiled, pleased. "It's just this weird thing—you ask people who slew Abel and they'll say Cain, but if you ask them who slew Cain, they'll say Abel." She had read about that somewhere but hadn't remembered where—just one of those random interesting facts that had stuck in her memory. It wasn't the first time she had used it as a conversation starter.

"It's kind of sad for Abel," said Ava with a slightly nervous laugh. "Don't you think?"

"It's the curse of having siblings," Lauren said. "You're always judged by their behavior. She's my sister," she informed the men, gesturing at Ava.

"So I assumed," the older man said. "The resemblance is striking. Are you twins?"

They both shook their heads and Lauren said, "Nope, she's older."

"You're at the firm, right?" Peter said to Ava. "I know we've met, but I'm terrible with names. Please forgive me. I'm Peter."

"Nothing to forgive. I'm Ava. This is my sister, Lauren."

"And I'm Tom," the older man said.

"Are you at the firm too?" Lauren asked him.

"No," he said cheerfully. "Just here for the free drinks." Up close he was clearly younger than his balding head and slightly stooped shoulders made him appear from a distance—closer to forty than to fifty.

"He's here with me," Peter added, with a proudly defiant tilt to his chin.

"Ah," Lauren said with a nod and raised her glass to her lips— but not without first shooting a very quick, very surreptitious, and very amused look at Ava, who returned it with equal amusement and a sheepish shrug.

"Next time you ask a cute guy to push an elevator button for you, check out his sexual orientation first," Lauren said after Tom and Peter had left them to go in search of food. The trays of smoked salmon sandwiches and chicken sates followed a path that bypassed their corner, and the men were getting hungry.

"Yeah," Ava said. "I'll do that. 'Fourth floor, and are you gay or straight?'"

"That's rude," Lauren said. "You should say, 'Fourth floor, *please*. And are you gay or straight?'"

A waiter came by with a tray that had some empty glasses on it and told them it was time to find their table and sit down for lunch in the big hall.

"Hold on," Lauren said as the young man started to move away. "I need your advice."

"Yes?" He turned back, smiling with polite attentiveness. He wore the white button-down shirt and black pants of the classic server, but his hair was appealingly tousled and his pants had slipped down a bit on his slim hips—no belt. She wondered if he knew that one shirttail had slipped completely out of the waistband in the back. It lent a charmingly roguish look to his standard-issue uniform.

She held up her newly filled wineglass. "Do I hold on to this during lunch?"

"Here," he said and held his hand out. "Give it to me. There are glasses already on the table and the first thing we're supposed to do is pour the wine."

"It sounds risky," Lauren said, moving her glass out of his reach. "What if no one comes to our table for a long time and I get thirsty?"

"What table are you at?" he said. "Even if it's not mine, I'll come by right away with a bottle. What do you like—red or white?"

"Both," she said and surrendered the glass. "What's our table number, Ava?"

"Fourteen," said Ava, who had checked and pocketed the little folded name card with their table assignment when they first arrived.

"Fourteen," he repeated. "My name's Diego, by the way."

"I'm Lauren."

"See you soon, Lauren." He moved on, stopping to tell the next group of people that it was time to find their tables, and the sisters followed the mass exodus of guests out of the foyer and into the dining hall.

Ava introduced Lauren to everyone at their table. Lauren's place card put her between her sister and a slightly geeky-looking lawyer named Richard who chatted with her about L.A. versus New York for a while, and then the table conversation opened up to a general discussion about which of the last group of summer interns deserved to be offered permanent jobs at the firm. Lauren listened quietly, smothering a yawn or two. She felt a light touch on her shoulder and swiveled around to see Diego the waiter standing behind her, a bottle of wine in each hand. "You're not my table," he said. "So I'm breaking the rules for you."

"You're an angel." She held out her glass.

"You do a good impression of one yourself." He had the easy

charm of a natural flirt, and Lauren felt like she was finally in the presence of one of her own kind.

Richard glanced up and tapped his own glass with an index finger. "Red, please."

"Sorry," Diego said. "Your server will be with you in a minute." He winked at Lauren and walked away.

"That was weird," Richard said, frowning at Lauren's filled glass. "Why'd you get wine and not me?"

"Diego and I are old friends," she said. "He was just looking out for me."

"Ah." He seemed satisfied with the explanation and returned his attention to the group discussion. Ava was making a point—something about how a candidate's individuality had to mesh with the firm's reputation without being smothered by it—and Lauren was impressed by how all the others were listening to her with real respect. Then she got bored again.

She sipped some more wine and looked around. The party seemed too sedate to her, like something vital was missing. It occurred to her that none of the kids who'd been fidgeting their way through the service and dashing through the foyer during the reception were anywhere in sight. So where were they?

She excused herself from the table, then wove her way through the room and back toward the double doors. Before she had even left the hall, she could hear the throb of loud music. She followed the beat of the bass line across the foyer, down a back hallway, and into a room that was smaller than the big hall but big enough to hold five round tables, a dance floor, a DJ, an enormous sound system, and what appeared to be several dozen thirteen-year-olds, every single one in motion, some dancing to the lilting sound of Rihanna's voice, some filling plates at the long buffet tables that lined one wall and were covered with kid-friendly junk food like chicken nuggets, pizza, and fries, some jostling to get in line at any of the three booths set up in one corner, and some just running back and forth between the different areas, screaming and calling to one another.

The room was alive with music, smells, screams, raw emotion, and total chaos, the exact opposite of the calm and quiet hall she had just left.

Lauren spotted the bat mitzvah girl for the first time since the service. She was wearing a white knit beanie hat embroidered with a red devil and the phrase "2 hot 2B 4 real." She and half a dozen friends were giggling and squealing and pulling at one another, moving around the room like one big, sprawling, very noisy, and potentially dangerous organism.

Her beanie was fantastic. Lauren wondered if she could get one for herself.

She spotted the beanie table, which was sandwiched between a T-shirt printing stand and a tattoo booth. She got into line behind an extremely short boy with a huge head of long frizzy blond hair that stood out halolike around his thin face and large dark eyes. He was talking excitedly to a girl who was about a foot taller than he was and who kept shifting from leg to leg, always raising the opposite one, like a stork. Her very adult halter dress, developed figure, and dramatic makeup contrasted oddly and strikingly with the braces she wore and the juvenile quality of her voice.

"Did you see Oliver last time?" the boy was saying to her when Lauren stepped in place behind him. "Did you see him at Autumn's party? He was like totally insane. I mean totally. Did you see him?"

"I heard about it," the girl said. "But I didn't see it. I wish I'd seen it, but my mom made me go to Aspen that weekend with my dad and his girlfriend."

"You shoulda seen him," the boy said. "He was totally insane. I think he's gonna do something like that again today. I bet he is. He is always totally crazy."

"Someone should tell him to calm down," she said. "Did you hear what Dr. Cryer said to his parents? She said she was this close to throwing him out of the school."

"They won't throw him out of school," the boy said. "His dad is like the head of a studio or something. You know that thing they're building at school? The—you know—the thing that they're building upstairs that we can't use those stairs for because they're building it and there's like construction stuff and shit that could fall on us and our parents could sue if it did?"

"It's like a student center or something."

"Yeah, whatever. Oliver's parents like gave all the money for it. I mean, it's going to be *named* after his parents. I mean, it's going to have their *name* on it. They'll call it like the Lightlinger Center, you know? So they'd never throw him out."

The girl tugged hard on her lower lip. "I heard Dr. Cryer said they might."

"They won't," the boy said. "But he's so unbelievably insane. Did you hear he threw a book at a teacher?"

"I heard it was a pencil."

"A *pencil*? Who told you *that*? It was totally a book."

Lauren tapped the boy on the shoulder. "Hey," she said, straining to be heard over the loud music. "Is Oliver here? Which one is he?"

The boy turned. "This room is for the kids," he said, eyeing her suspiciously.

"You guys have all the good stuff," she said. "The adults don't get beanies, but I want one."

The guy working the table overheard enough to glance over. "They're only for the kids," he said.

"Come on," Lauren said and gave him her cutest smile. "Please? Just one little beanie? For me?"

He shook his head. "I can't. The parents only bought enough for the kids."

It was like the whole world was conspiring against Lauren Nickerson's acquiring anything new to wear. "Fine," she said, a little petulantly. She turned back to the short boy. "So are you going to tell me which one is Oliver or not?"

"That's Oliver," he said, pointing to a kid who stood in the middle of a semicircle of boys on the dance floor, all of them laughing and shoving one another, getting in the way of anyone who was actually trying to dance.

"The dark-haired one?"

"Yeah."

"He doesn't look so crazy."

The kid didn't reply because it was his turn to order. He seemed mildly outraged when the beanie guy said he wouldn't put the word "suck" on a hat. "What's wrong with 'suck'?" the boy was saying as Lauren left the line. "'Suck' is like a totally normal word. My *mother* says 'suck.'"

Lauren stopped to steal a chicken nugget on her way out, cutting through the line to grab one with her fingers, which none of the kids seemed to mind.

She left disappointed. She hadn't gotten a cute beanie and Oliver hadn't done anything while she was there to live up to his crazy reputation.

When she got back to her table, there were plates of chicken and rice in front of everyone. One of the male lawyers was leaning across the table toward Ava and saying, "I can name five female lawyers in our firm who left within the last three years because they wanted to stay home with their kids. I can't think of a single man who left for that reason. Why *shouldn't* that factor into our hiring decisions?"

"Because it's punishing future candidates for choices other people have made," Ava said. She nodded a greeting to Lauren as she slipped back into her seat. "And I've known far more women who *haven't* left the firm after having kids than ones who have."

"I'm talking odds. If a man and woman are up for the same job, the odds are simply better that the man will stay at the firm."

"If men were as willing as women to stay home when their kids got sick, then women wouldn't feel like they *have* to choose—"

"Aha," he said. "So you admit men and women feel differently about parenting responsibilities?"

"Of course," Ava said. "But the solution isn't to stop hiring women—it's to get fathers to do as much as mothers."

"Good luck with that," Richard's wife said, and everyone laughed. Someone else commented on the food and the general discussion devolved into private exchanges.

"I didn't know you were such a feminist type," Lauren said to Ava.

"It just drives me crazy." She picked up her knife and fork. "I want to bring more women to the firm, but there's this general perception that none of us will last past our baby-bearing years. It's another excuse to keep the old boys' club intact."

"Do you think *you'd* keep working such long hours if you had kids? Honestly?"

"I hope so." Then, sighing, "I don't know. I'd try to do more work in fewer hours, I guess."

"Could you imagine coming home after school and not having Mom there to ask us about our day?"

"You're not helping women's rights," Ava said. "I mean, it could be a father too, right?"

"It could be," Lauren said. "But I could never have told Dad all about how Susie Krasgow went around telling everyone I was wearing a bra in fifth grade when I wasn't. Know what I mean?"

"Well, *Dad*," Ava said. "But—"

"Hi, there," a voice said from behind them. They turned. Diego crouched down between their chairs, and they shifted apart to make room for him. "I brought you something." He reached for Lauren's hand, turned it palm up, and dropped a small chocolate heart into it. "They're for the kids, but I had a feeling you'd want one."

"That's so sweet of you," Lauren said. "I mean that literally."

"I got you one too," he said to Ava and dropped a heart next to her plate.

"Thanks," she said, but he had already turned back to Lauren.

"You having fun?" he asked her.

"It's okay. I won't mind when it's over."

"Me neither," he said. "It's been a long day."

"You have big plans for later tonight?" she asked.

"Nothing I can't get out of," he said, tilting his head back a little to study her. "You like to dance?"

"Love to."

"Good. Write your cell phone number down. I'll come by and get it before you leave." He stood up. "I got to go now. I'm supposed to be clearing." He stopped. "You want to come too?" he asked Ava. "I could get a friend—"

"Sorry," Ava said. "I can't. I have plans."

"What plans do you have?" Lauren asked Ava after Diego had walked away.

"The I-don't-like-to-go-dancing-with-strangers kind of plans. Guess that would be more of a state of mind, come to think of it."

"You should join us," Lauren said. "It'll be fun."

"You don't even know the guy."

"He's cute. He looks like he'd be a good dancer."

"He could be an idiot. Or a jerk. Or a homicidal maniac."

"Oh, please. If it's not fun, I'll say I have a headache and go home. And if he murders me, you get to have the apartment all to yourself again."

"Seriously," Ava said. "Don't go anywhere alone with him. Not even his car."

"Yes, Mom," Lauren said. She popped the chocolate heart in her mouth. Someone clinked the side of a glass, and Brian stood up and said it was time for them all to watch a video about Sarah. The kids were ushered in from the other room and seated on the dance floor while a movie screen was set up. The lights were dimmed and the video, an expertly produced collage of photos and home movies, began.

When it ended a seemingly eternal twelve minutes later, people clapped and the lights came back on and Brian announced that some of Sarah's friends wanted to say a few words. Two girls got up and squealed for a while about how *totally awesome* Sarah was.

Lauren was moving restlessly in her chair and wondering if they could go soon when a tall dark-haired boy rose to his feet and said, "*I* have something to say about Sarah." A couple of the girls screamed "NO!" and tried to drag him back into a sitting position, but he shook them off and shouted, "Sarah smells like a dog fart after a rainstorm!" The rest of the boys screamed with laughter while Sarah and her friends just screamed, and Brian hastily shooed the kids off the stage with the announcement that an ice-cream-sundae bar had been set up for them in the back room.

"What was that about?" Ava said as they turned their chairs back to the table, and the servers started frantically passing out individual crème brulées. "Who *was* that kid?"

"That was Oliver," Lauren said, leaning back in her chair, helpless with laughter and delight. "He's *crazy*."

⟨ ● ⟩

That night, genuinely concerned about Lauren's safety, Ava decided she should stay awake and alert until her sister was home again.

She kept her vigil in the living room, sipping tea and catching up on TiVoed shows. She accidentally dozed off somewhere around midnight and was woken up by the ringing of the phone. The caller ID showed Lauren's cell phone number, and Ava's heart surged with an adrenaline rush of fear. She pounced on the phone.

"Hi," Lauren said with a sheepish giggle. "I'm downstairs. I forgot my keys."

Torn between annoyance and relief, Ava buzzed her in. She went to the apartment door and opened it, crossing her arms and leaning against the doorway as she waited. After a minute or two, the elevator opened and Lauren emerged.

"Hi," Lauren said, running up to her. "Sorry about that. Did I wake you up?" They went into the apartment and closed the door.

"I hadn't gone to bed yet," Ava said, which was true since she had fallen asleep in the living room. "How was your date?"

"Okay." She scrunched up her nose. "But not good enough to go for a repeat. I was right about him being an actor. He's a little too into himself. Plus he smokes. I can usually smell it on a guy, but he's not allowed to smoke on the job, so his work clothes were clean."

"What'd you do?"

"We went dancing first. That was kind of fun—I was also right about him being a good dancer. I was right about everything." Lauren yawned. "But then we tried to go somewhere to get a bite to eat and talk and that's when I got kind of bored—not to mention freezing cold because we had to sit outside so he could smoke the whole time. I've got to remember that guys who are too pretty are almost always a mistake."

"Yeah," Ava said, although overly attractive young men had not really been a big problem in her life.

Lauren spotted the teacup on the coffee table. "Did you go out at all tonight?"

"No," Ava said. "I just watched TV."

Lauren's gaze was a mixture of incredulity and pity. "Is this what your Saturday nights are usually like?"

"No," Ava said. "I have friends, you know. I do stuff. I just thought the bat mitzvah was enough socializing for one day. And anyway," she added, "it's not like *you* had such a fantastic time going out."

"You're right," Lauren said. "You're right. I'd probably have had just as nice a time staying here with you." But once again there was pity in her voice, and Ava suspected that Lauren was only saying that to make her feel better.

Chapter 7

When Ava returned home from work the following Friday evening, she found the apartment door slightly ajar. She kicked it all the way open and entered with an irritable "Why don't you ever remember to lock the door?"

And there was Russell Markowitz standing in the living room, looking over his shoulder at her. "Oops," he said. "That would be my fault."

Lauren was nowhere in sight, but there was a half-empty bottle of Pinot Grigio on the coffee table (Ava recognized it as one given to her several months earlier by Brian Braverman after they had successfully completed a project together), along with two used glasses. So Russell had been there long enough to sit and have a glass of wine. Lauren might at least have put out three glasses, Ava thought: she knew Ava would be home soon.

Ava dropped her briefcase on the floor. "That's okay—guests are allowed to leave the door open. But Lauren always forgets to lock it." Lauren also had forgotten to mention that Russell was coming to their apartment that evening. "Oh, and hi."

"Hi, yourself," Russell said. Once again, he was wearing a

beautifully tailored suit, in black this time. He gestured toward a painting on the wall. "Where'd you get this?"

Ava came and stood next to him, studying the painting as if she'd never seen it before. It was easier than making eye contact. The dinner at the restaurant had embarrassed her so much that she doubted she'd ever be able to look Russell Markowitz in the eye. "From my grandmother," she said. "My mother's mother. I always liked it, and when she moved to a smaller apartment she gave it to me. I made her put something about it in her will so no one would contest it after she died." Russell gave her a funny look and Ava reddened. "Oh, God, that sounded really mercenary. And lawyerly. In a bad way."

"No, you're right to think about those things," he said, a little dubiously. "It's best to be cautious."

"I've just seen so many legal battles that could have been avoided by the right kind of paperwork," Ava said. "Better to spell things out clearly ahead of time with wills and prenuptials and all that than have a huge fight later."

"I don't like the idea of prenups," Russell said. "They start a marriage off with an assumption of failure. Completely undercuts that incredible moment when you realize the marriage *is* actually failing." He rocked back on his heels and grinned.

"Not everyone ends up divorced," Ava said.

He heaved an exaggerated sigh. "Ah, to be young and innocent again."

"Why'd you ask me about the painting?"

"There's one in our office that this reminded me of. I was checking to see if they were done by the same artist, and they were. This J. J. Wilers guy is really talented."

"Yeah," Ava said. "He's great. He's also a woman."

"Really? I thought—" He stopped and threw his hands up in a gesture of despair. "Now I'm going to get lectured at, aren't I?

How about I just admit I'm a sexist pig and we skip the lecture?"

"I wasn't going to lecture you," Ava said. "I assumed it was an honest mistake." She turned and moved over to the sofa. "Where's Lauren?"

"Getting changed." He followed her toward the sitting area. "Apparently I caught her in her 'hanging-out clothes' and she needed to put on her 'dinner clothes.' Those are her words, by the way, not mine." He looked down at the elegant suit he was wearing and said, "I'm stuck in my work clothes, I'm afraid. No time to change."

Ava sat down. "What line of work are you in again?"

"I work for a womenswear label," he said, and she could tell from his slightly injured tone that he must have said something about it at dinner the other night, but the truth was she remembered almost nothing from that conversation except that she wasn't really part of it and just wanted it to end so she could go home and hide.

"He's being modest," Lauren said from the threshold where she had suddenly appeared, looking fresh and pretty in a low-slung flouncy skirt and a short camisole top that revealed a flash of rounded hip between the top of the one and the bottom of the other. Ava stole a quick sideways glance at Russell and could tell that he liked what he was seeing. She certainly hadn't seen the same expression on his face when she had walked in. Of course, the gray shirt-dress she was wearing wasn't likely to inspire a second glance. Nor should it, she added quickly to herself: she didn't need to impress people with how she looked, just with how she thought.

Lauren said, "It's not just any label, Ava, it's Evoque Knits, and Russell doesn't just work there, he's the managing director."

"Wow. I'm impressed," Ava said. "Evoque's a pretty upscale

line. Even *I've* heard of it, and I'm not a fashion expert like my sister."

"You own any of our clothes?" Russell asked. He stuck his hands in his pockets and jangled his keys.

"I bought a skirt once," she said. "At Loehmann's, I think."

"Next time, pay retail. A guy's got to eat. Only one skirt, huh?"

"But one of my senior partners wears your suits all the time. They're more geared for older women, aren't they?"

"See?" he said, taking his hands out of his pockets to gesture with a sudden passion. "That's exactly the misconception I was hired to fix. We make beautiful knit clothing for women of all ages. Our fit is very flattering—"

"Stop right there," Lauren said, perching on the arm of the sofa. "You might as well just *say* you're going after the geriatric crowd. I'm surprised at you, Russell. You should know that women don't want to be told to buy clothing because it will make them look less fat. They want to buy a dress because it will make them look *hot.*"

"I'm well aware of how to market to the American female," Russell said. "Which is why we hired Carson Flite to be the new face of Evoque Knits."

"Oh, right," Lauren said. "I've seen the ads with her."

"She's the one who was in the Lady Jane movies, right?" Ava said.

"Yeah. She's the one with the enormous—" Lauren weighed imaginary cantaloupes in both hands. "And the skinny little legs and arms."

"Amazing how some women can have such big breasts and still be so skinny," Ava said. "It's such a common body type in L.A. And yet one rarely sees it in other parts of the world."

"Carson Flite claims they're real," Russell said.

"And what does your friend Corinne say about *hers?*" Lauren asked sweetly.

"Lauren!" Ava said.

Russell just shook his head. "I'm not going to touch that. So to speak. Anyway, our ad campaign with Carson is amazing. It's going to reinvent the company."

"Did the company need reinventing?" Ava asked.

"Companies are like people—they can grow stodgy and set in their ways if they're not challenged."

"The ads have been out for a while, haven't they?" Ava said. "How's the response?"

"It's only been a couple of months." He leaned back, crossed his legs at the ankles, then immediately uncrossed them and leaned forward again. "It's a big change—we're completely reinventing the company—"

"You already said that," Ava pointed out.

He looked momentarily taken aback, but then he regained his confidence. "Yeah, well, that's because it's true. You can't expect people to immediately accept change. It takes time."

"Why don't you just wait for most of your clientele to die off?" Lauren said. "Given your demographic, that wouldn't take all that long."

"See?" he said. "Jokes like that are why I'm—" He stopped.

"Reinventing the company?" Ava suggested, and he shot her a look.

"Getting back to Corinne," Lauren said. "Where is she this fine evening?"

"I have no idea," Russell said calmly.

"Should we be worried about the future of your relationship?"

"Lauren!" Ava said again, even more sharply.

Lauren shrugged. "What? I'm allowed to be curious."

"You guys are funny together," Russell said, looking back and forth between them. "You have a lot of the same mannerisms and you look so much alike. But then you're really different in a lot of ways."

"Yeah?" Lauren said. "How so?"

"Put him on the spot, why don't you?" Ava said, but she was just as curious.

Russell pointed at Lauren. "You're the troublemaker." Then he pointed at Ava. "You're the conscientious one."

"What do you think?" Lauren asked Ava. "Do we give him that one?"

"I'm okay with it if you are."

"What else?" Lauren asked Russell.

"You're fearless," he said to her, then hesitated, looking at Ava.

"You're saying I'm a wimp, aren't you?" Her outrage was exaggerated but not entirely feigned.

"No, not at all. You're just not out there in the same way. You're more careful. It's a good thing."

"You're a *little* wimpy," Lauren said to her. "I mean, you're so easily embarrassed."

"Thanks," Ava said. "You sure that doesn't have anything to do with how often you've deliberately embarrassed me in public?"

"Nah, you were born that way."

"Learn to fake confidence," Russell said to Ava. "No one really feels secure deep down—most of us just get good at faking it."

"*She* feels secure deep down," Ava said, pointing at her sister.

Lauren put her hand on her stomach. "No, I think that's hunger. Can we go eat soon?"

"Sounds good to me," Russell said. "You guys want to pick a place?"

"Angela's?" Lauren said.

Ava shook her head. Angela's was a small, old-fashioned Italian joint that had been around for decades, nothing like the restaurant where they'd met Russell. "That's not going to be hip enough for him."

"I don't need hip," Russell said. "I think you guys have the wrong idea about me. I'm actually a pretty down-to-earth guy."

There was a beat. The two girls looked at each other and, at the exact same moment, with the same tossing back of their heads, they let out identical bleats of laughter.

Russell flushed and fidgeted. "Wow," he said. "You guys really are destroying me bit by bit tonight."

"Oh dear, are you losing your self-confidence?" Ava said. "Learn to fake it. Some people are very good at that, you know."

"Deep down, we're all insecure," Lauren added.

"Jesus," he said. "You girls are evil. Do you always gang up on your guests?"

"No," Lauren said, blowing a kiss at him. "Just you."

Lauren was in her element, making many lighthearted and flirtatious demands as they all studied the menu at the recently opened Indian restaurant they ultimately settled on. She declared that she didn't like vegetables but was willing to allow Russell one serving of something green so long as it didn't interfere with the three chicken dishes she wanted; she insisted that the others share a bottle of wine with her, even though Russell had already said he usually drank beer with Indian food; she preferred Russell's seat, which faced out, to the one she first sat in, and made him switch places with her. And so on.

Russell seemed amused by her demands. He teasingly told

her she was spoiled and then willingly catered to her every whim with the good-natured indulgence of a weekend father taking the daughter he rarely saw on a special outing.

"She was like this when she was little, too, wasn't she?" he asked Ava after he and Lauren had settled into their new seats, which now put him right across from Ava rather than next to her.

"Absolutely," Ava said. "She always got what she wanted. Still does."

"Typical female," Russell said fondly.

"If you want something, go after it," Lauren said. "That's my motto."

"I admire that," Russell said. "You and I will get along fine." To Ava: "You, I'm not so sure about."

"Why?" she said, a little too fiercely. "Because I'm wimpy and overly conscientious?"

"No," he said. "Because we're getting married. That never ends well for me."

Lauren laughed and stood up. "I have to go to the ladies' room. I'll be right back." She strode off, her flouncy skirt swirling cheerfully around her legs with each energetic step.

Russell gestured toward her retreating back. "Don't you want to go with her?"

"She's twenty-six years old," Ava said, taking a sip of wine. "I'm fairly certain she's mastered the more challenging aspects of going potty all by herself."

"Then why'd you feel the need to run after her when she went to the restroom the other night at the restaurant?" he said. "I saw you chase her down and then you both came back ready to leave. You had obviously gone there to talk—admit it."

"So?"

"So you shouldn't have gotten all sarcastic when I asked you if you wanted to go with her. Right?"

"I guess," she said.

The waiter came to their table and put down a basket of naan.

Ava said "I'm starving" and grabbed a piece, bit into it.

"Look at you go," Russell said, watching her. "Bet you don't eat like that when you're alone."

Ava blinked at him over the top of the naan. "Excuse me?"

"It's just something I've noticed," he said. "Women think men like it if they eat and drink like sailors on shore leave, so when you're with us, you all act like you just love love love to eat and never count calories or think about carbs or fats or any of that—and then you starve yourselves and exercise like maniacs in private so you can pull off all that eating when we're together and still look good."

"I eat the same amount no matter who I'm with." Although, having said that, Ava felt uneasily like maybe it wasn't *entirely* true. And hadn't an older cousin once lectured her and Lauren on the importance of skipping lunch on the day of a big date?

"My first wife got fat the second we were married," Russell said. "She kept up with my eating, but once we were spending all our time together she stopped doing whatever she'd been doing to control her weight when she was alone—"

"Throwing up?" Ava suggested sarcastically.

"Exercising," he said, not amused. "I like a girl with a hearty appetite, but she needs to balance that with some common sense."

"And so you divorced her? Because she gained a few pounds?"

"She gained more than a few," Russell said. "But that wasn't why I divorced her."

"Why, then? She put her lipstick on crooked one day?"

"She wasn't the person she was pretending to be," Russell

said. "Same thing happened with my second wife, only worse. They both acted a certain way when we were dating and then it all changed once they felt they had landed me." He sighed. "I've had some really bad luck."

"It's bad luck if it happens *once*. Did you ever think maybe you like the wrong kind of women?"

Lauren came back to the table and slipped into her chair. "What'd I miss?"

"'The wrong kind'?" Russell repeated, ignoring her. "There isn't a right or wrong kind. There are just women. And women will do whatever they can to land a man, especially one they think is rich and successful. They'll sell him a bill of goods—how they don't care about material things and they love to eat a big burger and fries and drink beer and there's nothing they'd rather do than go down to the gym and watch him work out for a while . . . and then they get that ring on their finger and suddenly they're spending all his money on really ugly jewelry and demanding mediocre but expensive restaurants for dinner every night and refusing to let him even see his buddies because they'd much rather spend Saturday night with *their* friends and their weasely little husbands." He plucked a piece of naan out of the basket and waved it at them. "It's the way of the world, girls. Women trick guys into marrying them because you're smarter than we are. And then we either have to give in and accept the fact we're married to someone who's deliberately deceived us or agree to pay her and her money-grubbing lawyers huge sums to get set free. That's just how it is. It's not pretty but it's true." He took a big, savage bite out of the bread and chewed it ferociously.

"Geez." Lauren turned to Ava. "Has he been like this the whole time I was in the ladies' room?"

"Yeah, pretty much."

"What?" he said, his voice thick with the bread in his mouth.

"It's true, isn't it?" He swallowed with an audible gulp, then thumped his chest a couple of times like something was stuck there.

"Sorry," Lauren said. "You lost me somewhere around the 'all women are evil liars' argument."

"Well, not *all* women," he said. "Present company excluded, of course."

The sisters shot him identical looks of disbelief. "Thanks for that," Ava said. "Personally, I find wavy-haired, overexercised, handsome young managing directors of womenswear lines to be wildly misogynistic." She waited a beat. "Present company excluded, of course."

"Cool," Russell said with a weak smile. "You think I'm handsome."

"Food's here!" Lauren sang out as the waitress arrived, and they all threw themselves on the curries and tandoori dishes with a relief that may have stemmed from hunger on Lauren's part but definitely came from desperation on Ava's.

Lauren worked hard to keep the conversation moving along with cheerful comments about the food, the restaurant, L.A., and movies she'd seen recently. Russell responded in kind, but Ava only contributed to the conversation when Lauren directly addressed her with a question or an invitation to contribute an anecdote, and even then she answered briefly and made no effort to be amusing. It drove Lauren nuts. It was like the night they met Russell in the restaurant all over again: Ava could be so funny and sharp when they were alone together or with good friends, but she could also clam up like this in social situations and become deadweight.

Lauren maneuvered her into the front seat for the ride back to her apartment in the hopes it would force her to be more outgoing, but Ava just stared out the windshield like she was half asleep, so Lauren leaned forward as far as her seat belt would allow, rested her elbow next to Russell's headrest, and kept the conversation going with tales of harrowing taxicab rides she had endured back in New York.

As they arrived at their building, Lauren asked Russell if he'd like to come up for a cup of coffee.

"I'd love to," Russell said. "But I have to get up early tomorrow—my trainer's coming at seven."

"I had a feeling you had a trainer," Lauren said.

"She only comes twice a week," he said, a little defensively. "The rest of the time, I exercise on my own."

"Your trainer's a woman?"

"Yeah." He flashed an unashamedly lecherous grin. "She's gorgeous too. It's very inspirational having someone with a body like hers run ahead of you. Gives you all sorts of reasons to catch up."

"Does she know you think that way?" Ava said.

"Of course. She doesn't wear teeny-tiny sports tops for no reason, you know." He tapped on the steering wheel. "Anyway, I've been shortchanging myself on sleep all week, so I'm ready to collapse, but I'll happily take a rain check if you're offering one."

"Absolutely," Lauren said.

"I'll call you." He glanced over at Ava to include her in the "you."

She didn't acknowledge it, just said a quick good night and slid out of the car. Lauren leaned forward to give Russell an air kiss near his cheek and said, "Talk to you soon," before getting out of the car.

Ava was already halfway across the lobby by the time Lauren caught up to her.

"That was fun," Lauren said, falling into step with her. "I hope when you guys are married you'll let me hang out with you a lot."

"Would you really wish that guy on me? On anyone you liked?"

"Sure. Why not?" The doors opened and they stepped in. Lauren immediately reached over to punch the floor button— she always tried to do it before anyone else. "What's your problem with Russell? He's a good guy."

"So all that stuff about how a woman will lie and cheat to get a man to marry her—that didn't bother you at all?"

Lauren thought for a moment, pulling her bottom lip into her mouth with her top teeth. Then she said, "That stuff was stupid. But it didn't make me mad at him. It felt less like he was a jerk and more like he was . . ." She thought again and said, "Damaged. He feels a little damaged to me. Not beyond repair, but like he's been messed up in the past. He hides it with all the jokes and stuff, but it comes out when he talks about women."

The elevator doors opened and they got out. "Yeah," Ava said as they walked in synchrony down the hall, their heels making quiet scuffing sounds on the gray and blue carpet. "I know what you mean. He probably *has* known some awful women in his time. But I blame him for at least part of that. He seems like the kind of guy who goes for looks. I mean, his job is all about clothes. And he has a trainer. And look at Corinne."

"Yeah, she's a mistake, no question."

"Exactly. You know, I've seen this before." Ava groped in her purse for her key.

"What?"

"Men who are like this. Women too. They have a certain

view of the opposite sex—a negative one—and then just keep confirming it by choosing people who fit that mold. They get what they expect to get. Oh, here it is." She pulled the key out and unlocked the door. She held it open for Lauren and followed her inside. "Like my friend Lisa. She always fell in love with guys who'd sleep with her and never call again. She would complain and complain that men were horrible and self-centered and cruel—and then she'd fall in love with another horrible, self-centered, cruel guy." She let the door swing shut behind them. "It was like she couldn't even *see* the good guys out there because they didn't fit her description of what makes a man a man."

"Yeah, I know what you mean," Lauren said. "And Russell might be a little like that—but all the more reason he *needs* to spend time with someone nice like you so he can learn the difference."

"Ah," Ava said. "My purpose in life is finally clear: I was put on this earth to teach Russell Markowitz to trust women."

"You do think he's cute, don't you?"

"Sure," Ava said with a shrug. "But I haven't had a man in my life for so long, *everyone* looks good to me. The UPS guy who comes to the office sets my heart a-pumping."

"UPS guys," Lauren said with a sigh. "I've never dated one. Flirted with a lot. Never dated. It's a goal of mine."

"It's good to have goals," Ava said with a gigantic yawn.

Two days later, when Ava and Lauren arrived at the house to have Sunday brunch with their parents, they found their mother still in bed, even though it was past ten and she was usually up by seven every morning. She raised her hand as they came in and then let it drop back down. Ava felt a little pang at seeing her usually energetic mother so listless.

A hoarse choking sound coming from the bathroom interrupted their greetings.

"What is that noise?" Lauren said, looking over. "Is that Dad?"

"Is he okay?" Ava asked as another loud cough echoed through the room. "Should we go check on him?"

"He's fine," Nancy said, unconcerned. "He's doing it on purpose. He read an article saying that if you think you might be having a heart attack, you can keep your heart going by coughing deeply at certain intervals—"

"Wait," said Ava. "Does Dad think he's having a heart attack?"

"No," Nancy said. "Of course not. But he decided that he should do it preventively. So every day—well, it's only been two days now—but anyway, he's been making a habit of going into the bathroom and coughing repeatedly in the morning."

"Does it work like that?" Ava asked.

Nancy sighed. "I seriously doubt it."

"He's insane," Lauren said. "We are all aware of that, right? I mean, it's a given that our father is certifiable?" There was another loud cough and the three women all looked at one another and then burst out laughing.

"He'll be done soon," Nancy said with the tolerant shrug of someone used to letting things run their course.

Ava sat down on the bed. Nancy turned to smile at her. There were dark purple shadows under her eyes.

"You okay?" Ava said. "Dad told me you threw up last night."

"It's just the chemo. No big deal."

Lauren said, "I thought the doctor said it wouldn't make you sick."

"He said it *probably* wouldn't." She moved her legs restlessly under the blanket. "I beat the odds."

Ava looked at Lauren. "Maybe one of us should call him, just to make sure it's normal."

"You don't need to call anybody," Nancy said, an edge to her voice. "I'm fully capable of monitoring my own health."

"I know," Ava said. "I'm sorry. I just worry."

"Well, don't. I'm fine."

Jimmy emerged from the bathroom, massaging his throat with his fingertips. "Anyone want to come with me to get bagels?" he said, a little hoarsely.

"I will," Lauren said. "Can we get some lox too?"

"I already took care of that. I went to Whole Foods last night."

"Really?" Ava said, surprised. "You went food shopping? All by yourself? That's not like you."

"I'm learning," he said. "I have to learn how to do these things. That's just the way it is."

Lauren linked her arm in Jimmy's. She was far more comfortable being physically affectionate with him than Ava was, and he tolerated her caresses with the not entirely displeased resignation of a family dog whose tail is pulled by its toddler owner and who knows he could make it all stop with one ferocious snap if he wanted to. "Don't forget to listen for the doorbell while we're gone," Lauren said as they headed toward the door. "Russell should be here soon."

"Who?" Ava said.

"I invited Russell Markowitz to join us," Lauren said as she and Jimmy left the room.

"Why did she invite *him*?" Ava said with mild horror. "Mom, if you're too tired to have company, I can make her call him back and—"

"No, it's okay," Nancy said. "I told her I wanted to see Russell again. I found him very appealing as a kid."

"Really? Why?"

"I don't know." Nancy hiked herself up into a sitting position. "I just liked the way he looked. He was a very clean boy. Very neat. His shirt was always tucked in. Sometimes he wore a belt." She smiled. "He even wore a bow tie to our house once for no reason."

"He's still a pretty clean guy," Ava said. "Wears nice suits and always looks very put together. Is that why you wanted me to marry him? Because he was so *clean*?"

Nancy pushed the covers back. "I think it was more because you were both so smart. His mother and I used to compete in bragging about you two and how well you did in school."

"Were you proud of me, Mom?" She knew she was fishing for a compliment, but her mother came through anyway, with a firm "Always."

Ava tried to repress the delight her mother's praise still gave her. She was a grown woman, after all. "So did you betroth Lauren to anyone?"

"Not that I remember."

Ava gave her a comical look of distress. "You thought *I* needed the help, didn't you? That I wouldn't be able to find a husband on my own? You weren't worried about Lauren, but with *me*—"

Her mother laughed. "Ava, you were something like seven years old. Trust me when I say that I wasn't all that worried yet about your marital status."

"Yeah, well maybe you should have been." She was joking, but Nancy took her seriously.

"I know it must be so hard to meet someone when you work the kind of hours you do . . ."

"I was just joking," Ava said. "Really. I'm fine."

"I could ask my friends if they know anyone."

"Don't you dare," Ava said with genuine panic. "I don't need your friends to start setting me up with their sons. I'm perfectly happy with my social life."

Her mother was following her own thoughts. "I could call Sylvia Alberts—she told me her nephew just got divorced and is moving to—"

"Stop that right now," Ava said. "I mean it, Mom. Stop it or I'll call your doctor and tell him how worried I am that you vomited last night."

"Fine." Nancy held her hands up in surrender. "No phone calls. Neither of us. But I still get to worry if I want to."

Ava rested the back of her hand briefly against her mother's cheek. "So do I."

◦◦◦

"Phew," Russell said when Ava answered the front door in response to his knock. "This *is* the right house. I wasn't sure." He kissed her on both cheeks in the European way, shifting the paper bag and bouquet of flowers he was holding to the side so he could get at her.

"Did you have trouble finding it?" Ava asked as she ushered him in.

"Only because your sister gave me an address that doesn't exist." He wore khakis and a dark blue sports coat over a crisp white oxford shirt that was unbuttoned at the neck. It bothered Ava that he had put effort into looking good on a Sunday morning, a time made for being comfortable and casual, but there was a tiny part of her that also thought he looked kind of cute. "The GPS system got very testy with me when I tried to enter it. I tried calling, but her cell phone wasn't on. And," he added with a slightly accusing tone, "I don't have *your* number."

"Never trust Lauren with things like phone numbers or addresses," Ava said. She gave the door a shove and it swung shut. "She thinks she remembers them correctly, but she never does. The downside of overconfidence."

"Now you tell me. Fortunately, she was only off by one digit and the house looked vaguely familiar." He handed her the flowers. "These are for your mother."

"How nice." It was an impressive bouquet—big fancy flowers like orchids and tiger lilies all draping over one another in an extravagant arrangement. She cuddled the flowers against her chest like a baby. "They smell wonderful. My mom will love these. She'll be down in a second."

"Where is Lauren, anyway?"

Ava let the flowers sag lower in her arms. It hadn't taken Russell long to start looking around for better company. "She'll be back any minute. She and Dad ran out to buy bagels."

"What?" He stared at her like she was nuts. "You're kidding me."

"Why would I be kidding?"

"Because Lauren told *me* to pick up bagels." He shook the bag he was holding. "I got three dozen."

"Three dozen?" Ava said. "That's a lot of bagels."

"I didn't know how many people were coming—didn't want to run short."

She flicked the edge of the bag. "No danger of that."

"Is Lauren always this flaky about things?"

"Only about things that don't matter," Ava said. "She's dependable when she needs to be."

"Is that true, or are you just being a loyal sister?"

"I don't know. She's just Lauren."

Nancy came down the stairs. "Russell!" she exclaimed with what appeared to be genuine delight as she joined them and gave him a big hug. "Look at you! You're a man now."

"Not even a young one," he said with a laugh.

"Young enough," she said and stepped back. "I mean, if *you're* not young, where does that leave me?"

"He brought you flowers," Ava said, rescuing him from answering. "Look."

"Oh, they're beautiful," Nancy said. "Thank you, Russell. You didn't need to, but they're lovely."

"He also brought bagels," Ava said. "And he *really* didn't need to do that, since Lauren and Dad are out getting some right at this moment."

"Lauren told me to," Russell said. "I swear."

"Oh, I believe you," Nancy said. "She's like me—completely disorganized. Go put the bagels and flowers in the kitchen, Ava. Russell, come with me." As she watched them leave the foyer, Ava saw Russell look down at her mother—he was much taller— and pat the hand that was on his arm with a warm smile that Nancy didn't even see but which made Ava suddenly like him more than before.

By the time she'd arranged the flowers in a vase (badly—she just shoved them in there with the elastic still holding the stems together) and rejoined them, Nancy had apparently already caught up on what Russell was doing and was moving on to the rest of his family.

"And Jonah? What about him?" she was saying as Ava sat down on the living room sofa next to her. "What does he do?"

"He's a guidance counselor at a high school in upstate New York."

"Good for him! It must be challenging, with kids bringing guns to school these days and selling drugs and all—"

Russell laughed. "He's a counselor at a small private prep school. I think his biggest problem is keeping the kids—and their parents—from freaking out when Harvard e-mails their rejections."

"Is he married?"

"Yes, to his college girlfriend. They've been together over a decade, which seems incredible to me."

"No wonder," Ava said. "I mean, only one marriage in all those years? What's wrong with the guy?"

He shot her a look. "I just meant that we're getting old."

Nancy touched him lightly on the arm. "I heard that your father remarried. Did your mother ever—?"

"No," he said. "She's much too busy being miserable to make time for an actual relationship."

"Do you like your father's new wife?"

He shrugged. "He seems happy."

"I'm glad," Nancy said. "People should be happy."

"Really going out on a limb there, Mom, aren't you?" Ava said. "You sure you want to take such a controversial position?"

"Oh, shush," Nancy said.

Russell said, "I don't know if I'm supposed to mention your health or not . . ." He looked at Ava, who looked at Nancy, who waved her hand.

"It's fine," she said. "*I'm* fine. I'm doing chemo right now, which isn't as much fun as they'd have you believe. But once that's done, I'll be as good as new."

"Better, if Lauren has her way," Ava said. "Lauren wants her to get new breasts," she told Russell. "Despite the fact she still has her old ones."

"Lauren thinks everyone should have new breasts," Nancy said.

"She's like the breast fairy," Ava said. "She wants to flit about the country giving beautiful new breasts to all the good little girls and boys."

"Really?" Russell said. "Boys too?"

"Maybe not them so much."

"And yet she disparaged Carson Flite's fake breasts," Russell said. "Oops—allegedly fake breasts, I mean. Anyway, I sense a discrepancy here. Might your sister be a tiny bit inconsistent in her views?"

"She might," Ava said.

"Just like every woman I've ever met," Russell said.

"Present company excluded?" Ava said, but she was teasing this time, not angry. The truth was, she was enjoying Russell's company. Somehow having her mother as the third rather than Lauren made a difference. For once, she didn't feel like she was losing a competition she hadn't entered in the first place.

"You took the words right out of my mouth," he said as the front door banged open.

"We're home!" Lauren called from the hallway. "We have fresh hot bagels!"

"So do we!" Ava called back, trying to ignore the strange pang of disappointment she felt at hearing her sister's voice. "We had a visit from the bagel fairy!"

"Do you have to call me that?" Russell said. "It makes me feel unmanly."

"I have a fairy thing," Ava said.

"I've noticed."

"It's not like I like them. Actually, they scare me, with their little wings and all."

Russell started to respond, but was interrupted by Lauren's sticking her head into the living room. "What do you mean, we already have bagels?" she said.

"You told me to bring some." Russell rose to his feet.

"Did I?" she said. Then: "Oh, right. I did. Where are yours from?"

"New York Bagel."

"Oh, good." She came into the room and gave him a friendly peck on the cheek. "Ours are from Noah's. We can do a taste test." She turned to her sister. "Hey, A, can you help Dad make the coffee? He asked me but I don't know how."

"How can you not know how to make coffee?"

"Duh," Lauren said. "Starbucks? Ever heard of it?"

"Yeah, I've heard of it," Ava said. "They charge like four bucks for a cup of coffee. That's another habit you need to break."

"Dad's waiting for you," Lauren said, and Ava got up and left the room. It wasn't like anyone needed her to make conversation now that Lauren was there and already chattering away about how ruthless the old ladies at the bagel place were about cutting the line.

She found her father standing by the kitchen counter. "Something's wrong with this machine," he said without looking up. He was punching at the button on the coffeemaker with short, angry jabs. "I keep trying to start it, but nothing."

"It's not plugged in," Ava said. She plugged it in and Jimmy pressed the start button again. The machine immediately started making brewing noises.

Jimmy said, "Why the hell wasn't it plugged in?"

"I have no idea. *I* didn't unplug it."

"Everything's falling apart around here," he said, putting the container of coffee back in the freezer and closing the door with an unnecessarily loud slam. "It's because your mother's not feeling well." Jimmy was built like a beanpole and was almost a foot taller than Ava and Lauren, who took after their petite mother, but today he suddenly seemed smaller to Ava, a little hunched over and shrunken around the neck and shoulders.

Ava thought maybe she should hug him, but they had never

hugged much. He wasn't that kind of father. So she twisted her fingers together and just said, "I hate that she's sick."

"She'll be fine," he said brusquely. "That's what matters. Get the orange juice out of the fridge, will you?"

They carried the food out to the dining room, where Jimmy instantly transformed into what teenage Lauren used to call "Social Daddy!" (and occasionally "SD" for short), smiling and clapping Russell on his shoulder and heartily welcoming him to his house. It amazed Ava how her father could turn it on like that, could suddenly become this cheerful, outgoing guy who charmed everyone he met. He wasn't like that when he was alone with the family: then he was moody, prone to quiet depressions and unpredictable irritability—and equally unpredictable bursts of kindness and generosity. Her mother, though, was pretty much always the same whoever was around.

"Those are some muscles you've got there," Jimmy said to Russell as they all sat down. "You work out?"

"He has a trainer," Ava said. "The kind who comes to your house."

"It's no big deal," Russell said quickly. "I'd go to the gym if I had time, but it's more efficient to have her just come to me—"

"It's an efficiency thing," Ava agreed. "Really, it's not self-indulgent at all."

"Hey, hey," he said. "Give a guy a break."

Nancy said, "I think it's great. If I had the time and money, I would have a personal trainer. And a masseuse."

"Do *you* have a masseuse?" Ava asked Russell.

"I don't keep one in my house, if that's what you mean." He picked up a knife and spread the cream cheese a little more evenly on his bagel. "But if the opportunity offers itself, sure, I'll have a massage."

"Who wouldn't?" Nancy said.

"You want one, Mom?" Ava said with sudden inspiration. "I

hadn't even thought about that. It might really relax you, help you sleep. We could arrange for someone to come here. My treat."

"You want me to call the woman I use?" Russell asked. He leaned back a bit and pulled his cell phone out of his hip pocket. "I've got her number right here."

"I don't know." Nancy looked uncertainly at Jimmy, who was putting lox on his bagel and didn't seem to notice.

"So you *do* have a masseuse!" Ava said to Russell. "And you keep her number in your cell phone? Is that in case of a sudden muscle spasm emergency?"

"I put every number I get in my cell phone," he said. "Lauren's number is in here. My travel agent is in here. The crazy guy I met at Starbucks who told me he's starting an Internet company—his number is in here, although I admit I meant to delete that one as soon as I escaped from him, but I forgot." He pointed at Ava accusingly. "*Your* number would be in here if you were ever to give it to me." He turned to Nancy. "So what time is good for you? You want to do it today? I could see if Summer Rain has any spots open this afternoon."

"'Summer Rain'?" Lauren repeated, her eyebrows soaring up.

"Hippie parents."

"It feels way too indulgent," Nancy said, still looking at Jimmy, who just took a bite of his bagel. "I don't know if I should do it."

"I mean it, Mom—I want it to be my treat," Ava said.

"Mine too," Lauren said.

"Oh, are you chipping in?" Ava said. "And the money for your part will be coming from—?"

"Shut up. I have enough for this—how much could it be? Seventy, eighty bucks? Split in half?"

"Um," Russell said. "She's a little more than that. A little more than twice that actually. But she gives you way over an hour and comes to your house, and she's really good. If you just give me a time frame—"

"I shouldn't," Nancy said. "It's too expensive. It's a lovely thought, but—"

"I want you to do it, Mom," Ava said. "Make the call, Russell."

"Yes, but *what time?*" he said.

"Jimmy—?" Nancy said.

Jimmy looked up from his bagel. "Do it," he said. "You deserve something relaxing like that with all you're going through. And I can afford it—the girls don't need to treat you." Ava started to protest, but he shook his head at her and she closed her mouth. "Any time after four this afternoon," he said to Russell. Then, to Nancy again, "That'll give you time to take a nap after brunch."

"All right," Russell said. "I'm making the call." He pressed a couple of buttons on his phone, then got up and went into the next room to talk. He returned in a minute, snapping the phone shut. "Done," he said. "She'll be here at five."

"Wonderful," Nancy said, beaming. "Thank you."

Russell slid his phone back into his pants pocket and sat down. "You'll love Summer," he said. "She's incredible."

"I know why he likes Summer," Lauren said.

"Why?" asked Ava.

"Because Summer is *hot!*" Lauren said with glee, and the others groaned in chorus.

On the drive back to the apartment, Lauren said, "See? Russell's a good guy."

"He's okay," Ava said quietly.

"The more time we spend with him, the more I like him.

That's a good sign. I think if you and he spent some quality time alone together—"

"I'm not his type."

"Did you notice he didn't even mention Corinne? I think she's out of the picture."

"Why don't *you* go out with him?" Ava said. "You guys are perfect for each other."

"I'm only interested in him for you," Lauren said.

"It's not going to happen," Ava said. "I'm not flashy enough for him. And I'm not sure I want it to," she added quickly.

Lauren was silent for a moment. Then she said, more to herself than to Ava, "I just need to get you guys to spend some time alone together."

"You don't need to *do* anything," Ava said. "Unless you want to date him yourself."

Lauren was studying Ava's face. "Would you let me do your hair and makeup the next time we see him? And pick out something for you to wear? I could make you look so great—"

"First of all," Ava said, "I think I look fine the way I am. Second of all, I don't want a guy who cares about how I dress and do my hair."

"What's wrong with you?" Lauren said. "I've never even seen you go shopping for clothes just for fun. Or fool around with different hairdos. Or put on makeup. Or buy shoes that look pretty but hurt your feet and it's worth it because it just *is*. Or—"

"Clothing should keep you clean and covered and presentable," Ava said. "All the rest is just fluff and expense and bother."

"And walls should keep the rain out," Lauren said. "All that art stuff people put on them is just fluff and expense and bother."

"That's different," Ava said.

"It's not."

Ava felt sure she was right, but not at all sure of the argument she could make to prove it, so she switched to a different point. "I'm not going to change myself to get a guy. I want to be appreciated for who I am."

"Yeah?" Lauren said. "Why don't you just grow a mustache and stop shaving your legs while you're at it? Any guy who falls in love with you then will be *really* great. Or blind." She snickered.

"I believe in being *hygienic*," Ava said. "That's a different issue."

"Oh, you're just making up distinctions now. It all falls on a sliding scale of trying to make yourself look good. Why not just slide a little further up the chain?"

"First of all, you're mixing metaphors like crazy. Second of all"—Ava pointed out the window—"it looks like the new Pinkberry is finally open. Should we get some?" Lauren assented enthusiastically, and pretty soon the girls were plunging into large scoops of frozen yogurt covered with fresh strawberries, their conversation forgotten.

That night, Ava clipped her shoulder-length hair out of the way to wash her face, then stopped and looked at herself. Feeling a little silly, she removed the hairclip, then experimented with pulling her hair back into a twist and clipping it into some semblance of an updo. It fell out immediately, so she tried pulling just the front pieces of hair back, the way Lauren often did, but no matter how she played with the different bits of hair or repositioned the clip, it always looked uneven and a little silly to her. She finally just pulled it severely back and out of the way again and scrubbed her face clean.

Chapter 8

Nancy met Lauren at the front door, purse already in hand, sunglasses pushed up on her head. "Let's go," she said by way of greeting.

"Am I late?" Lauren asked. It was Tuesday and she was picking her mother up for chemo.

"By most people's standards, yes," Nancy said.

"Time is relative, right?"

Nancy wasn't amused. "It tends to be fairly constant when you're talking about hospital appointments. We'll be okay so long as we leave right away and traffic isn't terrible."

"It's not great," Lauren said, having been stuck in it on the drive there. Nancy was letting her use her car so long as she made herself available to run errands on demand.

They headed down the uneven walkway and she had to resist the urge to reach out and support her mother's arm; she suspected that Nancy would only resent the attempt. "How are you feeling?"

"Better," Nancy said. "Really fine, at the moment. Just in time to feel worse again. That's the hardest part about going—knowing it will make me feel sick tomorrow."

"But ultimately it will make you better."

"One hopes."

Her mother's gloomy mood made Lauren feel guilty about the fact that she was kind of looking forward to going to the hospital. Looking forward to seeing Daniel again.

Being back in L.A. and living with her sister had been bad for Lauren's social life. She was used to going out a lot, either on dates or with friends, and all these evenings she'd been spending at home eating dinner and watching TV with Ava managed to be simultaneously quite pleasant and intensely boring—sort of like a walk down a tree-lined dead-end street.

Daniel had piqued her interest. There was something dark and angry about him that appealed to her worst instincts. She was well aware that those instincts were likely to lead her in a self-destructive direction—but she was *bored*. A small, manageable amount of self-destruction trumped boredom, in her opinion.

She had once been bounced right off a motorcycle by a date who had insisted on riding drunk and without a helmet. Since Lauren had also been drunk, she had willingly thrown on a helmet and joined him on the ride and had paid the resulting stupidity tax with a large portion of the skin on her right arm and thigh. Her date was less fortunate and ended up in the hospital for two weeks with a fractured skull. She waited until he had healed and then she broke up with him, making a silent vow to stick in the future to men who were clean-cut and well-scrubbed. And who didn't ride motorcycles.

Daniel was well-groomed enough, so that was good, and she doubted he had a motorcycle—he didn't have the oversized adolescent vibe peculiar to guys who rode bikes—but even so, she suspected he wasn't likely to be good for her emotional health. On the other hand, Lauren thought, to hell with health. She was spending her days being a dutiful daughter and a supportive sister, and she needed something risky to balance out all that goodness.

"We're going to be late." Nancy snapped the windshield shade down peevishly. "Look at all this traffic. We should have left earlier."

"Sorry," Lauren said. The car in front of her moved forward and she stepped eagerly on the gas but had to brake almost immediately as the other car stopped again.

"Don't lurch," her mother said. "It won't get us there any faster and it wastes gas."

"Backseat driver," Lauren muttered. But she was careful not to overaccelerate the next time the traffic started moving, just took her foot off the brake and let the car roll gently forward. The space between her car and the one in front widened, and another car suddenly darted in front, cutting her off so tightly that she had to slam on the brakes even though she was barely moving. The car that had cut her off made it through the next intersection just as the light turned from yellow to red. Lauren had to stop and wait. "Damn it," she said. "I could have made it if it hadn't been for that jerk."

"Calm down," Nancy said. "It doesn't do any good to get annoyed."

"You're the one who keeps telling me we're going to be late."

"I said that *once*."

The light changed again and Lauren quickly zipped through the intersection—only to be slowed to a standstill again half a

block later, within sight of the hospital. "L.A. traffic sucks," she
said. "I better drop you off before I park. That way you can go
up and get started." As Lauren pulled into the hospital drop-off
lane, she saw the car that had cut her off pulling away from the
curb, heading toward the parking garage—and this time spotted Daniel in the driver's seat. "I should have known," she said,
amused.

"What?" Nancy looked at her, hand poised on the door
handle.

"Nothing," Lauren said. She pulled up to the curb. "I'll meet
you upstairs. You going to be okay?"

"Fine," Nancy said. She got out of the car and Lauren watched
her walk up to the entrance. She looked a little more slumped
about the shoulders than usual, but she still walked with the same
fierce determination she'd always had. She passed a woman in a
wheelchair being pushed by a volunteer up the ramp, and Lauren
realized that the seated figure was Daniel's mother. She felt a
strange and uncharitable sense of relief that her own mother was
striding along on her own power when Daniel's mother couldn't
even walk the few feet, but then was hit by a sudden superstitious
fear that her selfishness would bring on her own mother's decline.
She shook her head to get rid of the thought.

She lingered in the drive-through for a moment, waiting for
Nancy to enter the front doors, and realized just in time that a
security guard was bearing down on her, waving his hand with
a "move along" gesture. She responded with a deliberately obtuse
cheery wave and pulled back out into the street. She continued
on to the parking garage but didn't see Daniel down there.

She had to go down five levels to find an empty parking space,
so by the time she made it up to the chemo ward, a nurse was
already settling her mother in the public reclining chair area.

"Actually, I kind of like it here," Nancy said when Lauren

wondered out loud whether there were any private rooms available. "If I get bored, I can look at the other people and decide whether or not I look better than they do."

"I can tell you right now you do," Lauren said.

"That's because they're all old." Once she was hooked up to the IV, Nancy closed her eyes with a sigh of exhaustion, then immediately opened them again. "I'm sorry. Did you want to talk? Something about being here always makes me so sleepy."

"Nah, I'm fine," Lauren said. "You relax. I'm going to go do a little exploring." She gave her a quick kiss on the forehead and walked over to the snack area.

And there was Daniel, sitting in a chair, leafing restlessly through a newspaper. The second she entered, he looked up and tossed the newspaper aside.

"There you are," he said. So he had been waiting for her. She was glad.

"Hi," she said. "Did you know you cut me off?"

"What do you mean?"

"In your car. You cut me off."

He stared at her. "I have no idea what you're talking about."

"Never mind. Is your mother all settled?"

"Yeah," he said. "We got a private room this time."

"So no yelling?"

"What do you mean?" he said again.

"You know. You were screaming at the nurses when you didn't get one last time."

"I wasn't screaming," he said. "I was just pointing out that they had promised us something and not delivered it."

"Very loudly," Lauren said. "It was very loud pointing out."

"I wasn't that loud."

"Not by monster truck rally standards." She sat down in a chair near him and blessed the addition of spandex to snug-fitting jeans as she crossed one denim-clad leg over the other. "Ready to play cards? I've been sharpening my skills by watching poker tournaments on TV all week."

"You have way too much time on your hands," he said. "You need a hobby."

"Watching TV *is* my hobby," Lauren said. "I'm very good at it. I may even go pro."

"I'm hungry," Daniel said, springing to his feet. "Can we get something to eat before we play cards? But not just cookies and orange juice. I didn't have lunch today."

"There's a cafeteria downstairs. According to the sign in the elevator they have chicken soup just like Mom used to make."

"My mother never made chicken soup."

"Maybe that's your problem." She meant it as a joke, but his expression darkened.

"What's that supposed to mean?"

"Nothing." She stood up. "Let's go get you some chicken soup."

Daniel said he had to check on his mother first, so they agreed to meet in front of the elevators in five minutes. Lauren got there first.

"Your mom okay?" she asked him when he joined her a couple of minutes later.

"Define 'okay'" was his response.

The elevator opened. It was already pretty full, but Daniel pushed his way in without hesitation. Lauren followed close behind, and people squeezed to the sides to make room for them. Once in, they turned and faced the front like everyone else. Lauren could feel Daniel's body close behind hers.

The passengers were all silent for the ride down, except for one old lady in front who kept saying to the young man with her—presumably her son—"Why are they so long? Why are they so long?" Lauren wondered what that meant. The son didn't answer, just patted his mother on the arm and murmured a weary "shush," with no apparent faith in his ability to silence her. They got off on the ground floor.

Three other people accompanied them the rest of the way down to the cafeteria, which covered the entire basement floor. Half of the room was devoted to tables and chairs, the other half was scattered with kiosks offering foods that ranged from sushi to subs to desserts to the famous Mom-like chicken soup. Several cashier counters bridged the two areas.

"What looks good to you?" Daniel asked as they scanned the room.

"Frozen yogurt?" Lauren suggested. Daniel made a face. "Wait," she said. "Don't tell me. Partially hydrogenated fats?"

"Not that I know of. I just don't like frozen yogurt. It's got that weird tangy flavor and a wimpy mouthfeel. Give me real ice cream or just skip the whole thing."

"I get that," she said. "Especially if you're talking Ben and Jerry's Chunky Monkey."

"Now you're speaking my language." He grinned at her and his face instantly transformed. He was a handsome guy no matter what—he had his mother's wide-set blue eyes and patrician bone structure—but there was normally something cold and grim about the set of his face. When he smiled . . . it got better. Good enough to make her glad they had some time to spend together. Too bad he didn't smile more often, Lauren thought.

On the other hand, maybe it was the rarity of the smile that gave it its potency.

They separated to get their food and reunited at the cash register. Lauren had scored a dish of chocolate frozen yogurt and Daniel a large Caesar salad. The cashier said, "You together?"

and Daniel nodded and handed her his credit card. Lauren let him pay for her without comment.

They settled with their food at an empty table. Lauren stuck her spoon into her frozen yogurt and twirled it around. "So how is it your mother lives in L.A. but you live in New York? Where'd you grow up?"

"New Jersey," Daniel said. He took his salad plate off of the tray and swiveled to drop the tray on the empty table behind him, then settled back in his chair. "Mom moved out here by herself about five years ago. She wanted to live somewhere warm—she's always hated the winter. She thought Florida was for old people and Arizona for crazy New Age types, and she already had a couple of friends who'd moved to L.A., so she came here." He picked up his plastic fork.

"Are her parents still alive?"

"No," he said. "But my father's father is. He's in a nursing home in Connecticut now, and all he says when I call him is 'It's not right that a father should outlive his son.' Can't say I disagree with him." He speared a mound of lettuce with a savage stab of his fork. "I'd trade the old son of a bitch for my father any day."

"It does go against the natural order of things," Lauren said. "But it's not his fault."

He glared at her. "Who said it was?"

"Relax," Lauren said. "We're in agreement here."

"Yeah, I know," Daniel said. "Sorry. I'm just in a bad mood. I hate hospitals. And I hate cafeterias."

"So you're *really* not crazy about hospital cafeterias," Lauren said. "I'm just guessing." She licked some yogurt off the back of her spoon.

"It's depressing here," he said, and looking around, Lauren knew what he meant—most of the people at the other tables were either doctors and nurses in their lab coats racing through a snack to get back to work or relatives of patients who ate without pleasure, the strain of dealing with illness showing in their exhausted faces. They all had the look of people who were only eating because someone had said they had to keep their strength up. You couldn't pretend you were in a regular restaurant: the mood was too dark.

Lauren didn't like feeling depressed, so she quickly turned her attention back to Daniel. "What would you be doing right now if you were home in New York?"

Daniel glanced at his watch. "It's after five there. I'd still be at the office, but working on finishing up so I could get home for a run and a shower and eventually a late dinner."

"Do you usually cook or go out to eat?"

"I never cook." He crunched on a crouton. "It's a waste of time."

"Cooking's not a waste of time," Lauren said. "What's more important than eating? I mean, without food we'd starve and die."

He snorted. "There are six restaurants on my block alone. I don't place starvation at the top of my worry list."

"You know what I mean: we *have* to eat, so we might as well figure out how to really *satisfy* our hunger and not just throw burgers down our throats."

"There are lots of kinds of hungers," he said slowly. "Might as well order in some takeout and spend your time satisfying the rest, don't you think?"

"Sure," Lauren said. "I'm all in favor of any kind of satisfaction." Their eyes met and held for a second. They were definitely flirting, but Daniel didn't smile or wink or even tilt his head toward her—he just watched her, like he was assessing her, doing some kind of metaphysical math in his head and trying to figure out whether she added up right or not. During the silence, a family dashed by their table, laughing, a father and his two small children. Their happiness seemed out of place until Lauren noticed that one of the kids held a balloon that read "It's a boy!" The one happy reason to be at a hospital, she thought, and gave them a big smile.

She turned back to Daniel. "What?" she said, even though he hadn't said anything.

He shifted suddenly in his seat. "You got any free time this weekend?" he asked.

Ava had given Lauren a brand-new American Express card shortly after she moved in, which surprised her since Carolina had instructed her to destroy all her charge cards. "It's in both our names," Ava had explained. "To buy necessities for the apartment. You're only allowed to use it at supermarkets."

Today Lauren had gone into Brentwood to shop at the Whole Foods there but decided to take a little walk first. It was a beautiful day, and it felt good to be out of the apartment. On one block, the window display of a clothing store caught her eye. She decided she should check out the merchandise, even if she couldn't buy anything. After all, she intended to return soon to her retail career, and it was important to keep up with the trends.

Inside, she moved idly around the store, fingering items and listlessly checking price tags. Without the thrill of the hunt, looking at clothing lost a lot of its appeal and excitement. She turned to leave.

And then Lauren spotted the World's Most Perfect Top.

The color was a dark turquoise that would, she knew, flatter both her skin tone and her hair color. It was cut long enough to wear over a pair of low-riding jeans but not so long it would hide the curve of her thighs. She loved the feel of the soft, silky fabric and the way the banded bodice was embroidered with delicate glass beads that caught the light and shimmered. It was sexy and classy and chic and she wanted it. Desperately.

She checked the price tag. It was ninety-five dollars, which seemed like a fair price to her—it would have been twice that in Saralyn's boutique. Lauren didn't believe in spending a lot on something you could get at the Gap, like a simple T-shirt or a pair of cargo pants, but this . . . this was a *transformative* top. She eagerly unhooked the hanger from the rack and . . .

Stopped. Stood there, holding it, suddenly despondent.

What was the point of trying it on? She had promised Ava she wouldn't buy anything that wasn't a necessity for six months.

By making her sign that contract, Ava had turned her into a child, someone who couldn't even buy something for herself— even something she *needed*—without a grown-up's permission.

She clutched the hanger, waves of disappointment, anger, and frustration crashing over her, each in its turn. She couldn't buy the top without Ava's knowing and Ava would never understand the importance of this one special purchase—Ava, who ordered frumpy wool skirts online and didn't care about shopping or owning beautiful things, who only cared about not being naked. She had no idea what a buzz you could get from the feel of something silky against your skin or from the looks of admiration you got when your clothes were tight enough in just the right places. She didn't get it and would simply think Lauren was being irresponsible and wasting money. In her blindness, she would never see the *necessity* of this top, only that Lauren had broken her promise.

Lauren hung the cami back on the rack with an effort that

was almost painful. Someone else would come along and buy it, she thought bitterly. Someone whose sister didn't interfere in her life. And she would wear it, and a guy—maybe a guy like Daniel—wouldn't be able to stop staring at her.

But it wouldn't be Lauren.

Chapter 9

When Ava walked into the apartment Friday evening after work, Lauren was busy switching purses, removing items from her large leather shoulder bag and packing them into a small glittery clutch. She was dressed to go out in tight jeans, black patent leather spike-heeled boots, and a silky black top.

"You look nice," Ava said. "Where are you going?"

"I have a date," Lauren said.

"Of course you do!" Ava said. "You just moved back to town and you don't have a job and you don't really know anyone here anymore, so it makes sense that you already have a date, whereas I—who've lived here for years and years and see tons of people every day—I have no date."

"See what I mean?" Lauren said. She pulled a used tissue out of her purse, made a face, and dropped it on a pile of similar items. "You're always putting yourself down."

"That wasn't putting myself down. That was being truthful. Well, sarcastic, but also truthful. Truthfully sarcastic." Ava eyed the growing pile of trash on the table. "You're going to throw all that out, right?"

"No," Lauren said. "I thought I'd sauté it with some soy sauce for dinner."

"Such a wit. It's no wonder the men flock to you." Ava dropped her briefcase on a chair, then thought better of it, pushed the briefcase off and onto the floor, and sat down on the chair herself. "So who's tonight's lucky guy and how did we meet him?"

"His name's Daniel," Lauren said. She took out her wallet and unsnapped it. "Look, Ma, no cards," she said, showing Ava. "I've cut them all into tiny pieces, except for the one you gave me for buying groceries, and I leave that at home all other times. Are you proud of me?"

"Yes, actually, I am. You need some cash for tonight?"

Lauren checked inside the wallet. "No, I have enough to pay for a cab if I get abandoned in a bad neighborhood. Just like Mom taught us."

"Good girl," Ava said. "You got some condoms in there too?"

"Mom never told us to carry condoms."

"Not directly, but she always left little brochures from the Women's Clinic lying around. What about money for dinner?"

"The guy always pays for dinner." Lauren pulled a few old receipts out of the wallet and added them to her discard pile.

"Not in my experience," Ava said. "But I'm willing to believe that in your universe they do. So how'd you meet this so-called Daniel, anyway?"

"At the hospital, when I took Mom in for chemo. His mother's going through it, too. We started talking and— What's so funny?"

Ava had let out a loud hoot of laughter. "Only you!"

"Only me what?"

"Only you could turn taking your mother to chemotherapy into the Dating Game. You're incredible. How do you do it?"

Lauren shrugged. "I'm just friendly. That's how you meet people, Ava. You act friendly. You should try it."

"I'm friendly," Ava said. "But I know that if I took Mom to have chemo, Mom would have chemo. And I'd probably get through a few more chapters in whatever book I was reading. I would almost definitely *not* end up with a hot date on a Friday night. He *is* hot, isn't he?"

"He's not unhot," Lauren said.

Ava reached forward and picked up a compact that had fallen out of Lauren's purse and absently pressed the mechanism that opened it. The makeup inside was dry and crumbly and some small chunks fell out. "Oops, sorry." She quickly closed it. "Maybe I should start taking Mom to the hospital—I mean, if the chemo ward is just one big singles bar . . ."

"Frankly, the martinis are a little weak." Lauren held out her hand. "May I have my compact back?"

"You need a new one," Ava said as she handed it to her.

"No duh. But someone said I wasn't allowed to buy anything that's not a necessity."

"Oh, right. Well, good for you for staying the course." Ava brushed the makeup crumbs off of the table with the side of her hand.

"Of course, if you want to buy me a new one as a reward for being so virtuous—" The phone beeped twice, which meant someone was at the front door. "That'll be Daniel," Lauren said. "Buzz him up, will you?"

"Oh, good, I get to meet him." Ava jumped up. "Hey, where's the phone?" she said. It wasn't in its base.

"I was using it before . . ." Lauren cast about vaguely.

"Do you ever put anything back where it belongs?" Ava spotted it over on the coffee table. "There it is." She went over and picked it up. "Come on up!" she said, and pressed the button to let their guest in.

Lauren went to open the front door. She glanced down the hallway, then let out a little "eek!" before quickly pulling her head back and closing the door. "Oops," she said, laughing. "I totally forgot."

"Forgot what?"

"I am so dumb. I already *had* plans for tonight—for you and me to do something with Russell Markowitz." She hit her forehead with the palm of her hand. "Can you believe it? I double-booked."

"*What?*" Ava said. "What do you mean? Russell's here?"

"Oh well," Lauren said, with a sudden, cheerful, and, to Ava, suspiciously quick reversal. "You and Russell will just have to figure out something to do without me." She went back to the door and flung it open before Ava could say another word.

"Welcome!" Lauren chirped as Russell came in. She pecked him on the cheek and then went back to the table to grab her clutch and a cropped wool jacket that was hanging on the back of a chair. "Don't get mad, but I'm actually on my way out. An out-of-town friend called me to say he's here for just this *one* day and tonight's my only chance to see him. Sorry I didn't let you know ahead of time, but you've still got Ava."

Ava covertly watched Russell's reaction. He stared at Lauren for a moment and Ava could have sworn that his expression darkened noticeably.

Great, Ava thought. *I'm not just a consolation prize—I'm a* bad *consolation prize.* "Sorry," she said. She could have *killed* Lauren, who she was sure had engineered the whole thing. Hadn't she said she wanted to get them alone together?

"No worries," Russell said with a start, as if it had suddenly occurred to him that his hesitation was rude. He came over and dropped a quick air kiss near both of Ava's cheeks, patting her absently on the shoulder at the same time. "Lauren's right—we'll have fun. You girls just don't give a guy time to get his bearings. I'm already confused and I only just got here." He was once again wearing a suit and tie and must have come straight from work.

"I better go down and wait out front for my friend," Lauren said. "You two have fun."

"We'll do our best," Russell said, and with a flurry, a quick rap of her shiny shoes, a good-bye wiggle of her fingers, and a big slam of the door, Lauren was gone.

There was a pause. Ava realized they were both staring at the door like they were waiting for Lauren to come right back through it and take charge again. She blinked and said, "I'm sorry. She only just told me—not just about her other date, but about this one, too. Not that I—" She halted. "It was just all a surprise. You know how it is with Lauren."

"Yeah," he said with a weak smile. "I'm the extra bag of bagels."

"No, no," she said. "The other guy's the extra one. You were the original bag."

"Doesn't seem to have mattered," he said. Then: "But it's fine, really. I'm delighted to have the time alone with you. Sometimes with Lauren around, it's hard for anyone else to get a word in."

"Really?" Ava said. "I think she's a perfectly good listener." *She* could criticize her sister, but there was no way she was letting anyone outside of her immediate family get away with it.

"I was just joking." There was another pause, a more awkward one. "So," Russell said, with a restless glance toward the doorway. "What shall we do? Dinner? A movie? Both?"

"A movie." Always her choice for a first date because it minimized the need to make conversation—not, she hastened to remind herself, that this *was* a first date. "Let's see what's playing." As she went to get the newspaper that was on the table, she noticed with no surprise that Lauren had left not only her everyday purse lying there but also the pile of garbage she had cleaned out of it.

They settled on a movie that was starting in twenty minutes in Century City, which meant they had to hustle to make it. Good, Ava thought as they nabbed the elevator down to the ground floor: they'd have no time to do anything other than buy tickets and go sit in a dark theater.

They spent the whole drive figuring out the best route to avoid traffic. But even so, their movie was sold out by the time they got up to the cinema, and so were all the other decent films.

"The fates are against us," Russell said, frowning at the scroll of movies and times flickering over the ticket counter. "But I'm getting hungry, anyway. Let's buy tickets for a later show and have dinner first."

Ava was still desperately scanning the list of movies. "It'll get pretty late if we do that."

"Or," he said, and the edge to his voice made her turn and look at him, "I could just take you home and not waste any more of your time. Would you prefer that?"

"Would *you*?" she asked, putting her hands on her hips.

"Not at all. I've been looking forward to this evening all week."

"Because you thought you'd be with Lauren." She hated herself for saying it, for her own perverse desire to force him to admit something that would only depress her to hear.

He wasn't honest enough to do that, anyway. He raised his hands in a supplicating gesture. "I'm thrilled to be out with you tonight, Ava."

"But Lauren's the one you made the plans with."

"So . . . is your point that you never intended to be part of them?"

"No, of course not," Ava said, frustrated—she was trying to prove that he didn't want to be there with her, and he kept twisting it back on her. "Once I knew about it, I was—" She stopped. What was she? "I was fine with the whole thing," she finished lamely. Then: "I just don't want you to feel like you have to hang out with me all evening if you really just wanted to be with Lauren."

"You know what?" Russell said.

"What?"

"I'm hungry. And it's making me irritable. And it's not outside the realm of possibility that hunger has the same effect on you. Can we please just go get something to eat? We'll hold off on the movie for now, see how we're feeling after dinner."

"Yeah, okay," Ava said.

He looked around. "Let's not do the food court thing. I desperately need to sit down and have a drink. It's been a long week."

"There's a Houston's downstairs."

"Perfect. They have a full bar."

There was a wait for a table at Houston's. The hostess said it would be roughly ten minutes and gave them a big square beeper. It was crowded inside the restaurant, so they went outside to wait. The evening was growing cold and Ava shivered in her thin top. In all the rush of trying to make the movie, she had forgotten to grab a coat.

"Here." Russell slipped off his jacket and held it out to her.

"That's okay," Ava said, hugging her elbows and huddling her shoulders. "I'm fine."

"Take it," he said and circled around behind her so he could drape it over her shoulders.

"Won't you be cold?" Ava asked.

"I'm never cold. It's a guy thing." He had on a long-sleeved oxford shirt and a T-shirt under that—you could see the outline of its shorter sleeves through the woven cotton of the shirtsleeves. His shirt still held the outlines of a good starchy ironing—the day's wearing had softened but not eliminated them—and was tucked neatly in at his narrow waist. Ava followed the row of buttons up to where the collar branched into two points and then up to his face. Their eyes met. She felt a weird jolt of familiarity, some sense of having known him when they were kids coming back to her as a brief moment of déjà vu. She didn't mention it, though.

Instead she said, "I have this theory that guys get just as cold as women but they think it's more macho not to admit it."

"*Now* who's generalizing about the sexes?" Russell asked. Stripped of the jacket, he looked younger and a little more vulnerable.

"Me," she admitted, and he nodded with a smile.

The jacket was blessedly warm and smelled nice. Russell didn't seem to wear cologne, so it must have been some other mild scent clinging to it—his deodorant, maybe, or his shaving cream, or some combination of various toiletries like those. Ava cuddled into its heavy, silk-lined warmth. "Thank you," she said. "For the jacket. I was lying when I said I wasn't cold."

He gave a slightly superior smile. "I know."

She leaned back against the mall directory, a heavy glass sign set in a concrete base. "So what made this week so long for you?"

"Work stuff." He twitched his shoulders, first one, then the other, rapidly. "A lot of people were yelling. At me. All week long."

"You're the managing director. Who's allowed to yell at *you*?"

"Angry members of the board," he said. "Meaning, primarily, the family who founded Evoque. They used to control every aspect of it. The mother designed the clothing, the daughter modeled it, the father ran the business . . . But a couple of years ago, everyone—even they—agreed it was time for a change."

"That's where you came in."

"That's where I came in." He absently rubbed his own arms.

"Why were they yelling at you?"

"Oh, you know. The usual. Earnings less than we'd predicted. Shares down. And so on." He made it sound like it was no big deal, but she suspected it took some effort for him to do that.

It seemed kinder to match his lighthearted tone than to express concern. "I thought Carson Flite was going to magically reinvent the company's image. I mean, Carson Flite and *you*."

"It takes time to do that," he said. "I need more time."

"There's no rush, is there?"

"Only if they're planning to fire me." He gave a little laugh.

"Is that likely?" and then she said, "Jesus!" as she gave a sudden jump.

"What's wrong?" Russell said, putting his hand out to her arm. "Are you okay?"

Sheepishly, she reached into the hip pocket of his jacket and pulled out the restaurant beeper, which was vibrating and lighting up. "Scared me," she said. "I thought something was attacking my leg."

"And I thought you were having a seizure," he said. "I was desperately trying to remember if I was supposed to put something in your mouth to keep you from biting your tongue or whether that's just a myth."

"I don't know," Ava said. "Does food count as putting something in my mouth?"

Russell took the beeper from her. "Let's go."

Once the hostess had seated them, Ava slipped her arms out of Russell's jacket, carefully folded it, and handed it back across the table to him. "Thanks," she said. "I'm okay now."

He put it on the booth bench next to him. "If you need it again, let me know."

"I will." They studied their menus. Ava looked up after a moment and said, "Oh, and I never got to say I'm sorry about all the work stuff."

He waved his hand dismissively. "It is what it is."

"I like that phrase," Ava said. "Or maybe I hate it. Either way, I admire its applicability. There isn't a situation in the world that can't be summed up by 'It is what it is.' But it doesn't actually *mean* anything, does it?"

"You think I should stop saying it?"

"Not at all. I just think it's important to acknowledge it's fundamentally meaningless."

"In other words," he said, "it is what it is." They grinned over the tops of their menus at each other.

The waitress stopped by the table to ask if they wanted to order drinks. Russell gratefully requested a martini made with Bombay gin, straight up, with a twist—but "not Sapphire," he instructed her. "That's important."

"I'll have one of those too." Ava leaned her head back to look up at the waitress. "But feel free to use Sapphire or any other precious gem. I'd never know the difference."

"Me neither," the waitress said and left the table.

Russell raised his eyebrows. "You normally drink martinis?"

"Nope," she said. "Can't you tell?"

"The precious gem thing *was* a tip-off."

"I don't 'normally' drink any hard liquor. Just wine. But I've been thinking I'd like to have a signature drink. Something I always get so when I walk into my favorite restaurant where everyone knows my name—that place doesn't exist by the way, but in a perfect universe it would—they'd immediately start making it and bring it over before I even sat down."

"I have a couple of restaurants where they bring me my martini without asking," Russell said. "Ones I go to for business dinners."

"So do you always order that drink?" Ava said. "The martini with the this and not the that?"

"Pretty much," he said.

"It's very James Bond of you."

"Thank you," he said. "I'm like him in other ways too."

Ava settled back against the booth. "How's that?"

"Devilishly good looks aside?" he said, and she laughed and nodded. "Well, I'm constantly doing battle with the forces of evil. And I have a bad habit of falling in love with beautiful women whose only goal is to betray and destroy me."

"I'm not sure you have the healthiest attitude about these things."

"Oh well," he said. "It is what it is."

"I can't stay out too long," Daniel called through the open car window when he finally pulled up, twenty minutes late. Lauren had expected him to be five minutes late, not twenty, and had therefore spent fifteen minutes waiting on the curb for him. She had received four offers in that time to jump into the cars of strange men and had declined them all, although she had briefly considered saying yes to one guy who was cute and clean-cut and driving a high-end Lexus, especially since Daniel was already twelve minutes late at that point. But in the end she had waved him on with a regretful smile.

"Why not?" she said, pulling the door open.

"My mother's not doing well tonight. I would have canceled, but she said I should get out of the house and do something on my own for once."

"It's nice to see you too," Lauren said as she swung herself into the car and flopped down in the passenger seat. "And I accept your apology for keeping me waiting."

"Yeah, sorry about that," he said. "So what do you want to do?"

"I don't know. Get a drink?"

He pulled the car back into the traffic, cutting off a driver who honked at him, which he ignored. "Sounds good to me. Tell me where to go—I'm new to these parts."

"You prefer funky and older, or hip and new?"

"I don't care. Like I said—just tell me where to go."

She directed him to a decent restaurant that had a large bar and was rarely so crowded you couldn't get a table at the last minute: she was hungry and hoped he'd be able and willing to squeeze in a quick dinner.

When they got there, the bar was standing room only, but just as Daniel was handing the bartender the money for their drinks, Lauren spotted a couple standing up to leave and ordered him to grab their table. A young woman approached just as Daniel did. She hesitated, tilting her head to give him a sweet "May I have this one?" kind of look. Daniel's response was to immediately slide into a chair, claiming the table for himself.

The girl looked momentarily stunned, standing there with her drink in her hand, but then she shrugged and rejoined her friends.

"You did that really well," Lauren said as she joined Daniel at the table with their drinks. "I'm impressed. Oh, and here's your change." She dropped it on the table as she sat down. "I gave the bartender a big tip."

"Did what well?" He didn't even glance at the money, just stuck it in his pocket.

"Grabbed the table before that girl did."

"Angelenos are such amateurs—any New Yorker can score a table around here. We're tougher and we think faster on our feet."

"Clearly you haven't been to the half-price sale at Fred Segal."

He grimaced. "Nor am I likely to go in the future."

"You might want to rethink that," she said. "You could use a little more style. You dress very 1980s Master of the Universe, you know."

He looked down at the khakis and V-neck sweater he wore. "What do you mean? This is what everyone wears."

"Exactly. Don't you want to stand out in a crowd?"

"Sure." He raised his drink—scotch on the rocks—to his lips. "But not because of my clothing." He took a sip and winced, the way people do when the liquor's strong.

"Why, then?"

"You care a lot about clothing, don't you?" he said, deliberately eyeing the fancy top she was wearing. She had pushed her jacket off and onto her chair back, the better to display the black silk camisole she was wearing and the pretty, strong shoulders it revealed.

"I have to," she said. "I buy clothing for retail stores—that's my job."

"Figures. And if you quit tomorrow, would you stop caring?"

"I quit weeks ago," she said, "and I haven't stopped caring yet."

"You quit your job?"

"It was in New York," she said, "and I wanted to come here and help with Mom, so I quit and moved out." It was basically the truth—the order in which those things happened may have been a little different, but none of it was a lie, except for the quitting part. "Eventually I'll need to find a new job here, once things get back to normal with my mom."

"What kind of job?"

"I don't know. Something in the same field, I guess."

"Does clothing count as a 'field'?"

"Fashion does. I like being a buyer. And I'm really good at it—I have an amazing eye for future trends."

"And you're modest, too."

Lauren flicked the side of her wineglass with her forefinger to make a slight pinging sound. "Just being honest. If you prefer, I could spend the evening telling you what I'm bad at."

"Which is what?" His lips curved a little, like he was anticipating a joke.

"Self-restraint, for one thing."

"Wow," he said and shifted abruptly in his seat. "That's a good flaw to have—or at least to claim to have. Guys like girls with no self-restraint."

"Don't get too excited," Lauren said. "I meant when it comes to spending money, not . . . anything else. Although . . ." She didn't bother to finish the thought.

Daniel narrowed his eyes. "You spend too much money?"

"More than I have."

"That's too much."

"I'm aware of that."

"Then stop."

"Easier said than done."

"Not really. Just don't do it."

"I'm trying," she said.

He flung his arm out almost violently. "I don't get it. I don't get why someone like you cares that much about what she puts on her body. You'd be a pretty girl if you dressed in a burlap sack."

"That's very Rei Kawakubo," she said with a snicker.

He ignored that. "If you were ugly, I could see how you might think that maybe clothing would add some style to the package, draw the eye away from the flaws. But you're not ugly. You could buy your clothes at Sears and still look better than most girls. Why waste your money chasing after fads?"

"Thank you," she said.

"That wasn't meant as a compliment," he said. "I was criticizing you."

"That made the compliment all the more sincere," Lauren said. "You weren't trying to make one."

"Whatever." He looked around the bar. "Everyone in this whole city is so goddamned pretty, always dressed up like they have to impress someone. I don't know how people can stand to live here."

"I grew up here," Lauren said. "It's not that bad."

"You fit in," he said. "You like to be pretty."

"First of all, that's not a sin. Second of all, there are plenty of good-looking people in New York too."

"It's not the same. They're not all soft and lovely and unthreatening."

"I loved New York for a while," she said. "But it's a harsh place. The people are harsh, the weather's harsh, the bartenders are harsh. L.A.'s easier."

"Yeah," he said with disgust. "It's all sunshine and puppies. Everyone gives you a big smile as he stabs you in the back."

"You definitely belong in New York."

He gave a short laugh. "Yeah," he said. "I'm harsh." He shifted again—he seemed to have a habit of sitting quietly for a few minutes and then suddenly and abruptly moving his whole body like he was going to explode if he didn't. Or like he *was* exploding. Then he'd be quiescent again. "I don't know," he said. "It's not all bad being here. It almost feels like a vacation. I get my work done early in the morning, then spend the day with my mother doing stuff I haven't done in years, like just watching TV or reading books. The weather's always beautiful. Sometimes we just sit on the deck and enjoy the sun. I could never be this—" He searched for the word. "This *lazy*, I guess, back home. In New York, there's an energy in the air—you feel like you have to keep moving. Here, you can just do nothing for days on end."

"Isn't that kind of nice? Can't you enjoy that on some level?"

"If I weren't watching my mother die, yeah, maybe." He picked up his glass and drank deeply. When he put it down, there was no more liquor left.

Lauren studied him quietly for a moment. Then she said, "Is she really dying?"

"I don't know." His tone ended the discussion. He put his glass down and did one of his explosive fidgets. "You hungry? Want to get some dinner?"

"Eventually," Lauren said. "No rush."

"Yeah, there is. I can't stay out too long, remember?"

"Oh, right." She raised her wineglass and drained what was

left of it—about a third of a glass. She put it down and wiped her mouth on a cocktail napkin. "Okay. Let's eat."

He gestured toward her glass. "That's a more impressive trick when it's tequila."

"I can do that too."

"You'll have to show me sometime."

"So long as you're prepared to deal with the consequences. Tequila"—she shook her head—"it makes you do strange things."

"Yeah," he said. "I've regretted a few things I've done under its influence."

"Not me," Lauren said.

"A woman of no regrets." Daniel stood up. "I admire that."

She stood up too. "None that are tequila-flavored, anyway."

They moved toward the restaurant.

Chapter 10

Ava was trying to convince herself that she wasn't having a good time. Which was harder than she would have expected.

It had been a long time since she had gone on a date with someone who was funny and smart and charming—and Russell Markowitz was, admittedly, all those things—and she was tempted to surrender to the pleasure of his company and the hope that maybe this could lead to something. But she fought the pull, frequently reminding herself that Russell was only out with her because Lauren had backed out of the evening's plans. Given the choice, he would have preferred to have Lauren sitting across from him: the expression on his face when he discovered they'd be going out alone said as much. And the truth was that a lot of what she was enjoying about Russell tonight—how he was less "on" than she'd seen him before, more subdued and introspective, less eager to show off—only underscored the fact that he wasn't as stimulated by her presence as he always seemed to be by Lauren's.

Besides, she reminded herself, the guy was hardly relationship material. His romantic history made it clear that he chose women based on a superficial appeal and then was surprised to find they lacked more worthwhile qualities. And her awareness that he tended to date model-pretty girls also meant that no matter what she thought of *him*, he wasn't likely to fall in love with *her*.

On the other hand . . . there was no reason to make them both miserable for the entire evening. Might as well relax—in a wary kind of way—and enjoy the conversation, which definitely got easier as dinner wore on and the martinis slid down.

Since he was older, Russell remembered more about her family than she did about his, so she bombarded him with questions about his parents and brother, curious about these people who had briefly been part of their lives.

She was a little nervous about bringing up his parents' divorce, but once the subject came up, Russell seemed comfortable discussing it. He explained that while his father *had* left his mother for another woman, it hadn't been for the one who later became his second wife. "I'm guessing that whoever he had the affair with was a stepping-stone," he said. "A way to get out of the marriage but not someone he ever wanted to commit to. I think my mother knows who it was but neither one of them's ever told me."

"Hey, maybe it was *my* mother," said Ava, who had drunk a good deal of her huge, icy cold martini and was slightly tipsy as a result.

"Wow," Russell said. "That would certainly make us look back on those family get-togethers with new eyes." They were sharing a grilled artichoke appetizer, and he reached forward and plucked out a leaf. "Just so you know, if that were true, I wouldn't blame him for a second—given the choice, I'd rather spend time with your mother than mine. She's nicer and smarter and prettier and—"

"Stop, please," Ava said. "Before you tell me my mother's sexier than yours."

"Oh, get your mind out of the gutter." He scraped the artichoke leaf between his even white teeth. "You know, it's actually possible. They were friends at the right time."

She instantly regretted making the joke. "It's not *really* possible," she said.

He dropped the furrowed leaf in the discard bowl and wiped his fingers on his napkin. "Why not? Parents have secrets too, you know. Even yours."

"My mother wouldn't do something like that. I know her well enough to know she just wouldn't." She leaned forward. "And don't start saying stuff about how all women are dishonest and betray men and you can't trust any of them or anything like that. This is my *mother* we're talking about and I know for a fact that she would never cheat on my father."

"Whoa." Russell put his hands up. "Back off. I was just joking. I didn't really think it could be your mother."

"Thank you," she said and settled back.

"Besides, I know it's not her, because my mother was thrilled to hear I had reconnected with your family. If your mother had been the other woman, I think I would have gotten a different reaction, don't you?"

"And also," she said, through exaggeratedly gritted teeth, "my mother *wouldn't have done that.*"

He laughed. "She wants to see your family, by the way."

"Who? My mother?"

"No, *my* mother. She's coming to town next weekend and was hoping I could bring her by your parents' house to say hi."

"Just so long as Mom's feeling up to it."

"Of course," he said. "Check with her first." The waitress came to clear away the artichoke, and he ordered another martini. "How about you?" he asked Ava. "You want another?"

"God, no," she said. "I can barely see straight as it is."

"I'd like to see you drunk," he said, studying her thoughtfully. "What happens when you can't be all careful and controlled?"

"When I drink too much, I fall asleep. Nothing more exciting than that."

"Too bad."

The waitress brought their dinners, a Thai noodle salad for Ava, grilled fish for Russell. Ava picked up her fork and poked at the noodles. "You know this contract thing Lauren keeps bringing up?"

"What contract thing?"

"You know. When our parents 'betrothed' us, or whatever you want to call it."

"Oh yeah." He cut into his fish with the side of his fork. "What about it?"

"Do you remember them talking about it when we were kids?"

"Vaguely."

"I don't really remember it, either," Ava said, "except there was one time when your father kept going on about how I was his future daughter-in-law and how lucky you were to have someone like me lined up, and I do remember just wanting to curl up and die."

"See?" Russell speared a green bean. "You really have always hated the idea of me."

"No, it wasn't that. I was just a little girl, for God's sake. *All* boys had cooties."

"I know," he said. "And I'm sorry about my dad. He had this

sick sense of humor. You should hear some of the stuff he did to *me* when I was little."

"Tell me." Ava was still idly twirling her fork around in the noodles. With the martini making her sleepy and sluggish, it seemed like too much work actually to try to get it to her mouth.

Russell chewed thoughtfully for a moment. "Well, there were the gay comments, for one. Constant little witticisms about how I was his homosexual son and Jonah was the manly one. Because I liked to do things like read and cook and cared about my clothing—"

"Not very enlightened of him."

"No kidding. I knew every gay slur by the time I was fourteen: 'queer,' 'sissy,' 'momma's boy,' 'fegolah' . . . Heard them all from my own father."

"Freud would say that explains the multiple wives and girlfriends. Yours, I mean. Not his." She considered. "Maybe both."

"Ha. Maybe. He always acted like he was joking, but I think it really bothered him that I wasn't more butch. Even now, he hates what I do for a living. He tells his friends I'm in management but won't say what kind of business I'm in. Anyway, the point is that that kind of thing was always passed off as a joke in our house. Never an open discussion or an honest question. Just little joking insinuations. Lord knows how I would have dealt with it if I had actually *been* gay. But he did worse things, too." He put his fork down and settled back in his seat, resting his hand absently on his martini glass. "Like once we were running errands on a Saturday morning, and at one store he tells me to get in line and hold his place for him while he looks for more stuff. So I do, and when our turn comes, I call over to him. And he kind of glances over and says, 'I'm sorry, little boy, but I don't usually buy things for other people's kids. Don't you have a daddy who can buy that for you?'"

"That's not very funny," Ava said. "How old were you?"

"I don't remember exactly. Eight or nine? Young enough to wonder whether they could arrest you for trying to make a purchase when you didn't have any money."

"What'd you do?"

"I just kept saying, 'Come on, Dad!' and he kept doing that 'Dad? I'm not your dad' thing. I was close to tears and all these people were waiting and the cashier was getting annoyed—in retrospect, they probably knew he was pulling my leg and were annoyed at *him*, but at the time I just thought they were all getting mad at *me*—and then finally he said, 'Oh, well, in the spirit of the holidays, I guess I could buy you something, kid—but next time, bring some parents with you when you go shopping.' On the way home, he kept talking about how funny it was and how I should have seen the expression on my face when he pretended not to know me."

"Couldn't he tell you were upset?"

He shook his head. "I had to pretend I wasn't. It was really a test. If I didn't shrug it off, then he'd just say I was a bad sport and didn't have a sense of humor. Trust me, it was always better to suck it up than risk having him say, 'What? Can't take a joke?' That was like the worst thing. It meant you were a crybaby *and* a loser *and* a bad sport." He sighed. "And in my case, probably 'queer,' too."

"You know, I'm starting to have a lot of sympathy for your mother."

"Don't." Russell sat up straight and picked up his fork again. "She could have defended us—stood up to Dad, told him this stuff wasn't funny, insisted that he knock it off. Instead, she'd laugh with him. Unless the joke was on her, of course, in which case she'd go apeshit on him. Which he probably got a sick kick out of."

"You know what's weird?" Ava said. "That you're so anti-women. I mean, I get that your mother drove you a little nuts now and then. But your father sounds really infuriating. So why don't you rant about men the way you do about women?"

"Well," Russell said with a slightly weary grin, "you can't hate *everybody*."

"I'm serious," she said.

He shrugged. "I don't know. For one thing, my dad's changed a lot. He's been a really different father to his second set of sons than he was to me and Jonah. A much better father."

"No more teasing?" Ava asked.

"Well, *less* teasing, anyway. He's just more accepting of them in general. I'm always waiting for him to make fun of them. Like the younger one's really into these Magic card things. He would have mocked me mercilessly for something like that— you know, because it's not manly and all-American like football. But with Farley he just laughs and seems to get a kick out of it. So he's definitely mellowed. I don't know whether it's because he's getting older or whether his second wife just does a better job of telling him to cut the shit than my mother ever did."

"Doesn't it bother you, though? That he's nicer to them than he was to you?"

"A little. But he's nicer to me now too. We have an okay relationship. Better than I would have thought we could ten years ago."

"Except he hates what you do."

He sighed. "Except he hates what I do. And, let's be honest— this improved relationship consists of maybe three or four days a year together."

"And have things gotten better with your mother?"

"Well," he said. "She lives there and I live here. So, in that sense, I'd say things have gotten better with her."

"I can't wait to meet her again."

"Keep your expectations low." He examined his plate of food, fork hovering expectantly.

Ava wondered if his mother was really as bad as he made out or whether his little barbed comments about her were simply a reflection of his general negativity toward all women. That uncertainty made her eager to meet Lana Markowitz and form an opinion of her own: it would give her some insight into Russell.

The restaurant told them it would be a fifteen-minute wait for a table, and Daniel said he was in too much of a hurry to stick it out. He suggested they grab a quick bite instead at the Wahoo's Fish Taco restaurant that they had passed on the way there. Lauren looked down at her dressed-to-kill outfit with a good-natured sigh and let him take her to Wahoo's. They ordered burritos and Coronas and settled down in a corner booth with their drinks.

Lauren looked around the room. "I feel unusually old," she said.

Daniel scanned the room, taking in the teenagers who were spread out around the entire restaurant, halloing to one another and touching fists and running from table to table. "Yeah. Me too."

"Would you want to be a teenager again?" Lauren said. "Hang out with friends, do homework, hate your parents, resent your teachers . . . the whole thing?"

"Are you kidding?" he said. "No one wants to be a teenager. That's the suckiest part of life."

A server came up to the table and presented them with two comically enormous burritos. They thanked him and he saluted them before rushing back behind the counter.

"I *liked* high school," Lauren said, studying her burrito, trying to figure out the best way to tackle it without making a huge mess. "I had great friends and played on a lot of sports teams and was totally happy."

"There's something deeply wrong with you."

"That makes two of us."

"Yeah, probably. But at least I didn't enjoy being a teenager."

Lauren picked up a plastic knife and cut a long slit into the burrito. "So what made those years so sucky for you?"

Daniel cut his own burrito in half, neatly, right across the middle. "Well, my father up and died, for one thing. Which, oddly enough, wasn't the worst part of those years. I mean, it was awful, but in a big, overwhelmingly tragic, everyone-feels-sorry-for-you-and-you-get-out-of-doing-any-work kind of way. It wasn't the soul-draining mind-suck of boredom and pettiness that the rest of high school was."

"Good times, good times," Lauren said jovially.

"Yeah, right."

She flicked through the burrito contents with her fork, seeking out the rare narrow strips of red pepper. "What did your father die of?"

"It was a stroke. Quick and painless. For him at least. Nothing like the shit my mother's going through now."

She raised her head to look at him. "It must be awful."

"It's fine," he said. He picked up a burrito half and took a big bite out of it, hunching his body forward over the table to get his mouth to it instead of raising the burrito higher.

"Come on," Lauren said. "You know it's not fine."

"What do you know about it? Miss Happy Cheerleader with

the perfect intact family?" He put the burrito down, wiped his mouth roughly with the napkin, and raised the beer bottle to his lips. "How could you possibly know what this is like for me?" He put the bottle down with a dull clunk on the hard table.

"I wasn't a cheerleader," Lauren said. "And my mother has cancer too, you know." She regretted the words the instant they left her mouth.

"Right," he said. "It's exactly the same. My mother's dying in front of my eyes, and your mother—it's awful, isn't it? She has to go to the hospital a whole bunch of times, right? And then it might be a few days before she feels okay again. And maybe even a couple of weeks before things are back to normal and she can take you shopping for new clothes again."

"You're right, it's different," Lauren said. "I'm sorry. I didn't mean to compare what our mothers are going through. I just meant I know what it's like to be worried about someone you love."

"Don't try to make us even in the bad luck department. I'll beat you every time."

"Want me to run out in the street and get hit by a truck?" she said.

"Aw, you'd do that for me?"

"No."

"Didn't think so." They ate in silence a moment. It was companionable at first but went on a little too long.

Lauren was just starting to say something about the song that was playing when Daniel shifted suddenly in his seat and leaned forward. She thought he wanted to get closer to her, maybe confide something personal, and moved forward to meet him halfway. Then she realized he was just extracting his cell phone from his back pants pocket. She quickly settled back in her seat. The cell phone was quietly vibrating. "I should take this," Daniel said, pursing his lips as he peered down at the screen. "Do you mind?"

"Go ahead."

Daniel got up and crossed the restaurant to a quiet corner where no one was sitting. He turned his back to the room so he was facing the wall and stayed like that for a while, hunching forward with the phone at his ear.

Lauren sipped her beer and pushed her barely touched plate away. She looked at her watch. Nine thirty-seven.

A sudden shout from another table got her attention. A teenage boy was leaping to his feet, his pant leg covered with a big wet spot. He shouted, "Fuck you, asshole! That totally drenched me!"

"Sorry, man," his friend said. Like the first boy, he was wearing a hugely oversized zip-up sweatshirt over exaggeratedly skinny-legged black jeans and colorful basketball sneakers. The sincerity of his contrition was questionable, given the fact he was doubled over with laughter. The two long-haired girls at their table also seemed to find the whole thing wildly amusing. "It was an accident."

"So's this," said the standing teenager and swatted the other guy's soda right into his lap. The girls hooted with laughter as their friend now leapt to *his* feet, swearing loudly. He swung his head around and noticed Lauren watching them. "Take a picture," he growled at her. "It'll last longer."

"All right," she said, and took her cell phone out of her purse, but the guys were now scuffling, grabbing at each other's arms, and the joke was lost on them. She stuck the phone back in her purse. She could have just taken her regular big handbag and saved herself the trouble of switching, she thought, snapping the fancy one closed with a sigh. The pretty little glittery clutch was completely out of place at Wahoo's Fish Taco.

Daniel came back to the table but didn't sit down. "I should go," he said, with a flick of his hand toward the exit.

Lauren stood up. "Is your mom all right?"

"I don't know—that wasn't her, and I'm worried if I call I'll wake her up. Her sleep's gotten pretty erratic lately. But I should get back and check on her." He reached for her plate and hesitated. "Are you done?"

"Yeah. But are you?" He still had more than half a burrito left.

"Done enough," he said and picked up both their plates. He dumped them in the trash can on their way out the door.

◦◦◦

Daniel surprised Lauren by saying the last thing she expected him to say as he pulled up in front of her apartment building: an amiable and somewhat clichéd "Thanks. This was fun."

"No offense," Lauren said, "but you didn't actually look like you were having fun."

"Really? I was enjoying myself."

"Enjoyment looks different on you than it does on most people."

"I'm not a big smiler these days," he said.

"That's putting it mildly."

"So are you saying *you* didn't have fun?"

She considered for a moment. "No, it was okay," she said. "You're not bad company." She hadn't been bored, she realized, and not just because the evening was short. There was a challenge in Daniel's company that intrigued her. Usually, men were so easy to please. "You could open up a little more, though. It's like pulling teeth getting you to talk about anything personal."

Daniel considered. "That's fair."

"Thank you," she said. "I try to be fair." She let her hand drop and turned back toward him, ducking her head slightly to the side so she could look at him through her eyelashes. "I guess it's good night then," she said, letting him know by her posture that she was in no rush.

He swiveled in his seat and leaned back against his door. The meaning of *his* posture was a lot less clear than hers: he was now facing her but had actually distanced himself an extra few inches. "Should we try this again another night?" he said.

"Do you *want* to?" she said. "Because I can't tell."

"Yes." He shook his head as if to clear it. "I'm sorry if I'm—" He let out a deep breath. "Look, I know I've been a little weird. It's just—this isn't my life. This is a break from my life. And the reason I'm here in L.A. in the first place is because I'm worried about my mother, so I can't just stop worrying about her because I'm going out to dinner. If I were back home and my life were back in place and my mother was healthy, then I'd—" He stopped again.

"You'd what?"

He sighed, his shoulders sagging. "I don't know. It's just a different life here for me and I don't always know what to make of it."

"It's not like you're from another *planet*," Lauren said. "Our dating customs in L.A. are fairly similar to those in New York. Except there's a lot less swearing at cabdrivers."

He laughed briefly and then there was a pause. He shifted and she thought, *He's going to kiss me now.*

But he didn't. Instead he faced forward in his seat again and gripped the steering wheel. "We'll be at the hospital on Tuesday afternoon. Any chance you'll be there too, so we can play some more cards? Maybe place bets on whose mother's IV bag empties first?"

"Sounds like fun. I'll try to be there around the usual time." Her hand found its way to the door handle. "I hope your mother has an okay night tonight," she said as she opened the door.

"Thanks," he said. "Good-bye."

She had stepped out of the car when she heard him say, "Lauren?"

She leaned back in hopefully. "What?"

He seemed to be about to say something, but then he stopped and shook his head again. "Nothing. Just . . . thanks for having dinner with me. Good night."

"Good night," she said. She stood another moment, waiting, but he didn't say anything else, so she pushed the door and it swung shut.

He drove off quickly, not waiting to make sure she got in safely. Lauren unlocked the front door to the building, biting her lip as she tried to figure out what exactly the story was with the guy. There was mutual attraction—that much she knew instinctively. And a fair amount of mutual wariness as well, which, she had learned from past experience, not only didn't dampen attraction, but often had a perverse way of increasing it. So why did she have the distinct sense that Daniel was pulling back, holding himself in check? She certainly wasn't asking anything more from him than a good time, but even that he seemed to begrudge her. And himself.

She strode briskly across the lobby. But then he had told her what the problem was, hadn't he? He was too worried about his mother to let himself have fun. Which was probably counterproductive: if his mother was anything like her own, she probably just wanted Daniel to be happy and would actually feel better knowing he had a reason to go out now and then, something fun in his life to balance out all the sick care. Hadn't he said she *wanted* him to go out tonight?

Lauren decided she would just have to work a little harder to help Daniel overcome the guilt and responsibility that were weighing him down and keeping him from pursuing anything more serious with her.

And that made her wonder.

If she had bought that beautiful silk turquoise top the other day . . . Daniel had been right on the edge of giving in to her tonight—she could *feel* it—and maybe that top would have made the difference. Maybe, if she had bought and worn it and shone with the confidence of knowing she looked as good as she could look—which was pretty damn good—well, maybe she wouldn't be going up to the apartment alone right now.

The next date she had with Daniel—assuming there was one—she had to at least give that top a chance, see if that gave her an edge that pushed him over *his* edge. Otherwise, she would never know for sure whether or not it might have made a difference, and a thought like that could plague you for the rest of your life.

Some things, Lauren thought as she punched at the elevator button with more force than was warranted, were more important than stupid homemade contracts forced on you by interfering sisters with no fashion sense.

Chapter 11

Russell insisted on paying for dinner. He said he owed her a meal since her family had had him over to brunch, and even though Ava pressed her charge card on him, he wouldn't take it. She tucked her card away again in her wallet, thinking of Lauren and her "the guy always pays for dinner," but she reminded herself again that this wasn't a date and that Russell had given her a logical reason why he should pay.

They walked out into the mall and headed toward the escalator that would take them back up to the cinema.

"Hey, wait," Ava said, touching Russell's arm. She pointed. "Isn't that your company's store?" She had passed it a million times without thinking about it, but suddenly the sign that said "Evoque Knits" had meaning.

"One of them, yeah." They drifted over to stand in front. "We mostly sell through department stores, but we have a few shops, more to increase visibility and name recognition than anything else. They don't turn a profit." He studied the window. "What do you think of the display?"

"Nice," she said with a shrug. She didn't really know what she thought of it. There were four headless mannequins arranged in various outfits all in the same brown and green color scheme. "I like that dress on the right," she added, feeling like she should sound more enthusiastic.

"Yeah, it's nice, isn't it?" he said. "Part of the more youthful trend—see how the neckline's low and the skirt's fairly short? That's all new." He glanced sideways at her, then back at the mannequin. "It would look good on you."

She gave an uncomfortable laugh. "I don't know. It's not really my kind of thing." It was a very revealing dress and looked like it would cling embarrassingly. Not her kind of thing at all.

"I assume this is?" He gestured at her current outfit.

"More or less," she said stiffly. As usual, she had dressed to look respectable in something she had ordered online at a price that was reasonable in colors that were serviceable and a cut that was unobjectionable. Today it was a light blue woman's oxford shirt over a black linen skirt that was, Ava realized as she now glanced down at herself, noticeably wrinkled after the day's wear. *They don't show you* that *in the catalogue*, she thought with a slightly tipsy sense of self-righteous indignation.

Russell studied her for a moment. "You could do better."

She felt herself flush. "Thanks."

"There's nothing wrong with that or that," he said, indicating the skirt and top in turn. "There's just nothing *right* about them."

"You sound like Lauren. She's always telling me I should be more fashionable."

"Why aren't you? More fashionable?"

"I don't know. I don't see the point, I guess. It feels like a waste of time to me."

"You prepare for meetings, right?" Russell said. "Write yourself some notes, read through the materials, think of the arguments you're going to make ahead of time?"

"Of course."

"So why not prepare *yourself* in the same way? Put a little effort in ahead of time, so all day long you feel confident and prepared and ready to impress people?"

"I'm not going out in rags," she said. "You make it sound like I'm running around town looking like Pigpen or something." She gestured toward herself. "This isn't scaring people off."

"Of course not," he said. "You look fine. Acceptable. It's just that you're young and pretty and you have a great figure and—"

"Don't," she said.

"Don't what?"

"I don't know." She wriggled irritably. "This conversation is annoying me. Can we just go see the movie?"

"No," he said.

"No?"

"I want to show you something."

"What?"

"It's a surprise. Come on." He turned around and headed back, not toward the escalator anymore, but across the mall.

Ava had to move quickly to keep up with him. She said, "The last time someone surprised me was when Lauren brought me to that restaurant to have dinner with you and your friends."

"That didn't turn out so badly, did it?"

She was tempted to tell him how miserable she had been all evening but refrained. "I just don't like surprises."

"You are the least girly girl I've ever met," Russell said, still walking briskly, forcing her to match his pace. "You don't like surprises, you don't like being fashionable, you don't like compliments, you don't like to talk about yourself—"

"Well, it all evens out," she said, slightly crossly. "You're the girliest man I ever met. You like all those things."

"You know," Russell said, pulling her onto another escalator with him, one that was going down into the parking level, "some men would be insulted by that."

"But not you?"

"I'm going to change your tone," he said. "Just you wait. You're going to thank me when the evening is over, Nickerson." They got off the escalator and he took her by the hand and led her to his car. Ava hadn't held hands with a guy in over a year and liked the feel of his fingers, which were warm and dry—but from the absent way he was steering her, she suspected the hand-holding was a practical rather than romantic gesture.

"Are you okay to drive?" she asked as they got settled in his car.

"We're not going far," he said, which didn't exactly answer her question.

But they made it safely out of the garage onto Constellation Boulevard and then down to Olympic, which they took into Beverly Hills. A few blocks up, Russell drove down into another parking garage, one where he had to punch a code into a keypad to open the gate. The garage was empty except for a couple of cars and a security guard sitting near the elevator who narrowed his eyes suspiciously at them until Russell flashed him the ID in his wallet. Then the security guard got up and stuck a key into the elevator button plate, and the elevator door opened. He gestured them inside.

"Wow," Ava said when they were in the elevator. "High-level security."

"Well, it's ten o'clock at night," Russell said. "Not exactly prime office hours."

"So this is where you work?"

"Yep." He punched the button for the seventh floor.

"You're not on the top floor?" Ava said. "I would have expected the managing director to get the best view."

"My office *is* on the top floor," Russell said calmly. "We're not going to my office."

"So where are we going?"

"You don't understand the concept of being surprised, do you?"

"I understand it conceptually," she said. "I just don't see the appeal."

"Get out," he said, shoving her gently as the elevator doors opened.

They emerged into a small foyer. There was one door in front of them. Russell pulled a set of keys out of his pocket. "It's good to be the boss," he said. He selected a key and unlocked the door, then gestured her inside.

"Well?" he said once they had both entered and he had flicked a long row of light switches to their on positions.

Ava looked around the now brightly lit room. "It's the world's biggest closet," she said. They were in a single large, industrial-looking room that was easily twice the size of her entire apartment, surrounded by racks of clothing and boxes of clothing and piles of clothing and even a semicircle of fierce mannequins wearing clothing. There was also an old velvet sofa and some matching chairs, presumably so one could just sit and stare at the clothing.

"We call it the Walk-In," Russell said.

"Cute." Ava wandered a few steps. She brushed her hand along a rack of dark blue skirts and looked back over her shoulder at Russell. "Is this where clothes come to die?"

"More like where they come before they've been born," he said. "Although I don't know how often things get thrown out, so if you made your way to the back, you'd probably find some pretty ancient items. Up here, though, it's samples from the upcoming seasons and from some of the current lines too."

"Is it your warehouse?"

"God, no. That's a thousand times bigger. And in New Jersey."

She bent down to stir a crate of silk scarves with her index finger. "So what do you use this for?"

"Different things. Publicity mostly—advertising layouts and magazine photo shoots and to show fashion writers what's coming next. We suits like to look through it now and then to remind ourselves what we're doing, compare our lines to what other companies are showing, check out how well we anticipated the trends and colors. And sometimes"—he sidled up to her and whispered in her ear—"sometimes we steal pieces to give to our friends who are in desperate need of wardrobe improvement."

"You wouldn't be talking about me now, would you?"

"Yep." He swept his arm in a big semicircle. "Look it over. What would you like?"

"I don't know." She glanced around the room briefly and gave a shrug. "It's all very nice, but I really don't need anything. Despite what you may think."

Russell groaned. "You're insane," he said. "Any other girl in the world—whatever the size of her wardrobe—would be running around this place like crazy, grabbing every piece in sight. Can you imagine Lauren in here? There'd be nothing left after she got through."

"She would love it," Ava agreed. "It's too bad she's not the one here right now. But I'm not like her. I don't get my thrills from shopping. I don't even enjoy it."

"Come on," Russell said. "This is fun. This is kid in a candy store time."

"Think of me as a kid with diabetes."

"I'm not letting you leave without picking something out."

"Fine. If it'll make you happy and get us out of here, I'll take a scarf." She bent over the box again and pulled out a large square of a patterned blue and dark orange silk. "This is nice."

"No, no, no," Russell said and tried to snatch the scarf away.

She pulled it back, out of his reach. "What? It's pretty." She figured she'd hang it on the back of a chair. It would dress up her apartment.

"Scarves are for women whose necks give away their age. Or for Frenchwomen who really know how to wear them." He crossed his arms. "You're definitely not old. Are you French?"

"Maybe," she said.

"Repeat after me: *Après moi le deluge.*"

"*Après moi le deluge,*" she repeated in her execrable high school French.

"Nope—you're definitely not French. Give me back the scarf." She surrendered it to him, and he dropped it back in the box. "Just hold on." He darted down a little alleyway between two racks and after a minute of rustling and clanging hangers, emerged triumphantly with a dark green dress like the one they had seen in the store window. "I know you like this—you already told me so."

"I said it was pretty. On the mannequin. But it's not the kind of thing I wear."

"Just try it on," he said. "I think it will look great on you. It's perfect for your coloring, and since you're pretty small, the sample size should work. But it's hard to tell without actually seeing it on you."

"Try it on?" she said. "Now?"

"Yeah."

"Where?"

He waved his hand airily. "Just go into a corner. I promise I won't look."

She looked around dubiously. "I don't know . . ."

"Oh, don't be silly," he said. "People try stuff on in here all the time. Most days you can't walk in here without seeing some model or another stripped down to her undies and sometimes not even that."

"Models also shoot heroin," she said.

"Here." He threw the dress at her and she caught it reflexively. "I'll leave the room, if that makes you more comfortable. Come get me when you have the dress on."

He headed back toward the door. Ava said to his retreating back, "I don't want to do this."

"I'm not letting you out of here until you do," he said, without even bothering to look back. "I'm going to drag you into the world of fashion, even if it's kicking and screaming." He left, banging the door unnecessarily loudly behind him.

Ava held the dress up and made a face at it. The whole thing was ridiculous—what kind of straight guy made playing dress-up part of an evening out? What kind of grown woman let him?

She couldn't remember when it was that she decided she wasn't going to care about clothing. As far back as she could remember, Lauren had been obsessed with her wardrobe and would beg their mother to buy her stylish things, but Ava simply wore whatever Nancy brought home for her from the Gap. When the time came to pick a college, she fell in love with Haverford, where the majority of the girls had long stringy hair and dressed in heavy sweaters and baggy jeans and argued about politics late into the night: it just felt like a place where she would fit in. Her last two years there, she had a fairly intense relationship with a guy who was a nature buff and an environmentalist. He criticized anyone who spent money or time on superficial things and reserved his greatest contempt for the kind of girl who wore nail polish (toxic) and makeup (tested on animals). He told Ava that her lack of vanity was what made her beautiful to him. They went hiking together and ate at vegetarian restaurants where the water was always served at room temperature and alcohol wasn't served at all.

Had Gabe influenced her more than she had realized?

Quite possibly—she had been madly in love with him. Unfortunately, he graduated a year before her and went off to study marine biology in Florida. He broke up with her by e-mail less than a month later. Ava wasn't as stricken as she might have been: a cute if slightly pretentious guy in her English class had been flirting with her and she hadn't gotten around to mentioning that she was in a committed relationship.

On her first date with the new guy, she ordered steak and ice-cold beer, and they both tasted great.

But even out with that guy she hadn't worn makeup or high heels, and didn't that mean it wasn't just Gabe's influence that had made her the way she was? That he had simply spoken to something that was *already* a profound part of her personality? When *hadn't* Ava believed that all the primping and the fussing and the accessorizing and the decorating were a sign that you weren't smart enough or confident enough to be truthful about who you were and ultimately appealed only to the wrong sort of guys?

But she was here now, slightly tipsy, in this crazy enormous closet, and the dress was pretty, and Russell had said she'd look great in it. He had also said he wouldn't let her out of the room until she tried it on, so it seemed to her she might as well get on with it.

With a weird sense of excitement, Ava pulled a couple of racks together to create a little dressing room. Hidden by the clothes, she stepped out of her shoes and unbuttoned her shirt, then slid the dress on before shoving her skirt down and off.

She had to contort herself to reach the zipper in the back. It was a struggle, but she finally got it zipped up and settled the dress into place. The neck was cut so low that it showed the plain white edges of her sensible underwire bra, and the skirt was shorter in the thigh than she was used to. With no mirror, she couldn't tell how it looked: it wasn't uncomfortable, but the fit was snugger than anything she was used to and she wondered if she looked bulgy.

She felt oddly nervous as she shoved her feet back into her Aerosole pumps and left the sanctum of the racks to let Russell in.

The second she pushed the door open a crack, Russell was pulling it the rest of the way open. "Let me see." He came in and studied her eagerly. She backed up a few steps and hugged her elbows, uncomfortable under his scrutiny.

"Very nice," he said. "Put your arms down, stand up straight, and turn around."

"I feel stupid."

"Just turn around, will you? I want to see how the back looks."

Ava had a tendency to buckle when given a direct order. She turned around.

"You look fantastic," Russell said, a little smugly, when she was facing him again. "I knew there was a great pair of legs under those dowdy skirts. You need a different bra, though."

Ava stared at him. "Are you sure your father wasn't right about you?"

"Just because I think about fashion doesn't mean I'm gay," Russell said. Then, considering, "Okay, maybe it should. But I'm not—which is a shame, because it would only be an asset for my career. I'm a regular guy who happens to like dressing women."

"Well, so long as *you're* good with that—"

He raised his chin. "I am, thank you. Although I'm not sure how I feel about being called the girliest man you ever met."

"I take it back," she said. "Aside from your interest in fashion, you're practically a Neanderthal."

"Thank you! That's the nicest thing anyone's ever said to me."

Ava looked down at herself again. "I couldn't wear this to work. It's too revealing."

"Sure you could. It looks great." He plucked at a thread on her shoulders.

"It's *tight*. No one would take me seriously."

"They'd take you *more* seriously," he said. "They'd think, 'A girl who's that savvy about clothing—'"

"See? I put the dress on and you immediately start calling me a 'girl.' I want to be seen as a grown woman."

"'Woman' I get," Russell said. "Why you want to be seen as an old and frumpy woman is beyond me."

"Oh, come on. My clothes are not that bad."

He just raised his eyebrows. Then he held out his hand. "Let me show you what a difference this makes. There's a mirror against the wall."

She put her hand in his and he led her across the room to a three-way mirror. It seemed to Ava that this time his fingers flirted more with hers, moving gently against them as he pulled her along, but he dropped her hand as soon as they reached the mirror, so it was hard to be sure. "Look," he said with a wave of his hand. "Really look."

Looking at herself never gave Ava any pleasure. She used mirrors to make sure that nothing was coming out of her nose or sprouting on her face, that her clothing wasn't stained or torn, that she didn't have food in her hair or crud in her eyes. But the surprise of seeing herself in a well-tailored formfitting dress startled her. She stared. "Wow," she said, then was immediately embarrassed by her own reaction. She quickly added, "The color is great in this light," so he would think she was admiring the dress and not herself.

From behind her, Russell's reflection said, "Behold the power of well-designed clothing."

Her waist was smaller than she had thought, her legs longer, her breasts rounder. "It fits well," she acknowledged, reluctant to give him more.

"No kidding. Unlike those *schmattahs* you were wearing before." She couldn't *see* him rubbing his hands together because her body hid his arms from her view in the mirror, but she could hear the *shush-shush* of his palms moving against each other. "Let's keep going. We're going to find you a whole new wardrobe tonight."

"No, really," she said, turning away from the mirror. "You don't have to. This is pretty, but—"

"I want to," he said and moved away, back toward the clothes. "It's a good thing you're a six," he called out as he flicked through hangers on a rack. "We only have twos, fours, and sixes."

"What about this?" Ava unhooked a hanger from a rack and held up a green wool skirt.

Russell glanced at it and rolled his eyes. "Oh, please," he said. "That's for the old ladies. When are you going to realize you're a pretty, young girl? Oh, sorry—I mean *woman*. A pretty, young woman. A pretty, young American woman." He returned his attention to the clothes in front of him and selected a pair of pants and a top. "Here," he said, rejoining Ava and thrusting the hangers at her. "Try on the pants and this top. I'll keep looking for more stuff."

"Okay," she said as she took the clothes. "But go wait outside."

"Come on," he said. "I think our relationship has moved beyond the waiting outside phase, don't you? You can trust me not to look." His eyes lingered on her body in its revealing dress for a moment. "I'm capable of resisting temptation. For a short period of time, anyway. But don't take too long. I'm only human."

Ava swallowed. He was *definitely* flirting with her now. She flushed, absurdly pleased, but the pleasure gave way almost immediately to doubt. Why was he suddenly flirting with her *now* when he never had before? Because she had changed into clothes he liked? Didn't that make him exactly the kind of man she had always despised, the kind who cared about the wrapping more than the contents?

Suspicion crept into her voice. "Oh, fine," she said. "Whatever." She grabbed the clothes from him and stomped over to her little V-shaped dressing room, where she struggled to unzip the dress before pulling it over her head. It got stuck for a moment and she felt panicky about how silly she must look with her head caught in the dress and her practical white bra and underpants showing. She finally wrenched herself free, tossed the dress to the side, and looked wildly about. The top of Russell's head was visible, but he was on the other side of the room and appeared to have his back to her. *So much for his stealing a look*, she thought, and relief that he hadn't spied on her was mixed with a slight disappointment that he hadn't *wanted* to.

She pulled on the pants. They were made of a fine silk/linen blend, very fitted at the waist and hips with wide, flowing legs—like something Katharine Hepburn might have worn on her day off. The top Russell had chosen to pair with them was a pure silk crimson tank with flat, wide shoulder straps. It felt lovely as it slid into place on her shoulders: soft and feminine and fluid. *Probably would need to be dry-cleaned regularly*, she reminded herself. She always tried to avoid clothes that were dry-clean-only and therefore liable to waste both her time and money.

"Okay," she said, raising her voice so Russell could hear her and resisting the urge to cry out, *Olly-olly-oxen-free.* "I'm dressed again."

"Let me see." She came out from behind the racks just as he reached them. "Terrific," he said with a nod. "You look fantastic."

"I think the top's too short. It shows my stomach."

"No it doesn't."

"Look." She raised her arms, which made the shirt rise and expose her midsection.

"Well, if you're going to do *that*. But it's not like you walk around all day with your arms raised, do you?"

"What if I want to wave hello to someone? Or hail a cab?" She feigned the motion, and the moment her hand was raised Russell reached out and stroked his finger across the inch of bared stomach. She instantly collapsed down and pulled away. "Hey!"

"Sorry. Couldn't resist." He flashed a mischievous grin.

She bit her lip. The brief touch had startled her, made her skin pulse. He was still standing closer than seemed necessary. She was suddenly very aware they were alone together in this big room, maybe even in the whole building.

He turned her gently around, put his hands on her shoulders from behind, and steered her back to the mirror. He stood behind her, his hands still on her shoulders, his mouth right at her ear. "Look," he whispered. "Look at the pretty girl in the mirror. Tell me that's not a welcome sight."

His breath in her ear made her feel a little shaky, and he was right that the outfit looked good on her, but she still refused to surrender the argument. "It's the same girl who's always in there," she said stubbornly. "There's a little extra icing, but it's the same girl."

"I never said it wasn't." His hands caressed her shoulders and slid down her arms.

Ava realized, with a slight sense of panic, that Russell was coming on to her for real now. That his hands were on the move and weren't likely to stop unless she stopped them.

This was not how she had expected the evening to go. He had been disappointed when Lauren ran out on them, so why was he suddenly making a play for *her?*

Any port in a storm, she thought. He was that kind of guy. And what about Corinne, anyway?

"What about Corinne, anyway?" she said out loud.

Russell raised his head to look at their reflection. His arms were still around her from behind. "Corinne?"

"Yeah, remember her?" She twisted out of his grasp and turned to face him directly. "Blond, thin girl, a bit younger than me? Very pretty?" *If you like that sort of thing*, she added contemptuously to herself, but had enough self-control not to say it out loud.

Russell dropped his hands to his sides. "Name rings a distant bell."

"Seriously," she said. "I thought you were a couple. What happened?"

"I'm just curious," Russell said with a sigh. "Have you ever gotten lost in the moment in your whole life?"

"I can be as spontaneous as the next woman when I choose to be."

"You do realize that's an insane thing to say, right?"

"You haven't answered my question."

"Corinne and I see each other from time to time, but there's no commitment there," he said. "I'm commitment-resistant at the moment. That okay with you?"

"I don't care one way or the other."

"Then why bring her up?"

There was a pause. Ava said, "It's getting late."

Russell didn't even look at his watch. "That's kind of the fun of it, isn't it?" he said softly. "That it's getting late? But we're still here, alone?"

She ran her hands nervously down the sides of the pants, then immediately worried that the sweat on her palms might have stained the beautiful fabric. They weren't even her pants. She curled her hands into fists. "I just meant I should probably go."

He moved closer again. "Now that you're all dressed up? You want to waste a good outfit on going home and going to sleep?"

"I was going to change back into my other clothes."

"We should go out," he said. "Go to a club. I could pick out something fun here for you to wear. Do you dance?"

"Not if I can help it."

He rolled his eyes. "Of course you don't. Puritans never do."

"I'm not a Puritan," she said. "I'm just not very good at dancing. I feel self-conscious."

"You need to get over that."

"I'll put it on the list," she said, almost sadly.

"Okay, no dancing." He stroked one finger gently down the length of her upper arm. "So here's a question. Once Pygmalion made Galatea come to life, what do you think they did together?"

"Wow," she said, twitching a little as his finger reversed itself, tracing a light path up toward her shoulder again. "Galatea. That's an awfully . . . uh . . . *classical* reference for someone like you."

"Someone like me?" he repeated. "What's that supposed to mean?"

"You know. Someone who likes fashion and hip restaurants . . . I wouldn't have expected you to know your Greek mythology."

He tugged gently on her arm, moving her closer to him. He let his fingers trail up along her shoulder, behind her neck, under her hair. "Don't forget that in my family, *I'm* the smart one."

She tried to sound relaxed, like his touch wasn't getting to her, which it was. "Only compared to your brother."

"Maybe. But I was more like you than you remember. That's why we're engaged."

"We're not engaged," she said, her voice a little thick. She made a token throat-clearing noise. Russell's fingers were twined gently in the hair behind her neck, the knuckles brushing against her skin. She closed her eyes, let herself relax back into him.

"Sure we are." He shifted so his body was against hers, his thigh brushing against her hip. "We've been engaged since childhood. Our parents looked at us and said, 'Those two—they belong together.' They must have known something, don't you think?"

Even with her eyes closed, she knew that he was bending over her, that he was about to kiss her on the lips, so it wasn't a surprise when she felt him there, though she breathed in sharply as if it were.

His mouth was warm and gentle, teasing hers open carefully and slowly, like he knew that if he went too fast, was too demanding, she'd be gone. *And I would, too*, Ava thought with a dreamy lack of conviction.

She hadn't even liked the last guy she'd kissed—a blind date her friend Anna had arranged with her chiropractor. His lips had been thick and clammy, his kiss unwelcome. She had extricated herself quickly from the embrace and never returned his calls. That had been over a year ago.

She had forgotten how good a kiss could feel, how the right touch against your tongue and lips could light little flares throughout the rest of your body, affecting distant areas like an acupressure map of the foot she had once seen: touch *here* and you'll feel it *there*.

Russell's hands slid around her waist and she let her head nestle into the crook of his shoulder.

His kiss moved from her lips to her temple and down to her ear. He murmured into it, "I think this is *exactly* what Pygmalion and Galatea must have done once she came to life, don't you?"

"Stone made flesh," she said, a little dazed, her eyes still closed.

"It'll be your epitaph," he said with a whispery laugh. She felt him lift the hair up off her neck, felt his mouth moving against the hidden skin deep under there and didn't want him to stop. Too soon, he was lifting his head. His arms still around her, he said, "Let's go."

"Where?"

"My place." He released her arms, took her by the hand, led her toward the door.

She felt drugged, stupefied by a long kiss and a romantic embrace. In her stupor, it was easy to let him lead her. He squeezed her hand and released it, leaving her at the door for a moment while he went back to gather up the dress he had found for her and the clothes she had been wearing all day, which she had forgotten about and would have left there. He plucked a few more items of clothing off of racks and out of boxes on his way back to her and piled them in his arms. "You can try this all on later," he said.

She stared at the mound of clothing he held until he nudged

her with his shoulder and indicated that she should open the door. She did. They went out and she pushed the button for the elevator.

"You're awfully quiet all of a sudden," he said when they were inside. The stack of clothing in his arms rose up to his chin. Ava wished he weren't holding them, that he was holding her. Bereft of his touch and the mild delirium it aroused, she could feel reason returning, and with it, cold hard doubt.

He was still watching her, his dark brown eyes searching her face from above his armful of richly colored fabrics. "Is every-thing okay?"

"I'm a little overwhelmed at the moment," she said, unable to meet his intense gaze.

"It's a hard transition," he said. "That stone to flesh thing."

"It's not that." The elevator door opened before she could explain—not that she really knew how to explain her sudden hesitation, anyway. They nodded at the security guard, who raised his eyebrows at the pile of clothing in Russell's arms but didn't say anything. Ava wondered if he noticed she was dressed in different clothes than she had arrived in, and what he would make of that if he did.

Russell dropped his bundle in the trunk of his car while Ava let herself into the passenger seat. He got in, closed his door, and looked at her for a moment, smiling. He leaned over to kiss her again, but she pulled back—just a bit, but enough to make him stop. "What's wrong?" he said.

"Nothing's wrong," she said, feeling in her strained cheeks how forced her smile was. "But now I'm thinking I should probably go home instead of to your place."

"Why?" he said. "You hear your mother calling again?"

"I need to think about this a little more."

"I thought you said you were capable of spontaneity."

"I am. But being with someone—" She hesitated. "You're going to make fun of me again, tell me I'm a Puritan. But it has to mean something to me."

"Hey, I gave you free clothing. Tell me that's not meaningful."

"I'm serious."

He pulled her hair lightly. "Well, don't be. Relax."

"I just *wonder*."

"What?" he said and, with an impatient sigh, let go of her hair and swiveled forward to start the car. "What do you wonder about, Nickerson?"

"Well," she said, "for one thing, you only seem to be attracted to me when I'm dressed a certain way. Your way."

"That's stupid," Russell said. "I'd be attracted to you no matter what you wore. In fact, you could be *naked*, Ava, and I'd be attracted to you. Really. I mean that."

She laughed in spite of herself, in spite of the doubt, in spite of the desire that his words sent twanging along her body. She squeezed her knees together. "That doesn't get at the root of the problem," she said.

"Does it matter?" He put his hand on her leg. "Man, that's quality fabric," he said, his fingers moving along the length of her thigh.

"I think I should just go home," she said, staring at his hand.

"You're making a mistake." He took his hand away and shifted into reverse. "Look," he said, "no pressure. We can go to my house and just talk, if that's what you want."

She studied the side of his face as he backed the car out of the space and drove out of the garage. She said, "If Lauren had come tonight instead of me, would you be inviting her back to your place now?"

"If Lauren had come instead of you, I'd never have gotten her out of the Walk-In," he said. "They'd find us there years from now, starved to death."

"Funny," she said. "But you're avoiding the question."

"Ava, what can I offer you to get you to come back to my house with me?"

"Not clothing."

"How about a wonderful evening of getting to know each other better in all sorts of ways?"

"You're very slick," Ava said. "You know that, don't you?"

"You say it like it's a bad thing."

She said drily, "I'm sure it has its advantages."

He glanced sideways at her, then back at the road. "What the hell happened to you? Fifteen minutes ago, you were my sweet Galatea come to life. What made you turn back into stone?"

"I'm just being careful."

He braked at a stop sign more roughly than was necessary. "Ever hear the phrase 'two steps forward, one step backward'? You define it."

"Yeah, well, maybe I'm right to be cautious. I'm not the one who's been divorced twice already."

He flinched. "Some might call that a low blow."

"I'm sorry," Ava said. She chewed on the side of her thumb. "I wasn't trying to be mean. But you can't blame me for being careful around you."

"Why?" he said. "You scared I might spring a surprise wedding on you? That I've got a judge waiting back at my place to bind us in holy matrimony against your will? I promise you, there is nothing I want *less* right now than to be married again."

"I'm just saying maybe you're not the one who should set the pace in a relationship."

He thought about that for a moment, then sighed. "You

might have a point," he said. "I don't particularly *like* your point, but I can't deny its validity."

"Thank you."

There was a pause. "So . . . back to your place?" He glanced over at her for confirmation.

She nodded.

"Oh well," he said. "At least I'll get a good night's sleep."

Ava had won the argument. So why did she feel so disappointed?

When Ava entered the apartment, a light suddenly went on and Lauren was sitting there, arm still raised, fingers on the lamp switch. "I hope you have an explanation for this, young lady," she said. "Coming home this late without so much as a phone call. I've been worried sick."

"No you haven't," Ava said. "And it's not that late." She was carrying the clothing bundled up in her arms. She dropped it all on the floor.

Lauren snuggled down into her blanket. "You're right. I wasn't actually worried at all."

"I thought you'd still be out," Ava said, coming over to her.

"Nope. Been home for hours." She narrowed her eyes. "Hey, why are you wearing different clothing than you left home in? Different and *nicer*? What kind of evening *was* it?"

She pulled her feet up to make room for Ava, who sat down on the sofa and told Lauren about the trip to Russell's office, about finding the clothing, about trying it on.

"Did he try to sneak a peek?" Lauren asked thoughtfully, like she was trying to figure something out.

"Of course not." A beat. "He *talked* about sneaking a peek."

"That sounds promising."

"Things got . . . interesting," Ava admitted.

"I knew it," Lauren crowed. "I knew if I pushed you two together, you'd catch on fire."

"That's overstating it," Ava said. "We kissed a little. That's all."

"Why was that all?"

"He wanted me to come back to his place. But I said no."

Lauren groaned and let her head fall back against the sofa with a thud. "Why? Why would you say no? You got something better to do? Like watching TV and sipping *tea*?"

"I don't know. It just didn't feel right."

"You like him, don't you?"

"Yeah, I do." She thought. "Most of the time." She thought some more. "Some of the time."

"That's good enough," Lauren said. "You should have gone back to his place."

Ava shook her head. "I don't trust him."

"Why not?"

"It's just . . . He didn't come on to me at all until I was dressed up in the clothes he'd picked out. Don't you think that's weird? Like it's either shallow or perverted?"

"Oh, relax," Lauren said. She wriggled up into a full sitting position. "Did it ever occur to you that maybe he just wanted to see how beautiful you are under those dowdy clothes you're always wearing? Or that he was having fun helping you try on clothes and that's what turned him on? Why do you always have to put a negative spin on things?"

"I'm just trying to be careful," Ava said. "The guy doesn't have the greatest track record with women. Remember Corinne? And the ex-wives? The fact that we were even out alone together was so random. I mean, if you hadn't bagged us . . ."

Lauren beamed. "That was brilliant of me, wasn't it?"

"I'm just not convinced he likes me in any deep, personal way. It still feels like we barely know each other."

"So?" Lauren said. "You can sleep with a guy you don't know that well—it's one of the best ways of getting to know him."

"I can't do that," Ava said. "I have to like a guy and trust him and feel like it could maybe lead somewhere—"

"You're a prude."

"No I'm not," she said seriously. "I like sex. It's just not casual for me, ever."

"Poor Russell," Lauren said. "He has such a long uphill battle with you. But he'll get there. How did you leave things?"

"Very awkwardly. We did the cheek-kissing thing and said we'd see each other soon. We're both busy this weekend, and then his mom comes into town, so we didn't actually schedule anything." She yawned. "Oh, that reminds me: he wants to bring his mother to visit Mom and Dad. Think they'll go for it?"

"I'll ask Mom on Tuesday." Lauren's eyes drifted over to the pile of clothing by the door. "Can I see what he gave you?"

"Sure."

Lauren slipped out from under the blanket and ran across the room. She brought the big pile back over to the sofa and held up one piece after another. She examined it all carefully and professionally. "He's got a pretty good eye. There are some nice pieces here. I don't like this one so much"—she tossed aside a chartreuse boatneck sweater—"it's a bad color for you. For anyone. But this sweater dress is fantastic. And what are those pants you're wearing? I noticed them as soon as you came in. They're gorgeous."

"I don't know. Pants." Ava put a pillow behind her head. "How was *your* date, by the way? You haven't said anything about it."

Lauren was folding the clothing neatly and swiftly. Ava had

noticed in the past that her sister always took good care of clothing, even though she could be a slob in other ways. "There's nothing to say. It was so short, I'm not sure it even counted as a date."

"Did anything go wrong?"

"No, he just had to go take care of his mother." She held up a skirt Ava hadn't tried on, a blue pleated miniskirt. "Hey, can I have this?"

"Sure. It's not my kind of thing."

"I wish I had gone with you," Lauren said, a little wistfully. "I mean, not really, because I'm glad the fix-up worked and I wanted you guys to be alone together. But I would have liked to have picked out some stuff for myself. Do you think Russell would take me back there another time?"

"Probably. Although he kept saying things about how his days working there were numbered, so you'd better ask him soon." Ava yawned again and stretched. "I should go to bed. You need the bathroom before I close the door?"

Lauren was still busy sorting through the clothing. "Don't like the way they finished the seams on this one." She held up a shimmery dark pink top. "Can I have this too?"

"Actually," Ava said sheepishly, "I was thinking maybe I'd wear that the next time I see Russell."

"Good girl," Lauren said. "Actually making an effort. Can I borrow it after that?" She held up another top. "And this too?"

"Why don't we just share it all?" Ava said.

Lauren gave a little leap of excitement and threw her arms around her sister. "You're the best," she said.

"But only when I share my clothes with you."

"Only when you share *these* clothes with me," Lauren corrected her.

Chapter 12

"How would you feel if Lana Markowitz came for a visit on Sunday morning?" Lauren asked her mother when they were in the car on the way to the hospital the following Tuesday.

"Is it a real possibility?" Nancy asked. "Or a hypothetical question?"

"Why?" Lauren asked. "Are they different answers?"

"Maybe." Nancy lolled her head back against the headrest and gazed absently at the windshield. "If it's hypothetical, then of course I'd love to see an old friend. If she's actually going to be in town, I'd have to think about it more carefully. As you know, I had mixed feelings about Lana."

"She'll actually be in town. Russell asked if he could bring her over—apparently, she really wants to see you. Maybe her feelings aren't as mixed as yours?"

Nancy was silent for a moment. "I think it would be nice," she said finally.

"Really?"

"Yes. For one thing, I'll probably be stuck at home anyway."

She sat up straight in the bucket seat. "And also, it's a weird thing, but I've been feeling kind of nostalgic lately. Something about being sick is making me think more about the past." She patted Lauren's knee. "I love my big adult daughters, but lately I find myself thinking a lot about you when you were little. And missing that."

"I could let you burp me now and then, if it would help."

"That's kind of you," her mother said.

"So somehow all this nostalgia means brunch with the Markowitzes?"

"Yes," her mother said. "Just make sure they bring bagels. Lots and lots of bagels."

"Very funny," said Lauren, who had personally bagged and frozen the three dozen leftover bagels from the previous brunch.

They drove in silence for a moment or two. Then Nancy said, "Are you going to introduce me to him today?"

"To who?"

"To whom," Nancy said. "That guy you've been hanging out with at the hospital when you think I'm asleep."

"You know what?" Lauren said. "You're sneaky. You're a sneaky mother."

"I wasn't asleep when you came home late at night during high school either," Nancy said. "All those years, I was up and listening to you as you stumbled around, drunk or wasted—"

"Mom!" Lauren said. "I never did stuff like that."

Nancy said calmly, "*Never*, sweetie? Really? Never?"

Lauren shot her a look—as venomous a one as she could manage without taking her eyes off the road for too long. "Infrequently enough to round down to never."

"Maybe it was just exhaustion?" Nancy suggested. "You were probably at the library studying until so late that your poor little eyes were worn out and that's why they were so bloodshot, and you were so tired from all that studying that you could hardly stand up, let alone walk straight—"

"Sneaky and a little bit nasty," Lauren muttered.

"It's the cancer talking," her mother said. "I'm really very nice, you know, but the cancer sometimes says these nasty little evil things. I just can't stop it from taking over now and then."

"Good thing we're going to the hospital to poison it right out of you, then."

"Once it's gone," Nancy said, "I'll go back to being the good, sweet, kind mother I really am. But until then—"

"Sneaky and nasty?"

"Learn to live with it." She touched Lauren lightly on her arm. "So are you going to introduce me to your friend or not?"

"Sure, I'll introduce you," Lauren said. "He's a weird guy, though. Don't expect too much."

"I'm just glad you've found someone to talk to at the hospital. It must be pretty boring for you, keeping me company there all these long, endless afternoons."

"I don't mind," Lauren said. "I'm glad I can do it."

"I hate that you have to." Her mother pushed the visor down in front of her with an irritated snap. "I hate that everyone's life is getting disrupted because of me."

"I like it," Lauren said. "Honestly, I do. I like getting you all to myself for a few hours. I've never had that before."

"You had three years alone with me after Ava went off to college," her mother said. "And you were rude and sullen the entire time. You never said a word to me except the occasional, 'Do you honestly expect me to eat that?'"

"I was a teenager," Lauren said. "I was just doing my job."

"You did it very well."

There was a pause. In the sudden quiet, Lauren could hear the car radio, very faintly—it must have been left on, but at a low volume. It sounded like someone was whispering secrets in the backseat.

Nancy broke the almost-silence. "Ava said you went on a date last weekend with the guy from the hospital."

"I can't believe she told you that!"

"Why?" Nancy said. "Isn't it true?"

"See, this is the problem with living with your sister. No privacy."

"*You* moved in with *her*. So how was the date?"

"It was okay."

"Ava said it ended very early."

Lauren flipped a lock of hair over her shoulder. She was wearing it long and swingy today: it had taken her half an hour to straighten it with the flatiron that morning. "You guys had a nice long talk about this, didn't you?"

"Do you like him?"

"I don't know. And I'm not saying that to be unhelpful: I'm just trying to figure him out. That's all. I honestly don't know if I like him or not."

"All right," Nancy said. "But when you do figure it out, will you let me know the verdict?"

"Probably not," Lauren said. "But don't worry—you can always ask Ava."

The chemo ward was a little less crowded that afternoon, and the nurses were able to put Nancy in a private room. Lauren got her settled, turned on the TV, waited until the drip was fully activated, and then prowled around the edges of the room until Nancy said, "I thought you were going to find your friend and bring him here for me to meet."

"You sure you're up to socializing?"

"Absolutely. It'll make a nice change from trying to pretend I'm interested in *that*." She jerked her chin in the direction of the TV, which only received three channels, all of which were currently showing daytime talk shows with guests who appeared to have been recruited from caves deep in the Ozark Mountains.

"I'll be right back," Lauren said and left the room.

Finding Daniel turned out to be unexpectedly easy: she spotted him the instant she turned the corner. He was just standing in the corridor, peering into his cell phone and pressing the keypad.

"Hello," she said as she came up to him.

He looked up and stared at her absently, as if he couldn't quite place her and didn't have the time or the inclination to work it out at that moment. But then he closed his cell phone. "Oh, hi. Where'd they put your mother?"

"Room 523," Lauren said. "Your mom in there?" She pointed to the door behind him.

"Yeah. She had a bad night and the nurse was a little worried about how weak she was today, so I thought I should probably stay close by. I only came out to make a call."

"Cell phone use is prohibited." She pointed to the sign that said so.

"They don't actually interfere with the machinery. It's all bullshit. Anyway, what's up?" He kept fingering the edges of his phone like he was anxious to get back to it.

"My mother wants to meet you," Lauren said.

He snapped his head back. "Why?"

"She just does. She knows I've been hanging out with you here and that I saw you this weekend—"

"How'd she know that?"

"My sister told her."

He heaved an exaggerated sigh. "And *you* told your sister."

"Yeah," she said, annoyed that he was putting her on the defensive. "Was I not supposed to?"

"I just don't see the need."

"It wasn't a need," she said. "It was a conversation. Anyway, will you come say hi to my mother? Just for a minute or two?"

"I'm not in the mood to make small talk with a stranger right now," he said. "I'll pass."

Lauren gave him an incredulous look. Then she shook her head. "Fine," she said, turning away. "Forget it."

"Hey." Daniel grabbed at her arm. "What are you acting all pissed off for?"

"You've got to be kidding me," she said, shaking his hand off. "*I'm* the one who's acting all pissed off?"

He took a deep breath and stood for a moment, his arms stiff and awkward at his sides. Then he said, "I'm sorry. Hold on a second. I didn't mean to be rude."

"You sure about that?"

He passed his hand over his forehead. "It's just . . . I didn't get any sleep last night. Mom was really sick. The worst I've seen her. She tried to get up to go to the bathroom and fell. Collapsed on the floor. Luckily I heard her. If I hadn't . . ." He shook his head. "And that was just one thing. She was in pain, too, even with the meds. And when I called the doctor this morning—" He stopped.

She immediately reached her hand out to him, concern replacing anger. "What?"

"Never mind. It doesn't matter. It's just—none of it's good news. Not that I expected it to be. But it keeps getting worse and worse. I was standing here feeling sorry for her and for myself when you showed up." He forced a smile. "It was bad timing."

"I often have bad timing," Lauren said. "And I totally understand. Can I do anything to help?"

"Yes," he said. "Don't make me meet your mother. I just can't be social right now. And don't resent me for not wanting to."

"Okay." A doctor in a white lab coat brushed by, making her step back out of his way. He didn't even make eye contact, just moved on in a rush. There was a stain on the back of his coat. It occurred to Lauren, not for the first time, that there were a lot of different stories going on at that hospital. She said to Daniel, "Don't worry about it."

"Hold on," Daniel said. "I was thinking—right now is kind of bad, but my brother's actually flying in later this afternoon—"

"Wow. All the way from Costa Rica, right?"

"You have a good memory. Yeah."

"So he came through in the end." Then, realizing how that sounded, she quickly added, "I don't mean the *end*. I meant finally." That didn't sound all that much better.

"I told him he had to come," Daniel said. "I didn't give him any choice. And he knows that—" Again, he stopped himself. "Anyway, the point is that he should have some time alone with Mom once he's here. Which means I could duck out for a cup of coffee or something later. Would you be up for that?"

"Sure."

"I'll call you. I can't say what time definitely. My brother's flight is due in at four this afternoon. It left on time, but you never know if there'll be a ground delay. Plus I'll have to get him settled with Mom, show him the routine and all that. But as soon as I know when I'll be free, I'll call you."

"Okay," she said. "I'll see you later, then."

"Yeah, if everything works out."

"Right." She moved off down the hallway.

He called after her, "Tell your mother it's not personal."

When she glanced back, he had already returned to thumbing his cell phone.

"I will," she said over her shoulder. But she was lying.

Her second lie was to her mother: she told her she couldn't find Daniel anywhere.

Nancy gave Lauren a big hug when they got back to the house. "Thanks for taking such good care of me," she said, and Lauren left feeling very pleased with herself. She *was* being a good daughter, and since that hadn't been her family role historically, she was reveling in its novelty and the sense of importance it gave her.

She got back in the car and drove straight to Brentwood—straight in a directional sense, anyway, but it was rush hour and traffic was atrocious. It took her five minutes to go half a block on Sunset and she felt briefly nostalgic for New York and its public transportation system. But then a song she liked came on the radio and she blasted it and sang along and danced in her seat and liked being in a car again.

When she did finally make it into the heart of Brentwood, parking was scarce and she had to circle around for a while. She ultimately found a space several blocks from her destination, and the walk back was long enough for a tiny pang of guilt to creep in. She worked on arguing it away. Sure, she had promised Ava she wouldn't spend any money on clothing—had even signed a piece of paper to that effect—but it was an absurd and unnecessary promise, one that she had been pressured into making. The ultimate goal was that she learn to be more *restrained* in her purchasing, and the last month had proven she could do that: she hadn't bought anything for herself that didn't qualify as a necessity. So for her to buy something now was no big deal: one new item of clothing a month was probably less than any other young woman in America was buying. So long as she didn't let the one purchase act like some kind of dam bursting and start spending money like crazy, there was nothing intrinsically wrong with it.

In fact, she thought, getting into her internal debate (which she was winning), you could even argue that the one purchase would prove how much she had changed. She was buying it not because she simply wanted to buy *something*, which was, admittedly, a pathetic habit that had needed breaking, but because she wanted this *one specific item*. And once she owned it, her wardrobe would be complete. She wouldn't need anything else for a very long time. Talk about your bargains.

With a determined jut of her chin, she shoved the door open, entered the store, and went straight to the turquoise camisole with the beaded bodice, which was exactly where she had remembered it.

The saleswoman admired the top on Lauren as soon as she emerged from the curtained-off dressing room to look at herself in the three-way mirror—"Oh my God, it fits you *perfectly*!"—and begged her to pair it with some jeans they had just gotten in that week. "You won't believe how good these fit," the girl said. She was dressed gamine-like in tight black clamdiggers and a short-sleeved black wool turtleneck, but the cadences of her speech were pure Valley girl. "Everyone who comes in here and tries them on loves them. And they'll totally work with that cami."

Lauren twisted her mouth to the side. "I have a lot of jeans," she said.

"But these have a curved waistline so they don't gape. You need that with this top since it has that loose drape—don't want the world to see your business every time you sit down, do you? Plus they have a trouser cut, which is so right when you need to be a little dressed up but can still get away with wearing jeans."

"That's a good point." She meant it. This girl was smart.

"Just try them," the saleswoman said. "You don't have to buy them."

The truth of that was inarguable. Lauren tried on the jeans. While she was checking them out in the mirror, the young saleswoman—Griffin, she had said her name was—returned to her side with a pair of high-heeled jeweled sandals. "These are too perfect," she said. "You have to try them on with that outfit. See how the beading kind of matches? You'd think they were made to go with that top. You're like a seven, right?" She bent down and put them on the floor in front of Lauren, all ready to be stepped into.

This time, Lauren didn't bother with demurrals, just slipped her feet into the sandals. The hem of the jeans had puddled on the floor before, but they were the perfect length with the sandals on. When she took a step, the tips of the sandals peeked out, girlishly pretty and satisfyingly shiny. She'd have to redo her toenail polish: the dark red she had on now was too obvious for these particular shoes. They needed something light and pearl-like.

She revolved slowly in front of the mirror.

"Wow," the salesgirl said. "That is an amazing outfit on you. Has anyone ever told you you look like Julianna Margulies?" She reached out and minutely adjusted the straps on Lauren's shoulders. She had been taller than Lauren a minute ago, but the shoes had given Lauren new height.

"God, I love this top," Lauren said, twisting so she could look at the back view.

"And the jeans fit you perfectly," Griffin said. "You have to get them. I wish they looked as good on me, but I don't have your figure."

She was clearly working on commission, Lauren thought, but that only made her feel warmly toward the girl—Lauren had worked on commission at previous jobs too. "I've been trying to cut back a little on my spending," Lauren said, raising her right foot so she could admire the way the jeweled strap curved across her instep.

"None of these pieces is all that expensive," Griffin said. "And you can wear them all separately or together. Honestly, you're going to get so much use out of all of these things—who doesn't need a really good, dressy pair of jeans? And the top will take you through every season—just throw a wrap over it when it's cold. And those sandals will go with everything. I have a pair of them and I wear them with skirts, jeans, you name it."

No you don't, Lauren thought with tolerant amusement. That was one of the oldest salesgirl tricks in the book: claiming to own the item you wanted someone to buy so you could extol its virtues and also subtly make the point that if even a low-paid salesgirl could afford it, then certainly her (almost definitely) wealthier customer could. Lauren had made that claim many times herself. Of course, she usually *did* own the item in question, having purchased a large percentage of her store's merchandise. And Griffin was admittedly well-dressed. A fellow spendthrift, maybe?

"I'll think about it while I get changed," she said, turning away from the mirror. "Try to make a decision."

"Take your time," Griffin said and moved off. Two new customers had just entered the store. "Give a holler when you're ready," she added over her shoulder.

Lauren undressed slowly, carefully arranging the straps of the top on the padded hanger and folding the jeans neatly and expertly. She put the shoes side by side on the floor and kept glancing at them as she pulled her own clothes back on.

If Ava knew how desperately Lauren wanted all three things—and how even so she was hesitating, not wanting to break her word or betray her sister's trust—she would *have* to feel progress had been made, have to know that Lauren had matured and changed. But Lauren couldn't risk telling her; if she bought something today, it would have to be a secret. Ava couldn't see into Lauren's heart and know how she had struggled over this, so she would simply assume Lauren was being her old extravagant self.

Lauren brusquely pushed aside the curtain, making the rings grate along the pole. She would buy only the top and the shoes. She had other jeans—although, sadly, none exactly like these, and she could really use them—she loved the way the waist curved with her body and the cut was just so modern—but she would resist—although the truth was she would probably get tons of use out of them, and they were the kind of thing she *should* be buying, pretty but also practical—

No. She was resolved: in spite of the many arguments in their favor, she would not buy the jeans.

And just a few short months ago, she *would* have bought the jeans, so she had every right to be proud of herself.

As far as Ava went . . . well, if she asked where the top and shoes had come from (which she probably wouldn't because when did Ava notice anything about clothes?), Lauren would simply tell her that the items predated the contract. It would be a lie, of course, and Lauren never liked to lie, only did it as a last resort and when she really needed a way out of a tough situation. And Ava was putting her in a position where she had no choice.

She soothed her conscience by promising it that these were the last things she would buy for a long, long time.

A pretty necklace hanging near the cash register caught her eye as Griffin totaled up her purchases, and Lauren scooped it up in her palm to examine it more closely.

"You want that too?" Griffin said, looking up. "It would go great with this."

"Not today." Lauren let the necklace drop back into place with a sigh. "Another time."

Chapter 13

"Hey," Ava said, walking into the apartment and tossing her briefcase on the side table. "Somebody looks awfully fancy tonight. You going out?"

Lauren looked up from the sofa where she was reading a magazine. "I think so, but I'm not sure when. Daniel's supposed to call."

"It's already past eight." Ava glanced at her watch to confirm it.

"Yeah, I know. He said it might be pretty late."

Ava thumped down on the armchair. "So what'd you do today?"

"Took Mom to the hospital. Watched her get chemo. Took her home again. Same old same old."

"How'd it all go?"

"Barrel of laughs," Lauren said. "As always."

"Meet any cute guys?"

"Not this time," Lauren said. "I hear all the good ones hang out at St. Vincent's now."

"You know what?" Ava said. "I'm going to go next time. I'll

just move some stuff around on my schedule. I should take Mom, at least once."

"Don't be an idiot," Lauren said. "There's no reason for you to have to stress about missing work when I have nothing better to do. I like taking her."

"That's not what you just said."

"It's fine," Lauren said. "Mom's a good sport and I like seeing Daniel when he's there." The mention of Daniel's name made them both check their watches again.

Ava said, "If he were smart, he'd call you sooner rather than later. The guy doesn't know what he's missing—that's quite a top." She meant it, too. Lauren looked great.

"It's nice, isn't it?" Lauren said, idly plucking at the hem.

"Very. Is it from your old store?"

"Yeah. I bought it a while ago but haven't worn it much."

"Well, I hope Daniel appreciates it." Ava reached her arms up over her head and stretched. As she arched her back, her stomach growled audibly, and she and Lauren both giggled. "Hmm," Ava said, dropping her arms back down. "It appears to be time to eat." She got up and went into the kitchen, emerging a minute later with jars of peanut butter and jelly and a bag of crackers.

Lauren's cell phone was lying on the center of the kitchen table, and as Ava picked it up to move it out of the way, it rang. She glanced at it, but Lauren was already on her feet. She pounced on Ava and grabbed the phone out of her hand, flipping it open and getting it to her ear with a single motion. "Hello? Oh, hi! I wasn't expecting it to be *you*. You still at work? . . . That sucks . . . Were you looking for—" She stopped and listened intently, then moved a few steps away and turned her back to Ava. "Yeah, I do," she said in a low voice. Another pause. "Close. That and a half . . . Right. Okay? . . . Okay. Good. So I'll see you soon?" Then she gave a flirtatious little laugh. "Too true. Okay, I better go. Bye." She flipped it shut again with a guarded look at Ava and shoved it into her back pocket.

"Who was that?" Ava asked.

"Huh?"

"Who was that?" Ava repeated, a little sharply.

"Oh. My friend Joseph. You know, from New York? He wanted to say hi."

"Really?" Ava said. "If he's in New York, why'd you say you'd see him soon?"

"Oh, you know. Habit. I always say that at the end of a conversation." She drew closer to the table. "Peanut butter and jelly—yum. I'll get the knives." She went into the kitchen, leaving Ava alone to chew on her thumb and think about the name she had seen pop up on Lauren's caller ID and wonder why her sister hadn't wanted her to know that Russell Marko-witz had called.

Daniel did call, but not until almost nine-thirty.

The sisters were watching a TV show, and Ava muted the sound while Lauren answered her phone.

"I'm sorry it's so late," Daniel said.

At least he had bothered to apologize.

"I was going to call you right after my brother got here, but my mother said she had some stuff she needed to talk to us both about immediately. It was—" He paused, then said, "It was kind of heavy. Not the sort of thing you walk out of to make a phone call."

"No worries," Lauren said.

"Anyway, Mom's asleep now and Matthew's here if she wakes

up. I know I said coffee, but I'm starving—you up for some dinner?"

"I kind of ate already."

"Make him come here," Ava hissed in her ear. "So I can meet him."

Lauren nodded. She was eager to get Ava's opinion of Daniel. So far, she had pretty much only seen him in a one-on-one vacuum, and maybe that was why she found him so enigmatic— maybe Ava, who was smart, would have some insight into him that was eluding Lauren. "Why don't you just come over to my place?" she said into the phone.

There was a pause. "I haven't eaten yet."

"I'll make you something here."

He was silent.

She said, "Or we can run out and grab something. Come over and then we'll decide."

That bought her a wary "Okay."

"There's wine and beer too," she said. "If you're in the mood."

"Okay," he said again, with a touch more enthusiasm. "I'll be there in half an hour."

Lauren folded up her phone and Ava said, "Do you have any idea how much that sounded like you were inviting him over to have sex? All that stuff about being 'in the mood' and having drinks?"

"Really?" Lauren said. "But you're here."

"He doesn't know that."

"Oh, right."

"He thinks you want to have sex with him."

Lauren grinned. "I'm okay with that."

"Because you do?"

"Because I don't mind his thinking I do. Speaking of hot sex, what's going on with you and Russell?"

"Not much," Ava said. "What's going on with *you* and him?"

"What are you talking about? I'm not the one who almost had sex with him a few nights ago."

"I'm so glad I didn't."

"Why are we suddenly down on Russell?"

Ava just shrugged and didn't answer.

"You're doing it again," Lauren said. "That thing you always do where you push guys away as soon as they start to like you."

"What?" Ava stared at her and then shook her head. "You're crazy. I don't do that."

"Maybe not consciously," Lauren said, "but you get suspicious when someone likes you—it's like you can't believe anyone *would*, so the second someone does, you stop trusting him, and you get all prickly and difficult and make it even harder for him. It's like he has to cut down all those prickles and thorns around you—like the guy in the fairy tale—just to prove to you he's worthy." She was pleased with her metaphor.

Ava didn't seem impressed by it. "That's the dumbest thing I ever heard," she said. "And I'd like to point out I've had plenty of boyfriends." She stood up. "Help me get the dishes into the kitchen."

"I never said you didn't." Lauren picked up the lid to the jelly jar and screwed it back on. "But it's like the way you won't make yourself look good for a guy—it's part of the same—oh shit!"

Ava glanced up, licking peanut butter off her finger. "What's wrong?"

"I got jelly on my new top."

"Serves you right," Ava said. "Teach you to try to psycho-analyze your big sister. And I thought the top wasn't new."

"I haven't worn it much yet—you know what I mean." Lauren ran into the kitchen and wet a dish towel, then wiped furiously at the dark purple spot right in front.

Ava came in with the rest of the dishes. "Is it coming out?"

"I can't tell. The water's making a bigger stain. Oh, God, Ava, I hope I haven't ruined it permanently." If she had spent all that money just to stain the top before anyone even saw her in it, she'd be beyond furious. At herself and the world. "I better change."

"That should make you happy," Ava said. "You love to change your clothes."

Lauren didn't respond to that, just left the kitchen and went on into Ava's bedroom. The clothes she had hanging in the closet were mostly dresses, too formal for tonight, so she looked through the box of folded clothes she kept under Ava's bed and rediscovered a dark gray jersey tank that had briefly been a favorite piece when she first bought it a few months earlier. It fit her well and was kind of sexy in a relaxed, tomboyish way.

The truth was that the other top had really been too dressy for what this date had turned into—which didn't exactly make her feel any better about having bought it in the first place. And once she changed her top, the beaded, glittery shoes looked absurdly prom-nightish, and so off they went too. (Maybe she could still return those? Except, on examination, the soles already had slight scuff marks, which could have been there when she bought them—she hadn't checked—but might even so give the store an excuse not to take them back or at least to insist on an exchange rather than a refund.) She thrust her feet into a pair of Kenneth Cole flats and consoled herself with the thought that at least she hadn't bought the jeans. She would probably be regretting that purchase right around now, too.

She made a face at herself as she passed the full-length mirror.

Remorse was a rare companion for Lauren, and she wasn't enjoying its current visit.

Daniel buzzed up about half an hour later. Lauren let him into the apartment and he pecked her quickly on the cheek.

Ava stood up over by the sofa, and Daniel spotted her. "Who's this?"

"My sister," Lauren said. "This is her apartment. She's letting me stay here." She flipped her hand back and forth between them. "Ava, Daniel. Daniel, Ava."

"Nice to meet you," he said with a lazy jerk of his chin in Ava's direction.

"Same here." She came around the sofa and leaned against its back. She was still wearing her work clothes, a navy skirt and a white blouse, but she had taken off her shoes, which made the already overlong skirt look even longer and dowdier. Every time Lauren looked at her, she had to fight the urge to pin her sister down and forcibly hem her skirt to a more flattering length. "Were you able to find parking?"

"Yeah," he said. "It's a barely legal space, but I think I can make a case for it in court."

"Let's hope it doesn't come to that. Lauren said you hadn't had dinner yet. Can we make you something?" Ava gestured in the general direction of the kitchen. "We've got eggs and pasta and sandwich stuff—we can make pretty much anything, so long as you don't start thinking beef Wellington or something like that."

"Huh," Daniel said with a clear lack of enthusiasm. "I'm okay for now."

"There's also a little Mexican grill within walking distance,"

Lauren said quickly. "The food's pretty good there and I think they're open late."

"Let's do that," he said, clearly relieved, although Lauren didn't know whether it was the idea of real food or the escape from her sister's scrutiny that appealed to him.

Ava didn't seem too offended by Daniel's eagerness to be gone. All she said was, "They have great margaritas too. Which makes it especially good that it's within walking distance."

"I'll get my jacket," Lauren said and went into the bedroom to find it. She could hear Ava asking Daniel how his mother was doing and winced, guessing he'd be annoyed that Ava even knew his mother was ill. She'd never met anyone as private as Daniel. But how could she *not* have mentioned his mother's cancer, since that was how they met? At any rate, he barely answered—just muttered a "Fine"—and then there was silence and then Ava said something about what a beautiful day it had been and Lauren quickly grabbed the nearest jacket and rushed back into the living room so Ava wouldn't have to struggle to make any more conversation. Daniel's rudeness had never bothered Lauren, since it came in bursts and was tempered by the occasional revelation of something softer behind it all—or at least more interesting—but to hear him not even make an effort to be pleasant to her sister was agonizing. She wanted Ava to like him. Ava's approval made a difference to her, even when she wished it didn't.

"I'm ready," she said, bursting back into the other room. "Let's go. I'll see you later, A."

"I'll probably be asleep when you get back," Ava said. "I'm pretty tired."

"I'll try not to make too much noise."

"Thanks. Have fun, guys."

"Good night," Daniel said.

"Night." She looked at Lauren and their eyes met briefly. Ava gave a minute shrug that said, *The jury's still out on this guy.*

At least she hadn't immediately written him off, Lauren thought as she followed Daniel out the door. Lord knew there had been plenty of times in the past when a roll of the eyes from one sister to the other conveyed a clear *Get rid of this jerk.*

In the elevator, Lauren said, "So what did your mother need to talk to you and your brother about?"

Daniel stared at the elevator wall over her shoulder. "I don't know. Stuff." Then, heavily: "She doesn't have a will. Never got around to it. So she wanted us to write some things down."

"My sister's a trusts and estates lawyer, you know," Lauren said. "If you need something drawn up, she could get it done quickly." Then, realizing the implication of that, she said, "I mean, if you want to get it settled while your brother's still in town."

He looked down at his hands, spreading the fingers out as if he were trying to locate something he'd lost between them. "It's okay. We'll work it out."

"You sure?" Lauren said. "She'd be happy to help."

He gestured impatiently. "I'm too hungry to think about this stuff anymore right now. I need a break from it all."

"Okay," Lauren said. "But you can come back up to the apartment after dinner and ask Ava any questions you might have."

"She said she'd probably be asleep."

"Then we'll just have to find something else to do up there."

For the first time that night, he looked her right in the eyes. He even smiled. He said, "Yeah, all right. I'll come back up."

The elevator doors opened and Lauren led the way out with a sudden exuberance.

They started with margaritas on the rocks, made with real lime, not mixer, and by the time Daniel's tacos came, they were both slightly buzzed.

It was the first time Lauren had seen Daniel drink enough for it to affect him, and she was amazed at the transformation. He relaxed visibly: his face lost its tight, defensive look and even his limbs seemed suddenly looser, as he sprawled out in the chair opposite her. She felt his leg touch hers and waited for him to realize it and move it, but he left it there and the spot on her calf where they were touching soon grew pleasurably warm. He laughed more easily too, and actually told her some stories about his family. He described the spartan existence his brother maintained in Costa Rica and how when he, Daniel, had visited there, he had spent most of his time trying to find an Internet connection. "Matthew said he had chosen that life just so he could escape from things like the Internet," Daniel said. "And I said that as far as I was concerned, it's not a life worth living if you don't have e-mail and Google."

"So what did he say to that?" Lauren slid down a little in her chair, which meant her thigh was now rubbing against Daniel's knee. She was fairly certain he was pressing deliberately against her, but it was hard to tell: the table was small and there wasn't all that much room under it. *She* of course was deliberately pressing against him. But that was her.

"He just kept saying I had to learn to relax. Which is impossible to do in Costa Rica, by the way, if you like coffee at all. The coffee there is phenomenal. I was averaging eight cups a day, which meant I was anything *but* relaxed." He poked his straw into the margarita glass, searching out more liquid. He had pretty much finished his second one. "At one point, I heard a noise in a tree above me and was in such a caffeine-induced state of nervousness that I actually jumped high enough to hit my head on a branch. I ended up with a huge scratch over my eye. My brother laughed so hard he almost threw up."

"What made the noise?"

"Howler monkeys," Daniel said. "Turns out they really do howl." He noisily sucked up the dregs of his drink.

"Does that mean that screech owls screech?"

"Yes." He set the glass back down with an unnecessary thump that suggested his hand control had been somewhat compromised by the margaritas. "And fire ants build tiny little campfires."

"Oh my God," she said, opening her eyes wide. "You just made a cute joke. I didn't think you were capable of that."

"I'm not. I can't believe I said that either. I must not be myself tonight."

"So who are you?"

"I don't know," he said. "But it's a relief to take a break from being me. Mind if I just forget about that Daniel guy for the rest of the evening?"

"Who, me?" Lauren said. "I've been hoping to ditch that loser for days."

"I don't blame you." He pushed his plate away. "He's a total downer." He flicked at an errant tortilla chip crumb on the tablecloth. "I wish this *were* my life. Going out for good cheap food and strong drinks with a pretty girl who's got an amazing smile. Nothing to worry about except paying the check when it comes. No sick mother, no life back in New York falling apart while I go crazy being stuck here. Just another L.A. surfer dude hanging loose."

"Hanging loose?" Lauren repeated, raising her eyebrows and trying to ignore the pleasure his tossed-off compliment had given her.

He scowled at her and looked like himself again. "Whatever. You know what I mean."

"Yeah," she said, leaning forward and resting her chin on her hand. "So tell me: what does Surfer Boy do for kicks when he's hanging loose?"

He met her eyes and answered the invitation in them. "He starts by getting the check." He signaled to the waiter without taking his eyes off of hers.

She had thought his eyes were pure blue, but there was gray in them too, she realized now—a narrow band of gray circling the pupils that flickered with the light from the candle on the table between them.

On the walk back to the apartment, he reached out his arm and she came into its embrace. He pulled her tightly against his waist. They walked like that, pushing their hips against each other and stumbling a little, laughing at themselves, the night air cool but bright from the streetlights and full moon above.

In the elevator, he stood behind her and folded both his arms across her chest, resting his chin on her head. Looking sideways, she could see their reflections in the mirror-lined wall, but his face was in shadow so she couldn't see his expression.

He released her when they stopped at their floor, and they walked out of the elevator separately, but he caught her hand in the hallway and held it against his stomach until they were at the door to the apartment. He let go so she could get out her key and let them in. She fumbled in her purse, hoping that for once she actually had her key and wouldn't have to wake Ava up in order to get in. Luck was with her: her fingers touched metal and she pulled out the key with a quiet crow of triumph.

She unlocked the door and pushed it open and was relieved to see that the living room was dark and quiet and the door to the bedroom was shut tight, no light peeping out from underneath.

"Oh, good, my sister's asleep," she said. Then, realizing how teenaged that sounded, she laughed and said, "And my mom and dad are out of town until tomorrow, so we have the place all to ourselves, Scooter."

"I bet you were just like that in high school," he said, catching her around the waist again. "Always misbehaving behind your parents' backs."

"Still am."

"I'm glad your sister's asleep," Daniel said and kicked the door shut behind them as he pulled her hard against him. He found her mouth quickly and the kiss went from tentative to intimate almost immediately. He bent over her, gently forcing her head back, making her throat curve until the part that was usually hidden under her chin became opened up and exposed, which made her feel vulnerable. That excited her. His hands moved from her waist up to her breasts, under her jacket but over the tank, which was tight and didn't leave much to the imagination. Neither did the thin cotton bra she was wearing. The palm of his hand curved around her right breast and his thumb played with the hardened tip of her nipple through the cloth.

Lauren let out a quick, hard breath.

"You like that, huh?" he said.

"What do you like?" She put an inquiring hand between his legs.

"That's a good start," he said in a voice that was suddenly thick.

Their clothing got shed—or at least the pieces that were in the way did. At some point they moved over to the sofa. They were cramped there, and along with the good sensations of her flesh being touched by a warm mouth and eager fingers were less pleasant ones of her neck being strained and her calf knocking against the coffee table.

Daniel had a condom in his wallet. "I'm impressed," Lauren said, watching him as he went to retrieve it, enjoying the shadowy sight of his almost naked body (he still had his shirt on), which was strong and in shape but in an athletic, healthy way, not with the overdone musculature of the narcissistic.

He looked over his shoulder at her. "It's a Boy Scout thing. Always be prepared."

"You'll have to restock."

"No rush," he said. "This one's been there for ten years."

"Don't tell me it's been that long for you."

"Since I've had a one-night stand, yeah."

For a moment, the words nagged at her. Was that what this was?

He dropped the wallet back on top of his pants and turned around with the condom package pinched between his thumb and index finger. For a moment, he hesitated, his face almost invisible in the dim light, the outline of his shoulders tensely hunched forward.

"Put it on," Lauren said, too aroused and drunk to think about things any more deeply. She held out her arms, arching her back a little, and he looked at the picture she made for a few seconds, then with a catch of his breath did as she ordered and came back to the sofa, where he covered her body with his in one swift motion.

He groaned loudly at one point and Lauren said, "Shh. Don't wake her up!" and he whispered, "This *is* just like high school, isn't it?"

"The good part," she said, sliding the palms of her hands down his back and gently digging her nails into his ass. "The part where sex is new and exciting."

He was too distracted to respond to that and pretty soon she was too, arching her back, rising up into his thrusts, and working hard to keep her own cries of pleasure reasonably quiet.

They both gave one last sigh as he shuddered into her, and

then there was a moment where they didn't make a noise at all or move, and then he raised himself on his arms and smiled down into her face.

"That was nice," he said and pulled out of her.

"Yeah," she said.

"Where's the bathroom?"

"Oh shit," she said. "It's through Ava's room. I'm sorry."

"Think I'll wake her up if I run through?"

"I don't know. Probably not."

Daniel rolled off of her and onto his feet. He was still wearing one sock, his shirt—partially unbuttoned—and the condom. Not an easy look to pull off, but Lauren felt she could happily have stared at his half-naked body forever. "I think I have to risk it," he said. "What's the worst thing that could happen?"

"She wakes up and sees you and screams and a neighbor calls the police and you get arrested for indecent exposure?"

"Okay," he said, instinctively covering himself with his hands at just the thought. "What's the second worst thing?"

"Here," Lauren said, sitting up. "Let me go first and make sure she's asleep." She still wore the tank top, but her bra had been unhooked at some point and pushed up out of the way so her breasts were no longer actually contained within the cups. She wiggled it back into place under the tank and reached behind to hook it up again.

"It would be a nice world if men and women never wore pants," Daniel said, studying her as frankly and admiringly as she had him.

"It would cut down on wars," Lauren said, shifting her legs and bending them slightly to give him the most flattering view of them. "Don't you think?"

"People would have to carry their own towels, though. Like in gyms. To put under them whenever they sat down."

"Definitely. Personal towel usage would be key." Her bra settled in place, she looked around. "Hmm. Where did my underpants go?"

He picked up her jeans and handed them to her. "They're still in here."

"You're an animal," she said and plucked them out, then pulled them on, twisting her body on the sofa as she maneuvered them up. She stood up. "Okay. Follow me."

She led the way to Ava's bedroom door. Daniel followed her, his pants clutched against his torso, covering his genitals. "You have a cute butt," he said.

She waggled it a bit for his benefit. "Thank you." She carefully turned the doorknob and pushed the door open a few inches. She peered into the room, which had just enough light coming in from the street to pick out the shapes of the furniture and reveal the doorway to the bathroom. She listened for a brief moment. Deep, regular breaths from Ava. Lauren gestured silently to Daniel to head toward the bathroom. He nodded and ran across the room, briefly mooning her before he was inside and the door was shut.

Lauren swiped a pair of sweatpants out of a drawer, very carefully sliding it open and closed so it wouldn't make noise. She carried the pants back to the living room, where she pulled them on and turned on the lamp.

Daniel returned a few minutes later, fully dressed except for his shoes, which still lay on the living room floor. He was also still missing the one sock. He closed Ava's door softly behind him. "That's the girliest bathroom I've ever seen," he said. "How many different kinds of hair products and lipstick can two women own?"

"Never enough," Lauren said. She didn't bother to point out

that almost all of the beauty products were hers. Ava basically owned a bar of soap, some shampoo and conditioner, and a bottle of sunscreen.

Daniel picked his jacket up off the floor and extracted his cell phone from the pocket. He flipped it open and peered at the screen. "Good," he said. "No messages."

"You'd have heard it ring, wouldn't you?"

"Not necessarily," he said, slipping it back in the pocket. "I was pretty distracted."

"I'm pretty distracting," she said with an exaggerated leer.

"Yes, you are." He dropped the jacket on the back of the sofa and looked at her. "Aw, you put on pants. I liked you without them."

"You put *yours* on."

"Still." He spotted his missing sock a foot or so away and picked it up before sitting down on the sofa. He pulled it on, then patted the space next to him. "Come sit."

"What now?"

"I'm sleepy." He closed his eyes. "Can we just sit here quietly for a few minutes?"

"Sure," she said, and they did. She rested her head on his shoulder and he put his hand on her knee and they stayed like that for a while. It was nice, Lauren thought. Almost as nice as the sex had been. She peered up at Daniel's profile. With his hair a little messed up and his eyes closed, he looked much more vulnerable and open than usual. She liked this softer version of Daniel. She liked him a lot.

They must have both dozed off because it was a couple of hours later when she became aware of feeling cramped and uncomfortable and wanting to stretch out. She squirmed out from under his arm and draped herself the long way across the sofa, putting her feet on his lap. She felt him shift under her, and when she opened her eyes, he was awake and watching her, his gaze unreadable in the dim light of the one lamp left on.

"You okay?" she said. "Want to lie down?"

"No." He passed his hand over his forehead. "I need a drink of water."

"In the kitchen." She curled up her legs so he was no longer pinned in place. "Glasses are in the cabinet."

He stood up and she lay there quietly while he was gone, listening contentedly to the sounds of his rustling around the kitchen.

When he came back over to her, she moved her legs to make room for him again, but he didn't sit. She opened her eyes. He was standing there, looking down at her.

"Everything okay?" she said.

"Not really."

She propped herself up on her elbows. "What's wrong?" She thought suddenly that maybe the condom had broken and felt a shudder of panic. *Calm down*, she thought. *That's why the morning-after pill was invented.*

"The thing is," Daniel said, "I shouldn't have done this."

"What?" she said, confused. "You mean the sex?"

"I didn't mean to. I had too much to drink. I wasn't thinking."

Suddenly wide awake, Lauren slowly sat up and planted her feet on the floor. "Wow. Nothing a woman likes to hear after sex more than a guy's regrets."

"I'm sorry."

Her voice grew sharper. "You seemed to be enjoying yourself. What's the problem exactly?"

He rocked back a bit on his heels. "The problem exactly," he repeated absently. "The problem exactly." Then, with a sudden clarity, like he had just woken up: "The problem exactly is named Elizabeth and she's in New York right now in my apartment."

"Elizabeth." Lauren took a pillow and held it across her chest with the sense she'd be needing a shield. "Give me a clue. Wife, daughter, dog, housekeeper?"

"We're not married yet," he said, and his flat tone took away any hope she might have had that he was joking. "But we live together. We've been living together for two years now."

"I see," Lauren said, and did. A lot of things made sense that hadn't before. "And yet somehow she never came up in conversation?"

"I'm sorry," Daniel said. "I should have—"

"All those discussions about your life back in New York," Lauren said. "Like what you did at night after work and what you ate for dinner—but you never mentioned a live-in companion?"

He stared at the floor. "I don't know why I didn't tell you about her."

"Maybe because you wanted to screw me?"

"I didn't want to," he said. "I mean, that wasn't what I—" He stopped again.

"You looked like you wanted to," she said. She felt queasy, like she could throw up at any moment. "Maybe it was the way you had an orgasm inside of me. Did I misread that?"

"Shh," he said.

"Don't shush me."

"I'm sorry. I'm trying to explain."

"You're doing a great job," Lauren said. "You asshole."

"Yeah, okay." He almost seemed relieved to have her swear at him. "We were only ever going to be friends," he said. "You and me. That was the idea. Cancer buddies. Both at the hospital because of our moms. It was nice having someone to hang out with there."

"I know," she said. "I thought so too. And if you had just *told me* you had a girlfriend—"

"I don't know why I didn't."

"You keep saying that. Isn't the answer obvious?" She gestured down at the sofa where just a couple of hours earlier they had been pawing at each other.

He said, almost sadly, "You think I meant to do this all along."

That was too obvious to even respond to. "No wonder you called me a one-night stand."

"I don't think I actually said that."

She put her head in her hands. "God, I'm an idiot!"

"I'm sorry, Lauren," he said. "I know you think I'm an ass-hole. *I* think I'm an asshole. People aren't supposed to act like this. And I don't normally. I've never cheated on a girlfriend before, ever." He opened and closed his hands around nothing. "But my life's been so fucked up since my mother got sick. I don't know where I'm living, I don't know what I'm supposed to be doing. Neither life seems real, not the one back in New York or the one here. I spend my days in a black hole, watching my mother get sicker in front of my eyes without being able to do anything about it, and sometimes I think I'm going crazy."

Lauren didn't say anything. Did he expect a free pass to be a total creep just because his mother had cancer?

"But I shouldn't have," he said after a moment of silence.

Her agreement came out as an angry exhale. She raised her head to glare at him. "You going to tell her? E-liz-a-beth?" She enunciated the name with exaggerated deference.

"I don't know," he said. "I've got to decide what the fairest thing is for her."

"Yeah," Lauren said. "You wouldn't want to do anything to hurt *her*."

"I swear I never meant to hurt you—"

"Oh, I believe you," Lauren said. "I'm sure you would have loved to have screwed me and not hurt me at all. That would have made everything easier for you."

He was silent again for a moment. Then he said, "I should go back home. My brother's not used to taking care of my mother."

"Go ahead," she said. "Nothing keeping you here."

He turned away, then stopped and turned back. "I don't know if I should even say this," he said. "Whatever I say feels like a betrayal to *someone*. But I didn't do this because I was looking to get myself off. I've kind of been falling in love with you in spite of myself. Wanting to spend time with you even though I knew it was risky and I shouldn't. And if this were really my life—if I didn't have a real life back in New York—I'd happily stay in love with you."

"That doesn't mean *anything*," she said.

He stood there silently.

"You were leaving," Lauren said after waiting a moment. "Don't forget your shoes."

He nodded, crammed his feet quickly into his shoes, picked up his jacket, and left the apartment with a last quiet "Goodbye."

Lauren let out a strangled and muffled scream of anger, but it didn't make her feel better. She slid down on the sofa until she was curled in a knot and played feverishly with the string that tied the waist of her sweatpants, pulling the ragged ends through her fingers over and over again, blinking her eyes against the hot, painful pressure she felt right behind them that wasn't tears but something angrier and more self-loathing than tears. After a few minutes of that, she stretched out into a lying position on the sofa and tried to will herself asleep but couldn't. She sat up again and suddenly the living room felt empty and lonely and sad and she didn't want to be in there anymore. She didn't want to be the kind of adult woman who lived in someone else's living room because she couldn't pay her own rent and who slept with other women's boyfriends. But that's exactly what she was.

She padded to the door of the bedroom on bare feet and went inside.

Ava was sleeping in the middle of the double bed, her dark hair tousled and sticking in patches to her cheeks and closed eyes.

"Ava?" Lauren whispered.

Ava stirred and made a little questioning noise and then was still again.

"Ava?" she said, a little more loudly. "Can I sleep in here with you?"

"Wha'?" Her voice was heavy with sleep. "Why? Wha's wrong?"

"I spilled something on the sofa," Lauren said. "Please?"

"God, you're a spaz," Ava said in that same thick, slurred voice. She slid over to make room and turned on her side so her back was to the empty side of the bed. "Go to sleep—don' bother me."

"Okay," Lauren said and slid in under the covers next to her sister. She lay on her back, staring up into the darkness. Then she whispered, "Can I say just one thing?"

Ava's voice was muffled by the pillow. "No."

"Even if it's that I'm sorry?"

Ava heaved a dramatic sigh and turned back toward her, her eyes still closed. "What are you sorry for?"

"Always telling you what to do when it comes to guys. Acting like I know so much when I don't know any more than you do. Less, probably."

"Did something go wrong tonight?"

Lauren wanted to tell her but hesitated, trying to figure out how much to say and what *not* to say, scared to let Ava know she had been stupid enough to sleep with a guy who was already taken—the signs had been there if she had bothered to look for them—but also desperate for solace. After a few minutes of struggling to find the right words, she became aware of the regular sound of Ava's deep, measured breaths and realized her sister had already fallen back to sleep.

But Lauren didn't go to sleep for a long time after that. She lay there wishing she had never bought the shirt she had stained that night or the shoes that would probably just lie there on the bedroom floor for days that would turn into weeks, waiting to trip her up just when she was beginning to forget about them.

Chapter 14

O n Sunday morning, they drove to the house, and Ava
went upstairs to find their parents while Lauren carried
into the kitchen the fruit and juice they'd brought.

As Ava came up the stairs onto the landing, she heard her
parents talking. She was struck by the unusually querulous tone
of her mother's voice and by the equally unfamiliar soothing
and patient sound of her father's. It all felt wrong and a little
fascinating, and Ava paused outside the partially open bedroom
door to hear more before going in.

"—sounds disgusting," her mother was saying.

"You need to eat something." Jimmy's voice.

"I'll throw it up."

"You might not. You're past the worst of it for this week. You
haven't thrown up on a Sunday yet."

"Force me to eat an egg and today will be my first time."

"At least drink something. I don't want you to get de-
hydrated."

"Why not? What's the worst that happens? You take me to
the hospital and they put me on an IV? I spend half my time

on an IV now—what difference will a few more hours and a few more holes make?"

"I could make you some hot tea. Or mix some juice with bubbly water. How does that sound to you? A cranberry juice spritzer?"

Her mother: "Will you just drop it? I don't want anything."

Ava drew closer to the door, waiting for the explosion from her father, who *always* exploded the second someone crossed or offended him in any way, which was why the girls in the family had learned to tiptoe carefully around him except on the rare occasions when they were fully armored and geared up for battle.

But all Jimmy said was "Just think about it. You need energy. We've got company coming."

"I don't know why I said yes to that. I wish I hadn't."

Ava peered around the door and saw them at that moment, her mother's face twisted and petulant as she plucked at the bed-sheet pulled up around her waist, her father's craggy features drawn with concern. He reached his hand out as if to pat her on the shoulder, but Nancy swatted it away with a noise of irritation. He folded his arms resignedly across his chest and said, "You'll get a burst of energy. You'll see. The girls always cheer you up."

"But Lana Markowitz? What was I thinking?"

"I don't know," said Jimmy, with a touch more of his usual asperity. "What *were* you thinking?"

"Thanks," Nancy said. "That's really helpful." She turned her shoulders away from him. As she shifted, she spotted Ava through the slightly open door. "Ava? What are you doing out there?"

"Eavesdropping," Ava said, coming into the room.

"Well, at least you're honest. I mean, in a deceitful, listening-at-doors kind of way." She said it jokingly, though, and sounded like her normal self again. So she saved up most of her anger and frustration for her husband, Ava thought. The girls only got to see the good patient.

It wasn't how she thought about her parents and their relationship at all. Her mother had always been the soother, her father the bomb that could go off at any moment. But here he was being gentle and here she was being difficult.

Jimmy said, "When did you get here? I didn't hear the front door."

"About five minutes ago. Lauren's putting out the food." She rested her hand on her mother's foot, which lay under the dark green wool blanket that covered her from hip to toe. "You want us to cancel this brunch, Mom? We can easily call and catch them before they get here. They'll understand."

"No, it's fine," Nancy said. "Really. I'm looking forward to it. I just like to complain so everyone feels sorry for me and I look noble for just doing what I was going to do in the first place." She held her hand out and Ava took it. "But it is hard," her mother said, gently swinging their linked hands, "to see an old friend when you look and feel awful. How am I supposed to impress her by how magnificently I've aged?"

"You look fine," Ava said. "Really, Mom. You may feel awful but you don't look it." That wasn't entirely true: at that particular moment, her mother looked kind of haggard. But she was pretty beautiful to begin with, so Ava figured her mother on a bad day still outshone most women her age on their good days.

"It's petty of me anyway," Nancy said, releasing Ava's hand. "Wanting to impress poor Lana Markowitz. I mean, any way you look at it, I've *won*. I have my husband and my wonderful beautiful girls, and until this stupid and minor cancer thing, I've been healthy and happy. A kind person would deliberately look awful so Lana could have something to feel good about."

"You couldn't look uglier than Lana Markowitz if you tried," Jimmy said.

Ava stared at him, astonished. Her father had just complimented her mother. That was a first—at least in her hearing.

"That's not fair," Nancy said. "Lana was very pretty underneath the clothes and makeup and that terrible haircut. We *all* looked awful in the eighties."

"You never looked awful," her husband said. "You haven't looked awful a day in your life."

Nancy minutely adjusted the blanket around her legs, a small smile on her face that Ava had never seen before. "Liar," she said.

But Ava looked back and forth between her two parents, stunned. They were actually *in love* with each other. It had never occurred to her before. She had always thought the main relationship in the family was the one between Nancy and her daughters. To have a family, you needed a father, of course, and Jimmy had played that role perfectly well, if you were okay with an old-fashioned interpretation of the job. But the Nickerson family was all about the women and their noisy, bickering, gossiping, interfering relationships with one another.

And now it seemed that maybe she had been looking at it all wrong. Maybe she and Lauren were just the icing, and the basic, underlying cake of the family was the couple in front of her who had a shared history she knew very little about.

She shook her head to clear it and said, "You should get dressed, Mom—they'll be here soon," hoping to bring things back to steadier ground.

"I'll go down and get things ready," Jimmy said. "Help your mother get dressed," he said to Ava before leaving the room.

Ava pulled the blanket off of her mother and Nancy swung her pajamaed legs over the side of the bed. "Pick out a shirt for me, will you?" she said as she sat on the edge of the bed, her hands gripping the mattress on either side of her knees.

Ava rifled through the tops in the dresser, then plucked out a dark green polo shirt and turned back to her mother.

"I'm going to put it on over this one," Nancy said. She was wearing a thin white T-shirt. "I'm too tired to start taking things off and on."

"Why not just start wearing housecoats like Grandma Ingrid used to?" Ava said. "Just a big old flowered muumuu to cover you from head to toe. Nothing simpler than that."

"I don't think I have what it takes to carry it off."

"Grandma Ingrid did. Of course the blue hair helped."

"And the support hose." Ava handed her the polo shirt and Nancy pulled it on. When her head emerged, she said, "I can't wait to get really old—so old I can be as eccentric and demanding as I want. I think I'll start some kind of worthless collection that takes up a lot of space and embarrasses you girls and runs through your inheritance."

"Like Hummel figurines?"

She shook her head. "Something worse—I want to make you both cringe."

"Men," Ava said. "Collect handsome young men."

"Don't you think your father might object?"

"All the more reason." She arranged her mother's hair with her fingers. The roots were starting to show, and it made her sad to see that her mother's natural color, once a medium brown, was now almost entirely gray.

"Can you tell it's thinning?" Nancy asked, peering up at her anxiously. "It feels like so much is coming out—I have to clean my brush every day. Do I look bald to you?"

"Not at all," Ava said. "It doesn't even look thinner to me. Did the doctor say it would fall out?"

Nancy waved her hand dismissively. "Oh, you know. He downplayed it all, said it wasn't likely, but a lot of women on this online cancer forum I looked at said it happened to them."

"Yours looks fine," Ava said. "Really."

Nancy looked skeptical but she dropped it. "Pick out a pair of pants for me, will you? And then help me put on just enough makeup to not look like death warmed over."

"You'll look like fresh death," Ava said as she went to the closet. "Nice, fresh, right-out-of-the-oven death."

"I did something wrong," Nancy said. "My children don't respect me."

Ava looked back at her mother over her shoulder and saw her sitting there on the bed in her pajama bottoms and double top, looking small and worried and sick despite the smile propped on her face, and even though they had been joking, she suddenly wanted to tell her that she had her daughters' respect *and* their love, as much as any mother could ever have, but hesitated, worried that the sentimentality would embarrass them both or, worse, scare her mother into thinking she was sicker than she was, and the moment passed with nothing said at all.

Ava came downstairs with Nancy after Lauren and Jimmy had already welcomed Russell and his mother into the house. In the flurry of greetings and kisses, Ava was able to avoid speaking directly to Russell, who kissed her enthusiastically on both cheeks the way he always did, although this time the kisses landed squarely on her skin and not in midair. She evaded his gaze and moved on. A moment later, he was embracing Lauren, who whispered something in his ear. He whispered back and then they separated, but not before Lauren had given him one last kittenish smile. Ava gritted her teeth and looked away. *It's good*, she told herself. *You need to be reminded. A guy like Russell would never go for you when a girl like Lauren's in the same room.*

Soon they were all sitting around the dining room table together.

Lana Markowitz seemed happy to be there: she hadn't stopped smiling since she first arrived, her lips curving up in a thin-lipped, bright red smile that Ava hadn't remembered she remembered until she saw it again. There was something generally familiar about Lana, although Ava couldn't have described what she looked like before her arrival.

Lana's bobbed chin-length hair was dyed a brown so dark it was almost black. Her eyes had that slightly off, tilted look that a surgical lift always seems to leave in its wake, and the skin on her cheeks and forehead was noticeably tighter and shinier than that on her throat. She wore bright Paloma Picasso–red lipstick and was way too dressed up for a relaxed brunch at the house of friends: the younger generation were all in jeans—even Russell for once—and both of Ava's parents were in relaxed, weekend clothes, but Lana wore a tight black skirt with high-heeled boots and a violet V-neck cashmere sweater that effectively displayed her still voluptuous chest.

Still voluptuous? Ava rethought that one. The breasts were firmer and higher than the forces of gravity would normally have allowed on a woman now firmly in her sixties. Lana seemed excessively proud of them, too: she frequently arched her spine and threw back her shoulders, aiming her chest most often in Jimmy's direction.

Unfortunately for her, Jimmy didn't seem the slightest bit interested in Lana Markowitz's breasts. He was politely genial to her but far more relaxed and jovial with Russell, who sat next to his mother and rolled his eyes and winced whenever she said something that embarrassed him. Which happened fairly often as the morning progressed.

"This is wonderful!" Lana said when they were all settled and served. She looked around the dining room and gave a girlish wiggle of delight. "I love that your house has hardly changed at all, Nancy. It makes me feel young again, being here, like no time at all has passed—except of course when I look around and see the grown-ups our little babies have become." She shared her narrow smile with everyone around the table.

Nancy said, "You hardly look a day older than the last time I saw you, Lana."

"Bless you," Lana said. "It's not true, but bless you anyway." She reached out to put her hand on Nancy's arm. "How are you, really? Russell has told me all about what you're going through."

Nancy patted Lana's hand. "I'm fine. It's all a huge pain and a little exhausting, but there shouldn't be any long-term effects."

"I'm so happy to hear it! I was afraid to ask at first. So often these days it's bad news with friends and family. Did Russell tell you about my parents?" Without waiting for a response, she said with a toss of her head, "Dead, both of them. Within three months of each other. It left me reeling. As you might imagine. I'm still recovering."

"That was over five years ago," Russell said.

"It can't possibly have been that long."

"It was early 2003," he said. "Well over five years."

"Anyway," she said, turning back to Nancy, "I had barely recovered from that—not really recovered, of course, but trying to pull myself together for the sake of the boys—when I get the news that Marcy has cancer. Horrible stage four lung cancer."

"How awful," Nancy said. Then, a little sheepishly: "I'm sorry, but who's Marcy?"

"Oh, you remember," Lana said. "My former sister-in-law. Sister of Lord Voldemort, as I like to call him." She gave a little laugh.

"Poor thing," Nancy said.

"Was she a smoker?" Jimmy asked.

"No," Lana said with some satisfaction. "Never smoked a day in her life. What do you think of that?"

"Kind of messes with your mind, doesn't it?" Russell said to the girls across the table from him. "We all want to believe that if we're good little boys and girls and don't smoke or hang out with people who do, we won't have to worry about lung cancer. Apparently it doesn't actually work that way."

"You mean we can't blame the victim?" Ava said. He smiled at her and she looked down at her plate again.

"Not even a little bit," Russell said. "And, by the way, Marcy ate all organic foods and did yoga every day."

"I'm going back to eating Twinkies." Ava poked disdainfully at the slice of melon on her plate.

"That's the obvious lesson here," Russell said.

"I never stopped," Lauren said.

"How's she doing now?" Nancy asked Lana.

"Oh, she's dead," Lana said cheerfully. "They caught it too late. We all went to the funeral. It was only right, even though it meant we had to see Lord Voldemort with wife number two and their sons. He's old enough to be their grandfather, of course."

"What's really weird," Russell said, again addressing himself to the sisters, "is that he named them Jonah 2.0 and Russell 2.0. It bothered us at first, but in the end Jonah and I decided that it's really a tribute to us. An *homage*, if you will."

"He's joking," Lana told the Nickersons. "They're actually named Brendon and Farley."

"Yuck," Lauren said. "They should have gone with the 2.0 thing."

"More original," Ava agreed. "Plus there'd be all those free upgrades."

Russell laughed, but again she avoided his eyes. He looked handsome this morning in a dark blue oxford shirt that was unbuttoned enough to show how much tanner the skin on his face was than his usually covered throat. Looking at him made her remember how closely he had held her the other night, and it seemed to her no good could come out of that since she was resolved not to let it happen again. What kind of guy secretly went after two sisters at the same time? It was, for want of a better word, *icky*.

"From what I've heard, they're very wild boys," Lana said. She pointed her breasts toward Jimmy, who was cutting a cheese Danish in half and didn't seem to notice. "Completely undisciplined."

"They're perfectly fine," Russell said.

His mother raised her penciled eyebrows. "That's not what I hear."

"I've spent a lot more time with them than you have," Russell said. "They're good kids."

"Oh, right," Lana said. "You always spend the holidays with them. Leaving your poor mother alone, I might add." She gave another little laugh.

Russell didn't seem to share her amusement. "I spent one Christmas with them," he said. "One Christmas. And that was two years ago. Every other major holiday, I've either spent with you or on my own."

"Are you sure?" Lana said. "Two years ago?"

"Yes. I remember because I was with—" Russell stopped. "Someone," he finished lamely, with an uncomfortable look at the girls across the table.

"Did you all know Russell's been married *twice*?" Lana said, opening her eyes wide. There was a bit of mascara detritus under the left one that Ava's fingers itched to wipe away. "Can you believe it? He's been divorced two times and he's not even forty yet. Sometimes I wonder whether Lord Voldemort and I set a bad example for our kids." She shrugged and her cleavage stayed put while her shoulders moved up and down around it. "Fortunately Jonah's marriage is holding steady at the moment, so maybe the fault lies"—her gaze fell on her son again—"elsewhere."

"Sounds like you've had some bad luck," Nancy said gently to Russell. "But they always say third time's the charm."

"There won't be a third time." Russell was jogging his knee up and down rapidly. "I've learned my lesson."

"The only woman a man can trust is his mother," Lana said. "That's what my mother told my brothers, and I've come around to thinking she was right."

"Ahem," Nancy said. "As the mother of two girls and a woman myself, I'd have to disagree with that one."

"Oh, it's an exaggeration, of course." Lana waved her hand breezily. "But I will say that I'm horrified by some of these younger women today. They'll say anything to trap a man as wealthy and handsome as—" She indicated her son.

"Hey, she sounds just like you," Lauren said to Russell, who shot her a dirty look in response.

"To be fair," Lana said, "it's hard for anyone to make a marriage last, even with the best intentions and all the love in the world." She waggled her finger back and forth between Nancy and Jimmy. "You two really beat the odds, you know. I'd love to know your secret."

"Lots of sedating drugs," Nancy said, and her daughters and Russell laughed.

"My parents were married for sixty-two years," Lana said.

"Can you imagine? Sixty-two years." She wiped her mouth daintily on the edge of a napkin. "Of course, they loathed each other."

"Kind of makes you feel all warm inside, doesn't it?" Russell said to the girls. "Sadly, I've never made it past the third year of loathing."

"Don't give up," Lauren said. "I have faith that you and Ava will one day celebrate your golden loathing anniversary."

"Him and Ava?" Lana said, looking at them. "Is there something we should all know?"

"Actually," Lauren said with sudden animation, "it's really funny. I found this contract that—" She stopped with a sudden yelp as Ava kicked her in the shin.

"Sorry," Ava said with a warning look. "Didn't realize that was your leg."

"That *really* hurt."

"What were you saying?" Lana asked Lauren.

Lauren pushed her chair back a little so she was out of kicking range. "I found this contract that you and our parents made when we were little. It said that Ava and Russell had to marry each other when they grew up."

Lana gave a little scream. It took Ava a few seconds to register it as mirth rather than distress. "Oh, my dear Lord, I had forgotten all about that!" she shrieked, holding her napkin in front of her mouth, presumably to preserve feminine modesty by hiding the interior from view. "But we *did* do that—I remember! No wonder Russell's marriages didn't work out! He was already promised to another! Oh, it's too wonderful." She dropped her napkin so she could grab onto Nancy's arm. "Why didn't we get these two together long ago? We've wasted so much time! Ava would have been the perfect daughter-in-law. Not like those other girls."

"Thank you," Nancy said. "I've always liked her."

"But not as much as me, right?" Lauren said, and Nancy gave her an admonishing look that was also amused.

"They make a gorgeous couple, don't you think?" Lana said, looking back and forth rapidly between Ava and Russell, who both shrank down into their seats.

The fact that Lana Markowitz thought she and Russell belonged together felt to Ava like the final nail in the coffin of her almost-relationship with the guy. The woman was five and a half feet of solid bad judgment.

"Imagine how cute the grandchildren would be," Lana added.

"Adorable," Nancy said, "but if I've learned anything over the past couple of decades, it's that we parents don't actually have much control over any aspect of our kids' lives, starting with toileting and continuing on to pretty much everything else, and *especially* not their love lives."

"But isn't that the shame of it?" Lana said. "We could choose so much better for them than they choose for themselves."

Russell raised his hand. "On behalf of the entire younger generation, I'd like to say that we appreciate your faith in us."

She shook her head at him, smiling. "Oh, you. You know what I mean. You can't deny you haven't made a complete mess of it all with your marriages and divorces and Lord knows what in alimony payments, and have you even learned anything from it all?"

Russell said, "No. I can't deny that. I can't even parse it."

"Don't you think Ava would have been a much better choice?" Lana said. "And don't go giving your father any credit for it—it was me and Nancy who came up with that idea, wasn't it, Nancy?"

"Yes, I'm afraid it was," Nancy said with a slightly apologetic glance at Ava. "But only as a passing joke. Who'd have thought we'd all end up sitting around our table talking about it decades later?"

A burst of a loud, unintelligible song interrupted the conversation. "Oops," Lauren said. "That's me." Her cell phone was lying next to her plate. She picked it up and looked at the screen. "It's Briana."

"Oh, how is she?" Nancy said at the same moment that Jimmy said, "Phones do not belong at the table when we're eating."

"I'll call her back later," Lauren said, pressing a button and putting her phone back down. "We're supposed to go for a hike later this afternoon."

"But you made plans to go hiking with *me* this afternoon," Russell said to Lauren, and Ava's heart gave a little painful hop. So that was the plan they had been making on the phone.

But Lauren seemed confused. "I did? Really?"

Russell grinned. "Nah, just joking."

"I would have believed you," Lauren said with a good-natured laugh. "I'm always messing up plans and double-booking."

"I've noticed," he said. "Hence the joke."

Ava looked back and forth between them. So that *wasn't* the plan they had been making on the phone? What was, then?

"I'm going to make some more coffee," Jimmy said, pushing back from the table. "Who wants another cup? Lana? Russell?"

Everyone said yes to another cup except for Lana, who said that she was cutting back on caffeine—"I'm jittery enough without it—at least that's what my doctor says"—and Nancy, who couldn't stomach coffee at all at the moment and had been drinking hot tea with lemon.

After Jimmy had left the room, Lana laid her hand across Nancy's pale wrist. "There's something I need to say." Everyone waited while she closed her eyes and took a deep breath. She opened her eyes again with a flutter of her heavily mascaraed eyelashes. "Nancy, I want you to know that I completely understand why you behaved the way you did back when things were so hard for me. I want you to know that I understand and I forgive."

Nancy looked down at the slashes of red lying across her arm. She said slowly, "I'm sorry. You forgive me for—?"

"You know." Lana's fingers flexed slightly so her fingernails dug gently into Nancy's skin. "For cutting me off when I needed my friends the most. Believe me, you weren't the only one. So many of my friends abandoned me after the divorce. And I was angry at first—I have to be honest and tell you that. I was just so hurt and lonely. With all I was going through those years, a phone call would have meant so much—" Her fingers relaxed and she tapped their tips lightly on Nancy's wrist. "But then I realized that none of you really understood the whole situation. In a way, it was *my* fault for always being so circumspect—maybe I should have confided in people more about what was going on, how he treated me . . ." She shook her head. "I don't know. It's easy to have hindsight. And of course I had to protect my boys. That was first and foremost. I couldn't say anything that might have come back later to haunt them."

"He didn't beat you," Russell said. "You're making it sound like Dad beat you or stuck you in a closet or something. He didn't. He didn't," he repeated to the rest of the room with a slight edge of desperation. The Nickerson women all nodded sympathetically.

"I never said anything like that at all." At least the interruption had made Lana take her hand off of Nancy's arm. For some reason, that was a huge relief to Ava. "All I'm saying is things went on in that house that no one outside of it could know about." She turned back to Nancy. "So of *course* you had confused loyalties. And later I realized you had also completely cut off my ex—never saw *him* anymore either—and let me tell you, that went a long way toward helping me forgive and forget." She sat back in her seat and flattened her hand expressively against her half-naked chest. "And today has completed the healing process. I feel whole again, thanks to you and your beautiful family and the warm welcome you've all given me this morning."

"Mom," Russell said.

"What?" She looked at him, her hand still glued against her chest.

"Nothing." He shook his head. "Nothing."

Nancy said, "I'm sorry I wasn't a better friend to you during that difficult time, Lana. I really am." She looked awfully tired, Ava thought, with a sudden flash of anger at Lana for wearing her mother out.

"You don't have anything to be sorry about, Nancy," Russell said. "We weren't even living here then. We *moved*, Mom," he said to Lana. "You can't blame people for not calling when you move out of town."

"Phones work long-distance, if I remember correctly." She removed her hand from her chest and daintily smoothed out a wrinkle in the tablecloth. "And I'm not blaming anyone for anything. That's my point. All is forgiven, all the wounds are healed."

"Oh God," Russell said and actually put his head in his hands. "Like these people need your forgiveness. Like anyone in the world needs Lana Markowitz's forgiveness."

"Someday, *you're* going to want exactly that," she said. "You'll want it more than anything else and just because of moments like this one—because of *all* the moments when you dismissed and belittled me—it will be too late." She appealed to Nancy. "It's life's great tragedy, isn't it? That we don't value our parents until they're dead and gone and nothing can ever be fixed."

"Oh God," Russell said again.

Nancy said, "Oh, don't be so sure of that, Lana. Look at us. My girls have been absolutely wonderful through my whole illness, helping out in any way they can. I don't wish an illness on you, of course, but I'm sure that your boys would be there for you in a second if you needed them."

"I'd have to be *dying* for them to pay any attention to me," Lana said.

"The temptation right now is to suggest it's worth a try," Russell muttered.

"You're so lucky you had girls," Lana said to Nancy.

"I am," Nancy said. "But if I had a son like Russell, I wouldn't throw him out."

"Thank you." He smiled at her and then pushed back his chair. "Mom, we should go."

"It feels like we just got here," Lana said and waited. When no one urged her to stay longer, she said, "But of course we shouldn't overtire you, Nancy. You have to promise me, though, that we'll do this again next time I'm in town."

"Of course," Nancy said, a little feebly.

Lana picked up her fork. "Just two more bites of my melon," she said gaily, "and I'll be on my way."

"Come on," Russell said to Ava, with a jerk of his chin toward the door. "I need to talk to you before we go."

Everyone stared at them both, and Ava flushed, but it seemed more awkward to protest than to comply, so she excused herself from the table and followed Russell into the front hall while the others settled back down at the table—although, now that she thought about it, her father still hadn't returned from making the coffee, which seemed a little suspicious. How long could it take to measure out a few tablespoons and pour some water?

A few steps outside the dining room, Russell halted, and so Ava did, too. He took her gently by the shoulders and turned her a little this way and that, eyeing her clothing, until she broke away, annoyed. She was wearing an old, loose pair of jeans and a Catalina Island T-shirt that had been a giveaway at her law firm's annual retreat. "You're not wearing any of the clothes I gave you," he said. "I'm disappointed."

"It's Sunday morning." She had abandoned her plan to wear the shimmering dark pink top when Lauren had gotten the call from him. She wasn't going to dress to please a guy she didn't even trust. "The clothes you gave me were pretty fancy."

"I know. But I wanted to see you in all your glory."

"There was no glory. Just me in nicer clothes."

"That's glorious," he said. "From where I'm standing."

Lauren emerged from the dining room and joined them. "Sorry to interrupt," she said, "but I've reached my limit. Your mother's a pain in the butt, Russell. No offense."

"Lauren!" Ava said.

"What? I said no offense." She was wearing a miniskirt with her go-go boots and a long top that was cinched by a narrow belt. She had pinned her hair up in an elaborate, puffy bun that Ava knew for a fact had taken her twenty minutes in the bathroom to perfect.

Russell certainly didn't seem offended. He laughed and said, "Did you see the clothes I gave Ava? Weren't they great?"

"They're awesome," Lauren said. "When do *I* get to go get some?"

"Greedy little thing, aren't you?"

She pouted. "I just want my fair share."

He shook his finger at her. "You dumped us for the evening. If you hadn't, you could have gotten some free loot too. That'll teach you to blow people off."

Lauren made her eyes wide and innocent. "I *wanted* to go. It's not my fault my friend came in that day."

Ava took a step back. They didn't need her for the conversation. But Russell noticed her retreat.

"Hold on," he said. "Don't *you* start going anywhere. I need to show you something."

"What?" It annoyed her that Lauren was grinning like she knew what he was talking about.

"Come here." He took her by the arm. "Cover for us, will you, Lauren?" he said over his shoulder. He steered Ava toward the front door and through it. "Think we could just make a run for it?" he said as he slammed it behind them. "My mother's plane leaves tomorrow at seven. If I could just hide somewhere until then—" He stopped.

"Then what?" Ava asked.

"I might actually keep my sanity." He was moving them forward, down the walkway, still holding on to Ava's arm in a way that was more authoritarian than romantic. "But it's probably too late for that, anyway."

"Where are we going?" she asked. "I should help clean up."

"Why are you always in such a hurry to get away from me?"

"I'm not."

"Anyway, we're here." They stopped at the side of his car and he dropped her arm. He got his keys out of his pants pocket and circled around to the back of the car, where he opened the trunk. Ava drew nearer to see what he was doing. He extracted a box and handed it to her. "For you."

"Shoes?" she said, examining the box. "*Prada* shoes?"

He nodded, brown eyes glowing with anticipation. "Open it up."

She took the lid off, pushed the tissue paper aside, extracted a shoe, and held it up. It was a black pump—shiny because it was patent leather—with squared-off toes and a touch of silver at the ankle. The heel was stacked and at least three inches high. "Wow," she said, for want of anything better to say. She would never have picked the shoes out for herself—the heel was too high, the toe too unusual, the price, she suspected, too steep.

Russell was watching her face eagerly. "I know you like pumps," he said. "So I thought I'd get you a pair to wear with those pants I picked out. They'll go fine with your work clothes—they're pretty sedate. But also fashionable." He nudged her arm briefly. "I thought about getting you a pair of leopard-print stilettos, but I didn't want to push you too far too fast."

"They're very pretty," she said, staring at the shoes.

"I asked the saleswoman for help. I described you."

"Yeah? What'd you say?"

"That you were a lawyer, a little on the conservative side but ready to branch out."

She wasn't sure he was right about that last bit, but let it pass. "How did you know my size?"

"Oh, I can tell a girl's shoe size with one glance," he said airily.

"Really?"

He winked. "Nah. I asked Lauren."

Realization dawned on her. And with it, the knowledge that she was a complete idiot. "Was that why you called her on Tuesday?"

"You knew?" he said. "I *told* her not to tell you. I wanted it to be a surprise." He scowled. "Trust Lauren to mess it up."

"She didn't. I just saw your name on the caller ID. She tried to keep it a secret and—" She stopped, realizing how stupid she'd look if she told him that she thought he and Lauren had been planning some kind of secret tryst. "She didn't tell me about the shoes," she said. "They're a complete surprise."

"Oh, good." He hesitated, watching her, but when she didn't speak again, he said, "So . . . do you like them?"

"I do," she said slowly.

"You need new shoes," he said. "To go with your whole new look." He tapped on the shoebox. "You're a diamond in the rough, Ava. I'm going to mold you into something beautiful."

"You don't mold diamonds." She struggled to keep her tone light despite the hurt his casual comment had just inflicted: he didn't think she was beautiful already; he thought she needed to be changed. "They're like the hardest substance on earth."

"Yeah, but you can grind them down with other diamonds."

"Is that what this is?" She let the shoe dangle from her fingertip. "Are you grinding me down?"

He laughed. "I guess so."

"To what end?" She wondered if he could hear the genuine pleading in her voice.

He didn't appear to. "It will make our married life so much more pleasant," he said jovially. He leaned down to kiss her.

Ava jerked her head away from his. "We should go back."

He peered at her. "You okay?"

"I'm fine." She moved away, out of the circle of his arm, and busied herself packing the shoes back up. "Just worried about my mother. She looked exhausted."

"Yeah, I know," he said, immediately contrite. "I'm sorry—I should get my mother out of here."

As they walked back up to the house, she could feel him watching her and knew that somehow she had disappointed him, that her reaction to his gift wasn't what he expected or wanted. *Fine*, she thought. *Being told I need to be ground down and altered to be at all appealing to you isn't what I expected or wanted, so we're even.*

"By the way," he said with an edge to his voice, when he was opening the door for her, "you're welcome. For the shoes."

She muttered a toneless "Sorry—thanks," and they walked in the front door just as Nancy and Lana emerged from the dining room. Ava quickly dropped the shoebox on the floor and pushed it to the side with her foot.

"I hope I didn't stay too long," Lana was saying. "It's just so hard to tear myself away now that we've reconnected."

"It was a treat to have such a nice long visit," Nancy said, but her smile looked effortful. "Jimmy?" she called, looking around for him. "Come say good-bye to our guests."

Jimmy emerged from the family room with a newspaper section tucked under his arm, closely followed by Lauren.

"Coffee brewed yet?" Nancy asked her husband sweetly as he joined them.

"Almost," he said with only a trace of a smile.

"You have to tell me who your decorator is." Lana tilted her head back to look up at the hanging light fixture in the foyer. "Your house is so pretty. I've been wanting Russell to do more with his little cottage—warm it up a bit. He did all the decorating himself, you know, and it's such a bachelor's pad. Or I guess I should say a divorced man's pad. Oh, look at those beautiful curtains!" She stepped toward the living room, but Ava quickly interposed her body and said firmly, "It was so nice of you to come."

"Our pleasure." Russell tugged on Lana's arm. "Come on, Mom. Let's go."

"It was lovely seeing you all," Lana said, clasping her hands as she batted her eyelashes at each of them in turn. "Really lovely. Your girls are absolutely beautiful, Nancy. What a wonderful family you have! You're very, very lucky."

"I am," Nancy said. "I really am."

Lana made kissing noises near everyone's cheek. "I feel like the past has been exorcised," she said. "Not 'exercised,' but 'exorcised.' You hear the difference, right?"

"Actually," Russell said, steering her toward the front door, "I feel like my past has gotten a real workout today. Which is good because it was getting flabby. You know how pasts get when they sit around watching TV all day." He opened the front door. "Good-bye, Nickersons, one and all. You haven't seen the last of us. Ava, I'll call you. Say good-bye, Mom."

"Good-bye," she said obediently. "Thank you all so much for your wonderful hospitality and the delicious food and for letting me spend a morning in your delightful home—" Even as she was talking, her son was propelling her firmly forward and down the front steps and onto the front walk, and she finally had to give up and just blow a final kiss in their general direction.

Jimmy followed after them, holding the door open as they went down the walk and calling out a cheery "Good to see you both!" Social Daddy gave one last wave and a shouted good-bye and then slammed the door and returned to being their father. "Never again," he said morosely and stalked off back to the family room with his newspaper, leaving the women to clean up.

Chapter 15

The next morning, Lauren examined the turquoise top she had stained. The water spot had dried, leaving behind a small dark wrinkled smudge. Staring miserably at it, she remembered how she used to stain her lips with berries when she was little and still forbidden cosmetics.

She decided to try removing the spot one last time on her own before sending it to the dry cleaners, where a top she had never even worn out of the apartment would cost her yet another five to ten dollars.

She had just squirted a dot of Woolite on a white rag when the apartment phone rang.

"Hi, Lulu," her mother said. "Just checking to see if you're still taking me tomorrow."

"I'm planning on it," Lauren said and realized she was, even though the hospital no longer held the allure of flirting with Daniel—in fact, she was desperately hoping to avoid running into him. But being Nancy's chauffeur and support had become a source of pleasure for her in and of itself.

A source of pleasure and of pride. For years she had been the prodigal daughter, and now she had remade herself into the responsible one. She liked that.

"When I'm done with all this, will you still come visit me once in a while, even if I'm the healthiest mother in town? Or will I have to go back to being grateful for one phone call every few months?" Nancy's tone was light, but Lauren got the sense there was a real question behind the joke.

"Don't worry," Lauren said. "You're not getting rid of me that easily. I'll even take you to the hospital now and then for old times' sake."

"I know why you want to keep going to the hospital. But you can find cute young men in other places too, you know. Have you ever, for example, tried going to a disco?"

"Very funny," Lauren said. "You're real funny, Mom. A little outdated, but funny. I'll see you tomorrow at one-thirty."

"Don't be late."

"I won't be."

"You always say that and then you're always late."

"That's not true," Lauren said. "I don't always *say* it."

"You're funny, too."

"It's the genes. I got your funny genes."

"We should take this show on the road," Nancy said. "Once I'm all better, let's put together a mother-daughter act."

"We could invite Lana Markowitz to join us," Lauren said. "I hear her stand-up routine kills."

Her mother laughed so hard at that she couldn't talk for a moment, but when she had regained her voice, she said, "So what's the story with Russell and Ava? I saw them slip out the door together and he said he was going to call her—"

"The guy obviously likes her," Lauren said. "And I think she likes him. But your oldest daughter's a psychotic mess when it comes to men. No offense."

"What makes you say that?"

"She was in a foul mood when we came back from brunch. You know why?"

"Why?"

"Russell gave her a pair of four-hundred-dollar shoes."

A pause. "She was mad about that?"

"Yeah," Lauren said. "Nothing pisses off a girl like an expensive gift."

"I don't understand."

"Neither do I. She's just weird."

"If you find out anything—"

"You'll be the first person I run and tell."

She had just finished her work on the top and was arranging it on a hanger, dubiously fingering the damp spot her ministrations had left, when her phone rang again. She didn't recognize the number, but as soon as she heard the voice, she knew who it was.

"Lauren?" he said.

She paused before letting out a wary "Hi." She hadn't expected to hear from him again. Run into him at the hospital by accident, maybe, but not get a phone call from him.

"I was wondering if I could see you," he said. "Just for a few minutes. I need someone to talk to." His voice had a strange quality—like something was flickering behind it, altering its rhythms in ways you couldn't put your finger on but that made him not sound like himself.

"Why don't you call Elizabeth?" She knew it was a snarky thing to say but didn't see any reason not to be snarky.

"She's a schoolteacher and can't take phone calls during the day." The blunt honesty of his response was so unexpected, Lauren didn't know how to respond. "Can I see you?"

Lauren tried to feel out her own emotions. Anger and hurt . . .

and curiosity. Why would Daniel call her after things had ended so badly? It wasn't like he could get her in bed again. He had to know that. You could only be betrayed once that way, unless you were a royal idiot.

"We can talk," she said finally, "but don't expect me to be particularly warm or sympathetic."

"I'll take my chances. Where do you want to meet?"

"Come here. My sister won't be home until late."

"Twenty minutes okay?"

She assented and Daniel hung up.

She didn't bother changing her clothes. She was done dressing for Daniel. She greeted him at the door in what she had thrown on that morning to do chores: red Juicy Couture sweatpants and a pink baby-doll tee that was frayed at the neck and bottom and said "Daddy's Little Princesse" in Olde English script. Lauren had bought one for Ava and one for herself as an ironic statement about their actual relationship with their father. Neither of them had yet dared to wear it in front of him.

Daniel was also in sweats—gray bottoms and a green Dartmouth sweatshirt. His pale feet were jammed into flip-flops and he still had on his sunglasses even though the hallway was windowless and fairly dark.

"Hi," he said. He didn't make a move to touch her.

Lauren stepped back. "Come in." She led him into the living room. "Do you want to sit down?"

He was turning his head from side to side, staring around the room, like he had lost something there the last time he had come in. Which, now that she thought about it, was eminently possible, given how they had flung their clothing around that night. But he hadn't said anything about that on the phone.

Now he just said, "Yeah, okay," and sat down hard on the armchair. After a moment, he seemed to realize he still had his sunglasses on and took them off, dropping them carelessly on the coffee table even though they were expensive Oliver Peoples aviators that Lauren had silently admired in the past.

Lauren balanced on the arm of the sofa, catty-corner to him, one leg crossed over the other so that foot swung freely about a foot off the ground. They were both silent for a moment. Daniel clasped his hands between his knees and stared down at them.

"You all right?" she said.

He hunched his shoulders forward. "I'm fine," he said with his old brusqueness. Then he shook his head. Then he put his hands on his knees and rubbed the tops of both legs in unison. Then he said, "We had an appointment with the doctor this morning. We're stopping chemo. I won't be seeing you at the hospital anymore."

"Is that—" She was about to ask whether it was a good or bad thing, but it was too obvious what the answer was, so she stopped herself. "What else did the doctor say?"

His voice was flat. "He said that it's time for hospice care. We've been making calls, filing paperwork . . . She's home for good. She won't be leaving again. My brother's with her now. But she's been sleeping so much. I'm not sure it even matters who's there."

"I'm sorry," Lauren said.

His face screwed up like something was hurting him, but then it went slack again. "The doctor said there was no point to continuing the chemo. That it was just making her weaker."

"I'm sorry," Lauren said again, because she didn't know what else to say. She was trying to hold on to her anger at him, but it was hard when he was so pitiful.

His eyes darted around, not meeting hers or alighting on anything. There was a blindness behind them for all their motion. "He said we should just make her comfortable. Not worry about how much pain medication we give her. The important thing is that she not feel any pain."

"That makes sense."

She could have said anything: he wasn't listening. "But all the meds—they keep her from being awake. She doesn't even talk to us anymore. She can't. She can't stay awake long enough to finish a thought." His face screwed up again, his mouth drawing up toward his nose, his eyes squinching half shut. Then his features fell back into place. It looked almost comical. "I thought when we got a time frame, we'd say, Okay, that's it, but at least now we know how much time we have together so we'll make the most of it. I didn't think she'd be barely conscious." He stared at Lauren's bare and slightly dirty foot that was dangling a few inches above his own pale toes. "When she finally stops sleeping, she'll be dead."

"You might still get some time," Lauren said. "If she rests up enough—maybe later there'll be some time when she's awake and can talk to you."

"Maybe," he said. "Maybe we'll have a few minutes." Then he said, "She's my mom," and his voice cracked on the last word.

"I know." Lauren slid down off the sofa arm and into a crouching position next to him. She put her arms around him. "I know."

He put his head on her shoulder and he cried—not the way Lauren cried when she felt sad, with tears choking in her throat and standing in her eyes, but big gulping, racking, wet sobs.

Like a little kid crying for his mother.

The rawness of it stunned Lauren. It made her realize that whatever she and Daniel had had—the flirting, the sex, the awkward dates—none of that had run very deep for either of them. They had gone through some motions, wondered if there were any feelings there, pretended for a few minutes maybe that there were, had some sex that was all the more exciting *because* they were really strangers.

But then you saw this—you saw a boy who was crying because the mother he loved was dying—and you realized the difference between love that mattered and a casual flirtation.

Seeing that made it easier for her to hold him. She didn't even feel angry anymore, just sad, although she couldn't have said whether she was sad for him, his mother, her mother, or herself, or for a world in which you had to watch your mother die because the only alternative sucked even more.

She patted his back and made soothing sounds.

Eventually he stopped and lifted his head. She released him and sat back on her heels.

"You got a tissue?" he asked, swiping at his eyes with his forearm.

"Yeah." She went into Ava's bedroom to grab some tissues from the box on her night table. When she came back, Daniel was standing near the window, his back to her. He held out his hand without turning around and she put the tissues in it.

He didn't turn back around until he had blown his nose and wiped his eyes. Then he faced her. "I'm sorry," he said, taking a deep, uneven breath. "I didn't know I was going to do that."

"You don't need to apologize for *that*," she said.

"Thanks for listening." He dropped the used tissues into the wastebasket near Ava's desk. "I needed to talk to someone. My brother's not the emotional type. I'm glad he's here, but he and Mom weren't all that close. It's not hitting him the same way."

"It will, though," Lauren said. "At some point. You can't just lose a mother and not care."

"He cares," Daniel said. "It's just different."

They stood there for a moment in silence.

"You want a cup of coffee or something?" Lauren asked.

"That would be nice." He glanced at his watch. "I should probably go home, though, in case she wakes up and has a few lucid minutes. It would kill me to miss that."

"You'll drive yourself crazy if you think like that," Lauren said. "You can't stay next to her bed twenty-four hours a day."

"I know."

"One cup?"

"Yeah. Okay." He followed her into the kitchen.

"Will your brother stay in L.A.?" Lauren asked as she poured water into Ava's coffeemaker. "Until—" She stopped. "Sorry. Is this bad to talk about?"

"No, it's okay," he said. "She's going to die. I might as well get used to the idea. Saying it out loud doesn't make it any more or less true." He stuck his hands in his pockets. "Just don't use any euphemisms. I hate when people talk about 'passing' or ask me how long it's been since I 'lost' my father. I didn't lose him: I know exactly where his ashes are." He gave a short laugh. "In my mother's linen closet—don't ask me why. And he didn't 'pass on' somewhere. He died. Avoiding the word doesn't change the reality."

"I know what you mean," Lauren said. But she couldn't bring herself to use the word even so. "How long do they think it'll be?"

"Couple of weeks?" he said. "Give or take a few days. My brother told me that hospice nurses sometimes slip a little extra morphine into the drip when the time is near just to speed it along, make sure it's painless."

"I wouldn't want that job." Lauren pressed the button on the coffeemaker and it immediately started gurgling.

Daniel raised his hands and pressed them up against the top of the doorway like Samson bringing down the house. His sweatshirt rose up and showed a few inches of his flat stomach. Glancing over, Lauren thought it was amazing she had ever slid her hand across his muscles, that they had once been that intimate, even if only for a drunken moment or two. "I don't know," he said. "I guess you just think of it as an act of mercy. Which it probably is."

"Think I could convince them to come over and give my father a quick shot?" Lauren said. "He's not sick or anything, but it might put me out of *my* misery."

Another ghost of a smile. "Sure," Daniel said and dropped his hands down to his sides. "Go ahead, Lauren. Make jokes about parents dying. Nothing funnier than that." At least he sounded a little more like himself.

"I'm sorry," she said. "It's a bad habit of mine. I get tactless when I'm nervous."

"It's fine. You should hear some of the jokes my brother and I have been making—some truly awful shit."

"Will you both stay in L.A.?" she said. "Until the end?"

"Yeah."

"And Elizabeth? Will she come?" No snarkiness this time: she really wanted to know.

"As soon as they can find a decent substitute." They were both silent for a moment. Then he said, "Thanks for letting me come over. After everything . . ."

"Guess I'm still your cancer buddy," she said with a lightness she didn't feel.

"I thought maybe I'd ruined that forever."

"You kind of did," she said. "But then you played the dying mother card."

"Clever of me."

"You only get to use it once, though."

"The thing is"—and his face was crashing again, crushed by misery and self-loathing and self-pity and despair—"the thing is that she would have been so mad at me for what I did to both you and Elizabeth. She would have said it showed a lack of integrity. That was the worst thing to her. It meant I had disappointed her in every way possible. If she knew—"

"She won't know," Lauren said. "She'll never know."

"That's not a consolation."

"I can't do better than that," Lauren said. "I'm not really in a place where I can tell you that what you did was okay."

"I know. I don't expect you to." He closed his eyes and took a deep breath, and when he opened them again he was once more in control of his features. "So where's my coffee?"

"Just about ready," she said and busied herself getting the cups out.

As they sat at the table, drinking coffee and not saying much, Lauren looked at him and thought, *In a different time and place, this could have worked.*

But then again, maybe in a different time and place he would have been just another rich, self-centered banker, no different from most of the Financial District guys she met when they ran into her boutique to buy gifts for their thin, self-centered girlfriends. Maybe that was who Daniel was when his mother wasn't dying.

She didn't really know him. He was a stranger. He had this whole life going on back in New York that she knew nothing about but was more real to him than anything here in L.A.

For years, maybe even decades, he'd look back at this time in his life and think, *Wow, those few weeks when my mother was dying were surreal.* He might remember that there was a girl during that time, maybe even that he had slept with her, but once a year or two had gone by, Lauren seriously doubted he'd remember her name.

She needed to talk to someone about what happened, so when Ava came home that night after a late client dinner, Lauren told her that Daniel had stopped by the apartment.

"Really?" Ava said. "So did you sleep with him again?"

They had both been curled up on the sofa, but that made Lauren sit up straight. "How did you know I slept with him?"

"I heard you. I was in the next room, remember?"

"We thought you were asleep."

"Do you have any idea how noisy you were? Crashing around, moaning, talking about condoms . . . Good for you, by the way— making sure he wore one. Made me proud of my little sister."

"Why didn't you tell me you heard us?"

"Well, you were *trying* to be discreet. It's not your fault the walls are thin. I figured you were entitled to your privacy."

"I don't think it counts as privacy if you just *pretend* not to hear." She slid back down so their heads were near each other. "Anyway, no, I didn't sleep with him again." She told Ava how Daniel was already living with someone back in New York but had waited to tell her that until after they'd had sex.

"Jesus," Ava said. "What a jerk."

"Yeah," Lauren said. "I hated him when he first told me. But today I actually felt kind of sorry for him. His mother's dying, Ava. She has probably less than a month to live."

"That doesn't excuse what he did."

"I know," Lauren said. "But to be fair, it wasn't like he ever claimed to be serious about me. The only thing we had in common was that our moms were sick. And, in the end, we didn't really have that in common because his was so much sicker."

"Thank God for that," Ava said. "Better his than ours."

"That's an awful thing to say."

"I know. I don't care. I want Mom to be okay."

Lauren remembered the look on Daniel's face when he first walked in, the blindness there, and the pain behind the blindness. She said, "Me too."

They sat quietly for a few minutes and then Lauren stirred and said, "By the way, I talked to her today. Mom, I mean. She wanted to know what's going on with you and Russell."

She could feel Ava stiffen into a more upright position next to her. "I hope you told her nothing's going on with us. Nothing at all."

"I told her he really likes you."

"He doesn't really like me," Ava said. "If he really liked me, he wouldn't always be working so hard to try to change me."

"He bought you a pair of shoes," Lauren said. "Any way you look at it, that's just *nice*."

But Ava's face remained stony. "I'm sick of him—and you, for that matter—telling me there's something wrong with me because I don't want to spend hours every day fussing over my outfit and worrying about whether my hair is ultra-thick and shiny or just *hair*. I'm happy with the way I look, and I think I'm the one making the right choices about this stuff, not you or the ten thousand women Russell's gone out with before me and the ten thousand women he'll go out with *after* me." Then she added hastily, "Not that there's a 'me' in his life in the first place. Just . . . Well, you know what I mean."

"Not really," Lauren said. "What's your point?"

"My point," Ava said, her voice going up higher than normal, "is that I don't want some stupid Prada shoes forced on me when I'm perfectly happy with the shoes I already have."

Lauren rolled her eyes. "You're not seriously mad at him about that, are you? You *can't* be."

"You don't get it," Ava said. She stood up. "You're incapable of getting it. You're just as bad as he is. Just leave me alone about Russell, okay? Every time I see him, I end up feeling worse about myself. It doesn't work."

"You're blaming him for something that's your fault. If you'd just—"

"What about 'leave me alone' don't you understand?" Ava turned on her heel. "I'm going to sleep. Don't make a lot of noise when you use the bathroom." She stomped off.

Lauren sighed and watched her go. For all of Ava's intelligence and professional success, she could be awfully stupid about some things. The girl needed help.

Chapter 16

Lauren was usually still asleep when Ava left for work, but on Thursday morning she came into the bedroom as soon as Ava's alarm went off.

"I planned an outfit for you," she said. "It's all laid out in the bathroom."

"Huh?" said Ava, who was sleepily fingering the snooze button. "You did what?"

"I want you to put on the clothes I picked out for you," Lauren said. "It's easier than not doing it, right? It'll take you two seconds to throw them on."

Ava was apparently too weary to argue because she just nodded, threw back the covers, and stumbled toward the bathroom.

Fifteen minutes later, she emerged with damp hair, wearing the black pants Russell had given her and a dark green top of Lauren's that had three-quarter-length sleeves and a scoop neck that dipped lower than anything Ava usually wore but which, even so, didn't reveal anything but the elegant hollow of her neck and a few inches of pale, smooth skin below and around that. "Perfect," Lauren said, with real delight. "Now give me your hand."

"Why?" Ava said, but Lauren had already taken her by the wrist and shoved four different silver bracelets up and over her fingers. "I never wear bracelets," Ava said, shaking them into place and studying them dubiously.

"I know. They look great. Come here."

"Why are we doing this?" Ava asked as Lauren pulled her into the bathroom.

"I'm proving a point." She put the toilet cover down. "Sit."

"I don't have a lot of time."

"This won't take long."

Ava sat and Lauren quickly and expertly brushed on some blush, eye shadow, and mascara—all belonging to her, of course—occasionally and indifferently swatting away her sister's protesting upraised hand. "I'd do more, but I know this is all you'll sit for," she said as she dabbed on some light lip stain. She put her head back and studied her sister's face. She nodded. "It works. Now put your head down."

"Huh?" Ava said again, and Lauren wished she had thought to brew her sister a cup of coffee before starting all this.

"Like this." She pulled Ava's head forward and thrust it down so she was staring at the floor between her knees, then grabbed the blow dryer and started working on her hair, using her fingers to flip it forward and down. A minute later, she said, "Okay, now sit up and twist toward the sink so I can get at your back."

"I'm hating this," Ava said, turning, her eyes shut against the dryer's blast. "I'll give you two more minutes. If you're not done by then . . ."

Lauren was using a brush now. "Okay, okay." She finished within the allotted time. It wasn't perfect, but at least Ava's hair looked sleeker and more stylishly groomed than it normally did.

Ava stood up and looked in the mirror. "Nice," she admitted. She peered more closely. "Too much eye shadow, though."

"I hardly used any. You're just so used to seeing yourself without anything, the smallest amount looks strange to you."

Ava turned to her. "And *why* do I need to be all done up today? Are you planning something I should know about?"

"Nope—I'm just proving a point." Lauren unplugged her hair dryer and wrapped the cord around the handle. "It took all of ten extra minutes—not even—to get you ready this morning and you look a thousand times better than usual."

"It's still ten wasted minutes. And I think 'a thousand times' is an exaggeration."

"How wasted?" Lauren asked. "What would you have done with those ten minutes otherwise?"

"I could have worked," Ava said. "I bill at three hundred dollars an hour."

"You spend enough time writing up contracts," Lauren said. "This is a better use of your time. Wait until the compliments come rolling in."

"No one will even notice." Ava walked out of the bathroom. She reached up to touch her hair, and the bracelets clinked gently against one another. "These are going to drive me nuts."

"Oh, please. Here, put these on." Lauren retrieved a pair of shoes from the top of the dresser where she had left them earlier that morning after discovering them stuffed way in the back of the closet.

Ava groaned. "Russell's shoes."

"Shut up and wear them and be grateful."

"I'll shut up and I'll wear them, but I won't be grateful," Ava said. She slipped her feet into them. "They're too high. I'll never be able to walk in them."

"Oh, stop whining. You'll get used to them. They make your legs look like they're a mile long. See?" Lauren closed the bathroom door so Ava could view herself in the full-length mirror. "A tiny bit of effort and you look fantastic."

"Don't be an idiot," Ava said and turned her back on the reflection. But she glanced at it again over her shoulder as she left.

People *did* notice. Ava wasn't sure she liked that. When Jeremy said, "Wow! Look at you!" she wondered whether all that enthusiasm meant he usually thought she looked awful. When a senior partner passed her in the corridor and then stopped and turned around and said, "I almost didn't recognize you, Ava. You look lovely today," she worried that his flattery came at the cost of some professional respect, that there was something dismissive in his tone. And when a wealthy client she had never met before came in to talk about the prenuptial contract she had drawn up for him and his soon-to-be fourth wife, she didn't like the way he gave her a real once-over look when she stood up (bracelets tinkling annoyingly) to greet him.

She knew that there were plenty of professional women—including quite a few in her own office—who were attractive and stylish and perfectly successful, that her experience and ability were what counted and that being plain had no more street value than being beautiful, and possibly even less. But the glances and comments still made her uneasy. She removed the bracelets midmorning—they just didn't feel like they belonged in a law office to her—and she considered washing the makeup off in the bathroom. Only her fear that it would come off unevenly and leave her skin patchy and her eyes raccoony kept her from scrubbing at it.

Well, that and the fact that when she caught sight of herself in the mirror, she liked what she saw there. Every glimpse gave her an equally quick jolt of pleasure. It was like spotting an especially good photo of herself in one of her parents' albums.

And when at lunchtime a random guy at the food court stopped to pick up the napkin that a gust of wind had blown off of her plastic container and returned it to her with a grin and a flourish, she raised her chin and smiled back at him with more confidence than she would have had on any other day.

All of which meant—

Ava had no idea what it all meant. No clear message was coming through to her, and since she liked things to be clear, she found that unsettling.

⟨●⟩

"Hey, Jeremy?" she said that afternoon after he had dropped some papers on her desk and picked up her outgoing mail. "What's this on my calendar?" She pointed at the screen. "It says I have a family dinner at seven-thirty tonight."

"Lauren was worried you'd forget," Jeremy said with a slightly patronizing smile. "She called yesterday to make sure it was on your schedule. Which it wasn't. But I put it on there for you."

"I don't remember anyone even telling me about it," Ava said, a little glumly: she had felt out of the family loop lately, since she couldn't spend her days chatting on the phone or running over to their parents' house the way Lauren could. When Lauren was living in New York, Ava didn't have to do much to be the better daughter—just show up for dinner now and then and remember her parents' anniversary and birthdays—but with Lauren back in town escorting their mother to the hospital on a regular basis, Ava's role as number-one daughter was slipping through her fingers. "Did Lauren say if it was the whole family?" If her mother was feeling up to going out on a Thursday—just two days after chemo—that would certainly be something worth celebrating. "What's the occasion?"

"I have no idea," Jeremy said. "Want me to get Lauren on the phone for you?"

"No, that's okay. Whatever." She had a lot of work to get through if she was going out that night, and Lauren had trouble keeping phone conversations brief.

A partner unexpectedly called her into a meeting at six-thirty and kept her in his office for over an hour, and there was an urgent phone message from a client waiting for her when she emerged, which she returned in the car on her way to the restaurant, blessing the invention of Bluetooth as she did so. She talked fast and wrapped up the conversation as she was pulling up to the restaurant, then snatched the valet ticket right out of the guy's hand and dashed inside. Her family had made comments in the past about her putting work ahead of them, and while she thought the accusations were unwarranted, she had to admit that at times like this—when she was half an hour late for a family dinner and hadn't had a chance to call ahead and apologize—circumstances conspired to make them *appear* well-founded.

As she entered the dark restaurant, the first thing she saw was Lauren walking toward her. She must have been waiting right by the door for Ava to arrive. An apology already forming on her lips, Ava raised her hand in guilty greeting at the exact same moment that Lauren saluted her.

And that was when Ava realized she was waving at *herself*—at her reflection in the mirror behind the bar. In the dim light, wearing the clothes Lauren had picked out for her, her face made up the way Lauren made up *her* face, she had fooled herself into thinking she was her own little sister.

She dropped her hand, embarrassed, and looked around quickly, hoping no one else had noticed.

But had she always looked so much like Lauren? And why did she think Lauren was so much prettier and thinner and sexier than she was, when her own quick glance couldn't tell them apart?

She postponed the question for later analysis, since the hostess was approaching her. She gave her last name and the hostess said, "I'll take you to your table," and led her toward the back of the restaurant. She looked for her parents and Lauren but didn't see them, thought maybe she was the first to get there—but that didn't make sense since she was late—and anyway the tables they were heading toward seemed too small for a big group—was turning to the hostess to question her—but the woman was already gesturing toward a table for two with an empty seat—and someone there was rising to his feet in recognition and greeting.

"There you are," Russell Markowitz said. "I almost gave up." He stepped forward and kissed her on both cheeks. He was wearing another well-tailored suit with his usual crisply ironed white cotton dress shirt and a dark blue paisley tie.

Confused, Ava accepted his kiss as she tried to figure out what was going on. Lauren must have invited Russell to join them. But where was the rest of the family? Had they been seated somewhere else? Or was it just a coincidence that Russell was at the restaurant, and the hostess was still going to lead her to her actual table? Except, no, that couldn't be it, because he seemed to have been expecting her. She turned to the hostess for elucidation. "Is this my table?"

"Is that all right?" the hostess said. "People usually like to sit back here, but if you prefer to be up front—"

"No, it's fine. It's just—"

The hostess pulled out the chair. "Let me know if you want to change," she said with a slightly impatient shake of the chair, and, obedient as always to authority, Ava sank into it.

Russell also settled back into his seat. "I don't get an apology?" He cocked his head at her. "You're almost half an hour late. I was ready to give up. I tried your cell but no answer."

"Sorry," she said. "Work went late and then I got stuck on a phone call with a client." She looked around. "Where is everybody?"

"It's a weeknight," he said with a shrug.

"What?" She realized he, like the waitress, had misunderstood her. "I mean my family. Where are they?"

"Did you invite your family to come?" Now *he* seemed confused. "We'll need a bigger table."

"It's a family dinner, isn't it?"

He gave her a funny look. "That's not how it was described to me."

It felt like the two of them were speaking different languages. "How *was* it described to you?" she said. "And by whom?"

Russell continued to stare at her for a moment. Then he put his hands flat on the table. "Okay," he said carefully. "Did you or did you not call me two nights ago and ask if you could take me out to dinner as a thank-you for the shoes I gave you?"

"I never called you."

He processed that. "You're serious, aren't you?" She nodded, and he said, "I got a call from someone—on *your* cell phone— who claimed to be you and who sounded like you, so either you were so drunk you don't remember making the call or—" He stopped.

Ava said grimly, "People used to confuse our voices all the time when we were teenagers."

"It was a quick conversation, too," he said. "Even so, I can't believe I fell for it. So you had nothing to do with any of this?" He gestured around them, at the restaurant's dining room.

"My assistant told me Lauren had planned a family dinner for tonight. That's all I knew."

"She said it was a family dinner?" He sat back and folded his arms, sinking his chin into his chest like a petulant child. "She must have thought you wouldn't have come just to see *me*."

Ava said irritably, "I don't know how her mind works. Don't read too much into it."

There was a pause. Then Russell said, "I was worried. At brunch the other day. You seemed kind of annoyed with me, but I couldn't figure out why. So when you called and sounded so happy about the shoes and wanted to get together—"

"That wasn't me."

"I know that now," he said icily. "I'm well aware of that." He fingered the martini glass in front of him. "I feel like an idiot."

"It's not your fault," Ava said. "Lauren and I have really similar voices, and if she was *trying* to sound like me—"

"Not just about that." He ran his fingers through his hair, made it stand up. "Everything I do with or for you seems to go wrong. You didn't actually like the shoes, did you?"

"They're pretty," she said. "Look—I'm wearing them."

He leaned over sideways, peering under the table, and she twisted her foot from side to side for him. "They look great on you," he said, and she could see the relief and satisfaction on his face. "So you do actually like them?"

"I do." It was true; at some point during the day of wearing them, she had come to like looking down and seeing the pretty tips of the shoes peeking up at her. The extra height they gave her was also kind of nice. She had felt more imposing all day.

"Those are the pants I gave you, too, right?" She nodded, and he smiled. "I'm glad you like them. You look fantastic. You know that, don't you?"

Of course she looked good to him. It was his taste she was showing off, not her own. "It was nice of you to give me all this," she said dully.

"I'm glad you think so. And glad to see you're making use of it all. Because, for better or worse, I brought you another present." He reached down to the floor and came back up with a flat box. "See? It's not so bad going out with me. You always go home with a party favor."

Ava raised her eyebrows. "*Another* gift?"

"Why not?" he said and handed it to her.

"I feel guilty. You keep showering me with stuff." But guilt wasn't actually the emotion she was feeling as she turned the package around in her hands. Did he think if he threw enough tinsel at her, some of it would stick?

He was oblivious to her discomfort. "I got inspired when you sounded so happy about the shoes on the phone. I mean, when Lauren did." He waved it off. "The point is, I *thought* it was you, and it got me excited about picking something else out for you. Open it."

She untied the ribbon and uncovered the box to find a pool of blue and orange silk shimmering in a familiar pattern. She hooked her finger into the shining fabric and lifted it a bit. "It's the scarf I liked."

"I remembered."

"But you said I wasn't a scarf person. That you had to be old or French to wear a scarf."

"I left out a category." He leaned forward over the table. "Stylish. Stylish American women can carry off a scarf, even at a young age."

"I'm not stylish."

"Ah, come on. Look at yourself right now."

She let the scarf slip back into the box. "This is all Lauren," she said. "She dressed me. She did my hair. She made up my face. She even set up this *date*. I mean, you're basically out with Lauren right now."

"Ha," he said.

But she wasn't trying to be funny. "Why aren't you?"

"Why aren't I what?"

"Out with Lauren right now?"

"What do you mean?"

"Well, she's your type, isn't she? More than I am?"

His smile was stiffening. "What's that supposed to mean?"

"You know." She closed the lid on the box, shoved it across the table. "She's pretty, dresses nicely, likes things like Prada shoes, probably knows how to tie a scarf—I mean, definitely knows how to tie a scarf, I've seen her—"

"Nothing wrong with any of that," Russell said. "Nothing wrong with Lauren, either." He drained the last of his martini. "And, much as I don't like the idea that I have a type, maybe you're right that I did once." He put the glass down with a sigh. "I'm getting old, I guess. My type is changing." He gave her a sideways look that was a little coy. "I think you might be my type now. If I haven't made that clear."

"Then why do you keep trying to turn me into Lauren?"

He recoiled. "I'm not. Why would you even say that?"

"The clothes," she said. "And the shoes. And this scarf. You're trying to make me more like her—change me into something I'm not."

"I've never tried to change you," he said. "Your clothes, maybe, but not you."

"I'm serious."

He shook his head slowly. "It's fun, finding stuff for you to wear. That's all."

"It changed how you felt about me. I put on the clothing and suddenly you—" She stopped and bit her lip, then picked up her glass and took a sip to hide her embarrassment, her unfinished sentence.

When she stole another very quick glance at him, Russell was drumming his fingers on the table, his face drawn tight. "How superficial do you think I am?" he said.

"I never said I thought you were—"

"That dress you put on that night?" he said, in a low, rapid voice. "I first spotted it on a hanger, and, God, that hanger looked hot. So when you refused to come home with me that night, you know what I did? Found another hanger with one of those dresses, took it home, and made passionate love to it all night long."

"Shut up," she said. "That's not what I'm saying."

"Isn't it?"

"I just think you're the kind of person who cares more about what people wear than about who they are."

"Thanks," he said. "I sure am one shallow guy, aren't I? And your theory explains my interest in *you* how? You're not exactly Coco Chanel."

"I don't know," she said soberly. "I can't figure it out. I mean, you clearly preferred Lauren to me at the beginning—"

"I *noticed* Lauren more than you at the beginning," he said. "Who wouldn't? She walks into a room with this 'Hey, everybody, look at me!' kind of attitude. So everyone looks. Meanwhile, *you* skulk around, practically begging people *not* to look at you. You make people work hard just to realize you're even there."

"Still, it was obvious you liked her—"

"Sure," he said irritably, cutting her off again. "Everyone likes Lauren—she's *likable*. And very easy to joke around with. But it took me like five minutes to realize she's a flake. You know that. I like Lauren, she's fun. But she's not someone you have a really meaningful or deep conversation with. I mean, come on—the girl can't even remember her own home address."

Ava always defended Lauren if someone outside the family attacked her. "It's not her fault—she hasn't lived there for a while."

"Oh, for God's sake," Russell said. "If I liked Lauren that way, I promise you she'd be sitting across from me tonight." He pulled at the collar of his shirt like it was choking him. "I'm not saying I'm irresistible, but I suspect a pair of Prada shoes would have gone a lot further with her than they did with you."

"Probably," she said. "She's the stylish one."

"And you assume that makes her more appealing to me? I think *you're* the one who's obsessed with what people wear, not me." The waitress approached them, but he gave her one savage look and she backed away. He leaned forward. "I've had a bad week, Ava. My mother was here crying every day and accusing me of neglecting her and my bosses were on my back, threatening to fire me, and I kept thinking, 'When I come up for air, I'll see Ava and that will make me feel better.' Because I really like being with you. More than I've liked being with anyone for a long time. But you know what?" He sat back. "You're not making me feel better. I gave you presents and you resented me for it. For no reason at all, you assumed my generosity was some kind of implied criticism and took offense." He held out his hands. "Look, maybe I was a little oblivious, but I only ever gave you stuff because I wanted to make you like me. To say my plan backfired is what you might call an understatement." He pushed his chair back. "I was so stupidly happy when I thought you'd called me, Ava. In spite of everything else that's lousy in my life right now, a girl I liked called me and wanted to have dinner and suddenly life was good again. But you *didn't* call me and you *didn't* want to have dinner with me tonight. It was all your sister's idea of a joke. You didn't want dinner, you didn't want shoes, you didn't want me." He stood up. "You'll be happier eating without me." He pulled out his wallet and threw down a twenty. "That's for my drink. Good night, Ava. Tell Lauren she should try minding her own business. If she's capable of it."

He walked away from the table. Ava stared after him a moment, blinking, her mind still twisting around what he had said. He was angry at *her*. How was that possible? Wasn't she the one who had been insulted and misused?

Sudden clarity hit her hard, leaving horror in its wake.

He was right. Russell was right.

Fear had made her stupid and insensitive. Fear of finding herself second to Lauren had made her reject Russell before he could reject her. Fear of being judged and found wanting had made her pass unfair and prejudiced judgment on *him*. Fear of being hurt had made her defensive and careful and closed off—and so she had hurt someone whose only crime was to pursue her.

Russell had reached his hand out to her and she had slapped him across the face in return.

She could have kicked herself—only she didn't have time. Russell was walking across the restaurant, and if he reached the door, he would leave. And if he left, she wouldn't be able to tell him she was sorry and try at least to make him see that she was stupid and blind but not cruel. Not deliberately cruel, anyway.

She pulled the scarf out of the box as she rose to her feet and ran after him. She stumbled briefly and wanted to curse her shoes because their heels were too high—but then she remembered that the shoes were also pretty and expensive and a perfectly lovely gift for a man to give a woman he liked, and if she slipped in them, it was because of her own clumsiness and not some fault of theirs.

She called Russell's name and he turned—as did several customers at nearby tables and the hostess who had seated her and a waiter who was trying to mix a Caesar salad on a rolling cart and the bartender who was arranging filled glasses on a round tray at the bar near the entrance.

"Russell, wait," she said, and Russell came back toward her with a tight *What now?* expression on his face. Ava clumsily scrunched up the scarf and pulled it around her neck, then tied it directly under her chin the only way she knew how, like she was tying a shoe, pulling the ends apart from each other way too hard and half strangling herself. "How's that?" she said, coming up close to him and throwing back her neck so he could see.

"It looks awful," he said, but there was amusement and anger and hope and confusion in just those three words.

"I know," she said, close to tears of sheer frustration because she didn't know how to tell him everything she needed to. "I can be an idiot about things like this."

"I've noticed," he said with a tentative smile. She managed a somewhat more tremulous one in return. He reached toward her. "May I?" She nodded dumbly and he deftly untied the scarf and slid it from around her neck. He gave it a quick hard shake so it was a square again. "This is why you need me to help you." He didn't fold the scarf or scrunch it like she had, just caught it around her neck, then neatly tied it in a loose and feminine knot off to one side, letting the ends fall onto her left shoulder. He shifted back to study the effect.

"How does it look?" she said in a voice that wasn't much more than a whisper. She had a dim sense of other people watching but didn't care.

"Old and French," Russell said.

"I'll wear it if you like it," Ava whispered. "I trust your judgment more than mine."

"Is that an apology?" he said, and she nodded, unable to say much more.

He put a hand on each of her shoulders. She reached up and touched his right hand with hers. And then he bent forward and kissed her on the lips, in front of all those people and the hostess, and the waiter making his Caesar salad and the bartender whose tray was completely filled now and who was just watching them.

And Ava let him.

No, she did more than let him: she kissed him right back and it was lovely.

A moment later, though, awareness returned, and embarrassment of course, and she ducked her head, blushing. She avoided looking at anyone around them, as if by ignoring them she could ensure her own invisibility. She caught Russell's arm and pulled him toward the back of the restaurant where their table was waiting for them, their napkins neatly shaken out and refolded and their water glasses refilled.

Chapter 17

She was no longer very hungry and neither, apparently, was Russell. They both ordered lightly and picked at their food, and he asked for the check as soon as their entrees had been bused. His cell phone rang as they waited for the waitress to bring back the credit card slip, and he took it out and peered at the number. "Corinne," he said with a grimace, pressing a button to ignore the call. He put the phone back in his pocket.

"She still calls you?" It occurred to Ava that she would happily pull out all of Corinne's highlighted hair. It wasn't the kind of thought she normally had. "I thought you'd broken up."

"It's hard to break up with someone when you were never a couple to begin with," Russell said. "At least, I didn't think we were. She seems to have a different opinion of the matter."

"What was the appeal?" Ava asked. "I mean, besides the way she looked?"

"There was a besides?" he said with a grin.

"Watch it." She fingered the scarf around her neck. It felt foreign there, strange and out of place—but not unpleasant. Silky.

"She made me feel like I was still in the game," he said. "That seemed important at the time. She impressed my friends."

"People like Cole."

He nodded. "Yeah. The old college buddies envied me. Especially the ones who were married."

"Because she was so pretty?"

"Well, it wasn't because she was so brilliant." He reconsidered. "Although the fact that she wasn't a rocket scientist actually had its charms. I always felt smart around her." He waved his finger at Ava. "Whereas with you, Nickerson, I'm always being outargued."

"I'm sorry," she said. "I've been a little rough on you, I know."

"Yeah, you have." He touched the back of her hand lightly. "But I kind of like it. You keep me on my toes."

"I still think I'll try being nicer to you."

"I like that idea," he said.

The waitress came back with Russell's charge card. While he signed the receipt, Ava dug out her own cell phone.

"Just remembered I have a call to make," she said and dialed Lauren's number. "Hey," she said all in a rush, when Lauren answered. "Listen, I am *so* sorry about missing the family dinner tonight. I tried but couldn't get out of work and totally forgot to call until now. Will you tell everyone I'm sorry? I'll see you later. Bye!" She hung up before Lauren could even say anything.

"That was evil," Russell said.

"How much do you want to bet she's going to call you in about five seconds?"

Russell's phone rang on cue. "What do you want me to tell her?" he said, holding it unopened in his hand. "Should I say that you and I had a date and you stood me up and I'm never speaking to you again? Or should I let her in on the joke?"

"Just don't answer it. Let her suffer a little while longer. She deserves it."

"Yeah," Russell said. "Look what she's done to us. The horribleness of her."

"She shouldn't have lied to us," Ava said primly.

"Yeah, but if she hadn't—"

"We wouldn't be here right now. I know." She shrugged. "But she pretended to be me on the phone. I can't let her get away with that."

"She's kind of brilliant," Russell said. "When you think about it. She maneuvered this whole thing, knowing it was best for both of us. She was one step ahead of us the whole way."

"For God's sake, don't tell her that. Her head is swollen enough as it is. If she decides she's good at running my life for me, I'm in deep trouble."

"It's nice to sit here talking about Lauren," Russell said, leaning forward with sudden impatience, "but—"

"Let's go," Ava said immediately, and they both rose to their feet without another word.

◦

Since they had come in separate cars, Ava had to follow Russell to his house in Larchmont Village. It wasn't easy keeping up with him. She lost him at a couple of lights—he had a bad habit of slipping through just as the yellow turned to red—but at least he had the grace to pull to the side of the road and wait until she could catch up with him again.

"You drive too fast," she said when they met up in front of his house, a small, neat ranch that wasn't too big for its lot, unlike most of the houses on his block. Russell had parked in the garage and walked down to meet her on the street.

"Sorry," he said. "I was in a hurry to get you back here." He took her by the hand and led her up toward the open garage. "Didn't want to give you enough time to change your mind again."

She stopped. "There's no danger of that," she said and pulled at the sleeve of his jacket for emphasis. "I promise."

"Good." He put his arms around her and held her against his chest for a moment. Ava closed her eyes and rubbed her cheek against his lapel and breathed in his scent, which was already familiar to her from when she had worn his jacket at the mall.

Russell's arms tightened briefly and then he released her and stepped back. "Come on, let's go inside."

He closed the garage door and they entered the house. The back hallway they were in was pitch-black, and the darkness made Ava bold: she was about to reach for Russell's hand when he flicked the light on. She dropped her hand in sudden embarrassment and stepped back.

"What's wrong?" he said.

"Nothing." She followed him into the nearby kitchen, which, like the house, was small but in perfect condition.

"You want something to drink?" He gestured at the snow-white cabinets and the stainless steel refrigerator.

"No, I'm okay."

"Then let's go into the living room."

The living room was decorated in shades of brown that ranged from chocolate to tan, with dark gold accents. Ava liked it, but its very perfection intimidated her. Her own apartment was an odd assortment of accumulated objects, and she had no color scheme.

Russell sat down and patted the sofa next to him. She came over, but remained standing, looking around, studying the room.

"You decorated this yourself," she said, remembering what his mother had said.

"You like it?"

Now that she was opening herself up to him, Ava could clearly hear the anxiety in his voice, the desire to please her and the fear that he might not. Why had she rushed to see him as overly self-confident, even swaggering, when he was so clearly the opposite? Hadn't he admitted to her and Lauren at the very beginning that he faked the appearance of self-confidence? Why hadn't she believed him?

"It's lovely," she said, and, to her now far less judgmental eyes, it was. He had done a wonderful job of keeping the house masculine enough for a bachelor without sacrificing warmth or comfort.

"Why aren't you sitting down?" he asked, reaching his hand up to her.

She took his hand and sat down at his side. "I'm a little scared," she said.

"Of what?"

"You know." She couldn't quite look at him, so she stared down at their linked hands. "I'm a slow starter. I need time to process all this."

"You've known me for over twenty years." His fingers moved among hers. "Isn't that enough time to get used to the idea of me?"

"It should be," she admitted. "Especially when you consider the fact that we've been engaged for almost the whole time."

"Hey!" He nudged her knee with his. "That's the first time you've ever willingly brought up the marriage contract."

"It's the first time I've ever felt glad it existed."

"So you're no longer horrified at the thought of being paired with me?"

"I'm getting there," she said and lifted her head.

He smiled down into her eyes and she looked right at him and she *knew* him. When hadn't she known him? With a little sigh of acceptance, she moved into his arms, meeting his eager kiss with a mouth that was just as greedy as his.

((◦))

What Ava had told Lauren was true: she wasn't a prude and she liked sex a lot, once she was comfortable enough to shed her clothes with someone.

When they were entangled on his bed, their clothing strewn about them, Russell said, "I told you I'd like the way you looked even if you were naked, and I was right."

"You do seem to approve." Her mouth was inches from his ear at that moment, so her whisper made him shiver a little, although the way her hands were moving along his naked shoulders and down his muscled back may have had something to do with that, too.

Meanwhile, Russell's mouth was now buried in her neck, so she could just barely make out his next words. "Think our parents would be pleased?"

"I guess so. This was what they wanted all those years ago, right?"

He raised his head and said, more clearly but somewhat hoarsely, "I'm not sure that *this* was exactly what they were picturing when you were six or whatever you were."

His shifting body extracted a moan out of hers. "Ah," she breathed. "Just as well they can't see us, then."

"That's kind of a given." He pushed up on his hands so he was in a plank position over her—a move that elicited another inadvertent noise of pleasure from her. "Can we stop talking about our parents now?" he said, his voice uneven.

It was all she could do to close her eyes and nod, and then she wasn't really capable of saying or thinking anything even remotely coherent.

"I should thank your trainer," Ava murmured a few minutes later into Russell's shoulder.

"Yeah?" He was lying on his back with her snug against his left side. He raised his right arm, made a fist, and studied his bicep muscle. "You like this?"

She nodded, a bit drowsily. "That and the whole package."

"Well worth all those hours of training, then." He dropped his arm. "I feel the same way about your package."

She made a face against his skin. "It doesn't sound good when you put it like that."

"You're right." He turned on his side so they were facing each other and stroked her bare shoulder with his free hand. "You're soft," he said.

"Thank you."

"Soft and real."

"As opposed to what? A blow-up doll?"

His fingers made circles on her skin that skimmed along her shoulder, then dipped down to her upper arm and across to her breastbone. She sighed with pleasure and rolled lazily onto her back. "It's just been a while since I've seen a real breast," he said. "One that doesn't stand up and salute you no matter what position its owner might be in."

Ava laughed. "Mine are definitely natural."

"You have no idea how appealing that is." He bent over her and gently rubbed his nose against her nipple.

"Hey!" she protested, pushing him away and pulling the cover up over herself.

"What? It feels so nice. Soft and real."

"Stop calling me soft."

"It's a good thing."

"Yeah? You want me to call *you* soft?"

He lay back and flexed his arm muscle for her again. "How could you possibly call *this* soft?"

"You're a man of steel," she said.

"Better believe it."

His cell phone rang. "Who calls you so late at night?" Ava asked with another spasm of jealousy.

He leaned over the side of the bed to extract the phone from his pants pocket and collapsed back onto his pillow as he squinted at the screen. "Your sister. She's probably worried I'm still waiting at the restaurant for you."

"I should let her know I'm here," Ava said. "It's not like I'm in the habit of staying out late. She may actually be pretty worried."

"I'll take care of it," Russell said, and did by answering the phone and telling Lauren that Ava was there with him. It was clear she was peppering him with more questions because after listening for a moment—while grinning at Ava—he said, "You can ask her yourself—later. We're a little busy right now."

Ava could hear the hoot of delight on the other side of the line.

Russell hung up and they were both quiet for a moment. Ava pushed her foot against his. He pushed back in a friendly way. They lay quietly again. Then Ava yawned and shifted. "I need to run to the bathroom." She sat up, holding the blanket modestly to her chest, scanning the floor for something to throw on for the short walk. "Mind if I borrow your shirt for a second?"

"Be my guest."

She reached down to scoop up the white dress shirt that had

been abandoned by the side of the bed. Turning her back to Russell, she slipped it on and quickly buttoned a few of the buttons before sliding to her feet. The tails came down to her thighs.

"Nothing more appealing than a cute girl wearing your shirt," Russell said, lazily putting both hands behind his head as he regarded her. "And you all know it, too. I can't tell you how many shirts I've lost to—"

"Don't tell me," Ava said, putting her hand up. "Seriously, I don't want to know."

"Hold on." In a sudden transition from inertia to movement, he leapt over to the side of the bed and got onto his knees in front of her. Ava couldn't help glancing down between his legs and grinning. "Hey," he said, "watch where you're looking."

"I can't help myself," she said. "Men are made funny."

"Come closer, will you?"

She obediently moved closer to the bed and he reached out to her. She thought he was going to embrace her and leaned forward, but his hands went up to her neck instead.

"The collar's all messed up," he said, frowning and fiddling with it. She couldn't see what he was doing, but could feel the stiff shirt collar being pulled out from where it had apparently been caught inside-out against her neck. He flipped it back into place, smoothed the points down, arranged her hair on her shoulders, then unbuttoned another button at the top of the shirt. "Looks better a little more open like this," he said. "I get to see more of the good stuff." Proving his point, he buried his face briefly in the soft skin just below her collarbone and then kissed her lightly on the chin and sat back with a nod of approval. "There," he said. "All fixed. You look perfect now."

"You can't just let me be, can you?" Ava said, crossing her arms. "You're *still* trying to pretty me up. It's never going to stop with you, is it, Markowitz?"

Russell put his hands up in remonstration. "I'm not trying to change you, I swear. If you prefer that button buttoned—" He reached for it again, but Ava stopped his hand by taking it in hers.

"It's okay." She squeezed his hand. "I think I could learn to like it when you make me look good. I mean, what's the downside, really?"

"You look good no matter what I do," Russell said and pressed her hand to his lips. "Better than good. I'm just gilding the lily here."

"I'm a lily?" Ava said and her heart beat fast with sudden delight.

"Of *course*," he said. "Haven't you noticed yet?"

"Well, then gild away," Ava said. She pushed him down and fell on top of him. "Gild away."

⌒●⌒

She never intended to spend the night at Russell's, but between drowsing and cuddling and drowsing and having sex and drowsing and getting something cold to drink and drowsing and talking . . . somehow the sun was on the verge of rising before Ava realized she still hadn't gotten herself out of there.

"I've got to get back to my place before I go in to work," she said when she realized how late it was.

"I should get up soon, too," Russell said, although he was lying on his back with his eyes shut tight and didn't look like he was going to be going anywhere in the near future.

Ava got dressed and dropped one last kiss on his forehead. He half opened one eye. "Call me?" he said sleepily. "Have dinner with me tonight? And then spend the whole weekend with me?"

"Yeah, okay," Ava said. "All of the above. Go back to sleep."

"I should work out," he said, but his eye had already closed again. He'd be asleep before she left the house, Ava thought affectionately.

On her drive back to the Westside, one half of her brain kept ticking off her agenda—drive home, park, shower, get dressed, go to work, finish the Brodericks' will, and so on—and the other half was singing some lively old rock song about love that she couldn't completely recall because the tune slipped away from her whenever she tried to focus on it.

The sun was in the sky when she walked into the apartment, making the yellow-green living room drapes glow. Ava tiptoed across the floor and was about to open the door to her bedroom when a loud "Aha!" made her jump and scream.

"Jesus, Lauren!" she said, collapsing back against the door, clutching her heart. "Was that really necessary?"

Lauren had reared up in the sofa, the better to scare Ava apparently, but now she collapsed back down in laughter. "Oh my God, you should have seen your face!" she chortled.

"If only there'd been a mirror nearby," Ava said.

"Yeah, then maybe you'd also notice that you're wearing the same clothes you were wearing when you left the house yesterday morning!" Lauren said. "The clothes that *I* picked out for you, I might add."

"I know. I'm on my way to change."

"Get over here and talk to me first. Come on, Ava, you're doing the Walk of Shame! That can't happen to you very often. You've got to tell me what went on last night."

"I don't have to tell you anything," Ava said, but she came closer.

"Yes you do." She bounced excitedly on the cushions. "Did

you meet him for dinner or not? I'm all confused about that and Russell wouldn't tell me anything on the phone."

"I met him," Ava said. "And I was really pissed off at you for lying to us both, by the way. If you ever pretend to be me again—"

"Yes, yes," Lauren said, impatiently waving her hand. "Whatever. So you went straight to his house afterwards?"

Ava leaned her hip against the armchair. "Yeah. We had to take separate cars, though. I thought about just leaving mine, but I wasn't sure what the valets would do with it after the restaurant closed—"

"Fascinating," Lauren said. "Tell me more about the cars. And about the valets. What color are their jackets? And how much did you tip them?"

"Shut up," Ava said. "The answer is yes, we went back to his house."

"And—?"

"And it was nice."

"Nice like watching TV and ordering in Chinese food with a good friend? Or nice like wild sex all over the house?"

Ava looked up at the ceiling. "Well," she said. "We weren't about to order in Chinese food. We'd just eaten."

Lauren pumped her fist triumphantly. "I am so glad I set this whole thing up! You totally needed a good screw. No offense."

"None taken." She reconsidered. "Well, maybe a little bit."

"I'm so brilliant," Lauren said. "Admit it. Admit I'm brilliant. First I introduce you two and then I make sure you keep seeing each other, because you're such an insecure mess that you'd have driven him off right away if I hadn't forced things along. No offense."

"Will you stop saying offensive things and then saying 'no

offense'? I'm not an insecure mess. I'm just cautious. Something you wouldn't know about."

"Call it whatever you want." Lauren peered up at her. "You like him, don't you?"

"I do," Ava said.

"Which means you owe me, because if it hadn't been for me you wouldn't have met him. Or given him a fair chance."

"I probably wouldn't have met him," Ava said. "As adults, I mean. Anyway, I'll give you that."

"Good." Lauren sat back and took a deep breath. "I'm glad you owe me, because I have something I have to confess to you. It's been weighing on me and I was waiting for the right time. Given your happy post-sex mood at the moment, this is probably as good a time as any."

"Oh no," Ava said. She lowered herself into the armchair. "What did you do, Lauren?"

"It's not *that* bad," Lauren said. "I didn't murder anyone or anything like that. I just bought some clothes. I know I promised I wouldn't and signed that stupid piece of paper, but there was this top—"

"The one you were wearing the night Daniel came over?"

"Yeah. The shoes were new, too."

Ava shook her head. "I knew you looked too good that night. And you were so upset when you stained the top that it made me wonder. But I wanted to trust you." She chewed on the side of her thumb. "Why is it so hard for you to control what you buy, Lauren? It hasn't even been a month since you signed that contract."

"I don't know," Lauren said. "I thought I was being pretty good, actually. It's just . . ." She thought for a while, rocking gently, knees to chest. "Honestly? It was kind of wrapped up in the whole Daniel thing. I wanted to make him really notice me. I thought maybe the right clothes would make a difference."

"One top isn't going to change how someone feels about you," Ava said.

"Maybe not. Anyway, I was also kind of mad at you for making me sign that thing in the first place. Buying these things was my way of rebelling."

"Very mature."

"Fuck mature."

"That's what he says in *Diner*."

"I know. It was a quote."

"I thought the contract would help you stick to your resolution," Ava said. "I was just trying to help."

"It's hard to be the one who always needs help."

"We take turns at it," Ava said. "Haven't you noticed?"

Lauren clasped her hands together. "So . . . Does that mean you forgive me?"

"What choice do I have? I can't exactly cart you off to fashion jail." Something occurred to her. "How did you pay for all that stuff, anyway?"

"Used the household AmEx."

"Didn't you think I'd notice the charge?"

"Why?" Lauren said. "Do you actually read through your statements?"

"Of course I do," Ava said. "Don't you?" Lauren shook her head and Ava said, "Well, that's part of the problem right there. You need to learn to monitor that stuff. And I expect you to pay me back once you're earning money again."

"I will."

"Which reminds me: you need to start earning money again."

"I'll start looking today. I told Mom I'd bring lunch over and hang out, but the rest of the day is free."

"It's nice that you're spending so much time with Mom," Ava said. "I'm a little jealous."

"I'm a little jealous you spent the night with a great guy," Lauren said. "You owe me for that one. Actually," she said with sudden excitement, "when you think about it, it's because I spend too much money that you ended up with Russell."

"Excuse me?" Ava said.

"No, really. If you hadn't annoyed me by making me sign that contract, then I wouldn't have hunted down Russell because of the *other* contract. So you should really thank me for not paying my bills."

Ava stood up. "That is the dumbest thing I've ever heard."

"Say 'Thank you.' Say 'Thank you, Lauren, for not paying your bills.'"

"I'm going to take a shower," Ava said and went into the bedroom.

Lauren called after her, "If you don't say 'Thank you,' I'm going to tell Mom on you."

Ava just shut the door. She went to run water for her shower but stopped at the sight of herself in the mirror. You could tell she had just had sex, she realized with amusement. All the classic postcoital signs were there: flushed cheeks, overly bright, almost feverish eyes surrounded by smudged mascara (thanks to Lauren), wavy, tousled hair, lips that were dark red and swollen from a night of kissing . . .

She stood there and she looked and she smiled and she thought, *Now there's a pretty girl.*

About the Author

I grew up and went to school in Newton, Massachusetts. Back then my name was Claire Scovell. A few months after I graduated from Newton South High, my parents dropped me off in Harvard Yard. They picked me and my dirty laundry up about four years later. Once my laundry was done, I left home to seek my fortune.

The eighties were a decade of bad hair, bad clothing, and bad judgment, and the less said about them the better. Happily, I survived, emerging with a new last name and a new state of residence.

Just to be clear, my tenure as a Californian is temporary. I'm only staying here long enough to bring up my kids and grow old in the sunshine and be buried next to Marilyn Monroe, and then I'm moving right back to the East Coast. Leave a light on.

I'm the youngest of five and my husband is the youngest of four, and together we have four children—three boys and one girl. This is the fourth book I've had published and my third novel. My fourth child celebrated his fourth birthday on the fourth day of the fourth month in the year 2004. None of this is significant.

I feel very lucky that I get to do what I love and still be home every day to greet my kids when they come home from school. How *they* feel about it will eventually come out in therapy.

Claire

Since this book is about **sizters,** here are five of my own favorite famous sister groups:

1. The March sisters

(Meg, Jo, Beth, and Amy) from Louisa May Alcott's novel *Little Women*

—Coming upon my sister reading *Little Women* for the very first time, my aunt instantly warned her not to get too attached to Beth. Where was she when I was reading *Old Yeller*?

2. The Bouvier sisters

(not Jacqueline and Lee, but the really famous ones: Marge, Selma, and Patty)

—The blue-haired Bouviers prove that sisters *can* sound identical. Of course, it helps if the same person is actually providing the voice for both or all of you.

3. The Brontës

(Charlotte, Emily, and Anne) There were originally two more Brontë sisters, but life was hard in the early part of the nineteenth century, and they died young.

—Brilliant? Yes. Crazy? Almost definitely. They wrote story after story about imaginary worlds in teeny-tiny handwriting. On the other hand, TV hadn't been invented yet, so what else were you going to do on a long winter's evening?

4. The Bennet sisters

(Jane, Elizabeth, Mary, Kitty, and Lydia)

—If you're a woman and you like to read, then you already know and love the Bennets. Elizabeth is always torn between loving her family and being deeply embarrassed by them—and if you don't relate to that, you probably don't have sisters. Or a family.

5. The Gorgon sisters

(Medusa, Stheno, and Euryale)

—Tough and mean, with hair that'll take on any flatiron and win, these women-beasts redefine what it means to be female, and you've got to love them for that. From a distance.